Palo Alto City Library

SMOKE-FILLED ROOMS

ALSO BY KRIS NELSCOTT

A Dangerous Road

SMOKE-FILLED ROOMS

Kris Nelscott

St. Martin's Minotaur ≋ New York

www.minotaurbooks.com

Library of Congress Cataloging-in-Publication Data

Nelscott, Kris
    Smoke-filled rooms / Kris Nelscott.—1st ed.
        p. cm.
    ISBN 0-312-26265-5
    1. King, Martin Luther, Jr., 1929-1968—Assassination— Fiction. 2. Private investigators—Illinois—Chicago—Fiction. 3. Children as witnesses—Fiction. 4. Political conventions— Fiction. 5. African American men—Fiction. 6. Chicago (Ill.)— Fiction. I. Title.

PS3564.E39 S66 2001
813'.6—dc21
                                                                                    2001019269

First Edition: August 2001

10 9 8 7 6 5 4 3 2 1

For Steve Braunginn
who made my days in the trenches
some of the best of my life

ACKNOWLEDGMENTS

A number of people helped with this book by providing information when I most desperately needed it. Thanks to Don McQuinn, Bill Fawcett, Steve Braunginn, Richard Gilliam, and Dean Wesley Smith.

I also owe a debt to Kelley Ragland and Paul Higginbotham, whose suggestions greatly improved the manuscript.

Thank you all. I couldn't have written this book without you.

[Chicago] is the city that invented the smoke-filled room, that locked-door cliché of cigar-chomping politicians bent on shifty deals.

—JACK SCHNEDLER,
Chicago

Repression turns demonstration protests into wars. . . . It forces everyone to pick a side.

—JERRY RUBIN

The people of Mississippi ought to come to Chicago to learn how to hate.

—MARTIN LUTHER KING, JR.

ONE

I had been in the Loop all morning. I had found a seat on the concrete steps leading up to the "L," and no one had asked me to move. Dozens, maybe hundreds of us crowded the steps. For an hour, the trains hadn't stopped and the platforms above me were closed, although policemen patrolled them.

They were searching for snipers.

The year of assassinations continued.

I hadn't told anyone where I'd gone. I wasn't talking much these days. I no longer felt as if I had anything valid to say.

It was September 4, 1968, only a week since the entire city of Chicago had erupted into chaos. Only a week since I had made a choice I couldn't have contemplated a year ago.

Only a week since everything had changed. Again.

The street was eerily silent. Hundreds of thousands of people gathered under the steel-and-concrete skyscrapers and didn't say a word. Police and National Guard, their rifles ready, kept the crowd on the sidewalks. Squadrols— paddy wagons in any other town—were on side streets, waiting in case last week's riots started anew.

I had no real idea why I had come. I'd felt drawn here, as if this place, these people, this moment could give me some perspective.

There were very few black faces in the crowd. We stood out so dramatically that the police gave us special attention. I sat so that no one realized how tall I was or how broad. My very size intimidated people. And I kept my hands in view at all times. I didn't want to start anything, even inadvertently.

Chicago had witnessed enough violence in this long hot summer.

I'd witnessed enough violence—caused enough violence—to last an entire lifetime.

I had embraced darkness because it was the only choice left.

The year of assassinations continued.

And in the midst of all these thousands of people, I was more alone than I had ever been.

TWO

It all began with the dreams. I had the first one on the night of August twenty-first.

I dreamed I was back in Korea, toward the end of the war. Our trench was waist-deep and not very wide, certainly not the kind required by regulations. It was on a lower hill, about eight hundred yards from the nearest Chinese trench. In that eight hundred yards there were higher hills and rice paddies, frozen over in the cold.

The enemy hills had no vegetation at all. The First Marine Air Wing had destroyed all of it, making the vista on moonlit nights eerie and unnatural.

The cold was unnatural too—biting and harsh, worse because nothing protected us from the wind. We patrolled and listened to the sounds of our unseen enemies digging in the frost-bitten earth. With each scrape-scrape-scrape of their shovels, the tension rose.

One day, we knew, we would fight them. One day, we would kill them.

The tension, the cold, the feeling that something horrible was about to happen were so strong that I could barely breathe.

I woke then, cramped onto the narrow couch at Franklin Grimshaw's, covered with sweat on that hot August night, the nap of the couch sticking to my back, and yet feeling so cold it seemed like I would never warm up.

The apartment was large, but the heat gathered in there like a live thing. The open windows didn't help—all they did was let in the noise of the street. Summer noises: people shouting, a radio blaring down the block, the roar of an engine, each sound magnified in the humidity, as close as the air.

I was used to heat—Southern heat—but somehow this Chicago weather was worse than any I'd experienced. Perhaps it was just the way I was living. For more than three months, I'd slept on that threadbare couch, forced to wake up whenever someone passed through the room. I had no privacy unless I went out onto the fire escape, and even then I had to share myself with the city.

Chicago. It was not my home. I hadn't even been to the city before May first, when Jimmy and I finally decided to find a permanent place to stay. Jimmy was ten and needed more stability than a life on the road could give him. But he was afraid to settle anywhere, and I wasn't sure there was any safe place for him to go.

I got off that couch and went into the apartment's only bathroom, leaving the door open as I splashed cold water on my face. The water smelled of rust, tasted of it too, but I drank, not wanting to raid the Grimshaws' refrigerator more than I had to.

I'd been living on their charity for too long. I'd known Franklin in Memphis. We'd been friends for years when he decided to take Althea north for a better life. In 1958, Chicago had looked a lot better than Memphis. Now I wasn't so sure that this city was better than any other.

Even though I'd paid a minimal rent to salve all of our consciences, money wasn't the problem. Space was. The apartment had three tiny bedrooms. Franklin and his wife, Althea, shared one, their three daughters another, and their two sons—along with Jimmy—had the third.

I leaned against the sink, feeling the warm condensation on the cracked porcelain, and wondered why I was dreaming of Korea.

And why it left me so cold.

That morning, Jimmy and I had an appointment to see a new apartment. I included him in all of my decisions. No one had ever done that before, and his reaction varied from gratitude to exasperation, depending on what I interrupted in order to bring him along.

He'd had as rough a night as I had. He was grateful to be looking for someplace new.

I gave him a once-over before we went out. He had put on weight since we'd moved to Chicago—Althea's meals were large and plentiful—but he also had deep circles under his eyes.

He hadn't slept well since the night Martin Luther King, Jr., had been shot. Jimmy had witnessed the assassination. He'd also seen the assassin—and it wasn't the man they'd arrested in June.

That night, I'd gotten Jimmy out of Memphis. It was the only way I could save his life.

He wasn't my child by blood, but he'd become my family. By the time we got to Chicago, we were telling people that we were father and son.

I adjusted his short-sleeved shirt, made sure his pants were clean, and double-checked his shoes. I knew we had a better chance of getting the apartment if we both made a good impression.

Jimmy squirmed under my administrations. "I dressed up, Smokey, and I'm hot. Let's go 'fore I start looking sloppy."

I smiled at him. He wanted to be out of here as much as

5

I did. We were both loners in our different ways, and living in such close quarters with so many people was driving us both crazy.

"All right." I stood and put my hand on his back, happy that I could no longer feel his bones through his skin. "Let's go."

Jimmy opened the door and we stepped into the wide hallway. It was high ceilinged and clean, despite the number of tenants in the building. The Grimshaws lived in a nice area. Still, I had to lock three dead bolts before pocketing the keys.

Marvella Walker was coming up the stairs. She wore a halter top and tight shorts that showed every curve. She looked cool despite the heat.

"Hey, Bill," she said, calling me by the name everyone in the building used. Franklin had told them that I was his cousin from Memphis. He never used my last name, and at my insistence he called me Bill in public. My legal name is Billy Dalton, although I've been called Smokey since I was a little boy. Smokey was too obvious and easy to track, I thought, and Billy no longer suited the man I'd become. So Bill it was.

Jimmy had stopped at the top of the stairs. He had never liked strangers, and that trait had gotten worse since the assassination. He'd become close to most of the men in the building, but he still had trouble with women—a fact I blamed on his abusive, neglectful, mostly absent mother.

I came up beside him. "How're you doing, Marvella?"

She let out a small sigh and gripped the thick wooden railing, as if she suddenly needed it. "I swear if this heat don't end, I'm gonna melt."

I gently moved Jimmy toward the wall. I knew better than to try to get him down the stairs while she was on them.

"Yeah," I said. "Sometimes I think it's hotter inside than it is outside."

6

She smiled at me. Her smile lit up her dark eyes, brought her regal cheekbones into focus, and accented her narrow chin. I thought if she cut her hair short instead of ironing it smooth and forcing it to curl along her shoulders, she'd look like one of those busts of African princesses sold at that imports store near Washington Park.

"I'd think you'd be used to the weather," she said.

"It seems hotter here."

Jimmy looked up at me, unable to hide his pleading look. He wanted to leave.

Then her smile faded. She looked to either side, as if she didn't want anyone to hear what she was going to say.

"Bill." Even her voice was soft. "You're not one of those outside agitators, are you?"

Beside me, Jimmy froze. I could sense him, a rabbit in the headlights.

"Outside agitators?" I knew the phrase, but it meant many things in many places. In Mississippi, during the height of the civil rights movement, the cops were using the phrase to imprison white civil rights workers, saying they were communists.

She shrugged, sheepishly, it seemed to me. "You know my cousin the cop, right?"

Franklin had told me she was related to a cop. Unlike Memphis, where the police department was just starting to become integrated, Chicago's force had had black cops for more than a hundred years.

Jimmy was shivering. I put my hand on his shoulder, partly to hold him in place, and partly as comfort. "I've never met him."

"Well," she said, as if my knowing him really didn't matter, "he says that potential troublemakers are being followed by undercover cops and the FBI."

I felt my breath catch.

"You're not a troublemaker, are you, Bill?"

I made myself smile. "Just a poor working man. Why?"

Her voice got even lower. "I thought I saw someone tailing you yesterday. He was doing his best to stay out of your line of vision, which didn't make sense to me."

I tried to remain calm, even though I felt my brain kick into high gear. I'd been on alert since April for just this kind of moment.

"It makes sense to me, Marvella," I said. "If they're following potential troublemakers, they're not going to want to be seen."

"No, that's not the point," she said. "My cousin said they *do* want to be seen. So that these guys know they're being watched and so that they don't try anything when the Democrats come to town."

The Democratic National Convention wasn't going to start for another four days, and even before this conversation, it had become the bane of my existence.

"Are you sure they're looking at me?" I asked. "I thought Mrs. Witcover upstairs had a grandson in the Blackstone Rangers."

Jimmy was shaking so violently that I was sure Marvella would notice. I tightened my grip on his shoulder.

"Maybe that's it," she said. "It just seemed odd to me and I thought you should know."

"I appreciate it," I said. "You only saw this guy the once?"

She shook her head. "He's been outside a few times. Not too obvious, but there. He was black, Smokey. My cousin says most of these guys are white."

"So that they wouldn't blend in."

She nodded. "He was staring at Franklin's place."

"And you thought of me? Not Franklin?"

Her laugh was hardy. I liked a strong laugh in a beautiful woman. It made her more human somehow. "Franklin?

He's as innocent as they come. You don't look innocent, Bill."

"No," I said, "I don't suppose I do. Thanks for the tip, Marvella."

I started down the stairs, bringing Jimmy with me. A knot, solid as a fist, filled my stomach. How had they found us so soon? Or was this just paranoia in a hot city, rife with tension?

"We gots to get out of here, Smoke," Jimmy said when we reached the bottom of the stairs. Fortunately the lobby was empty. Circulars lay on the floor beneath the metal mailboxes, always a signal that the mail had arrived. The front door itself was closed and latched, and the lobby was stifling hot.

"We are, Jimmy," I said, keeping my voice down. Sounds echoed upward from this lobby. It was not a private place.

"No, I mean this town. They—"

I put a finger over his lips. "We have to get to the car. We're going to be late."

Then I opened the front door and stepped onto the wide porch. The apartment building had been built in the 1920s out of brick, the only wood on the interior. The lack of wood, I'd learned, was a strangely Chicago fetish—apparently no one had forgotten the Great Fire a hundred years before. City ordinances insisted that no buildings in the city limits be made of wood.

Sometimes that gave Chicago a grandeur it didn't deserve, especially in the poorer neighborhoods. This one, just south of Hyde Park, was considered middle class, although by whose standards, I wasn't sure.

There were a lot of people on the street, most of whom I recognized. The other buildings on this block looked the same—white brick with tan trim, wide porches, and broad expanses of sidewalk leading to them. The grass was untended, and the shrubbery overgrown. The buildings themselves went up four and five stories, and the wealth of the inhabitants marked itself in the curtains (or lack thereof), the items left on the porches and fire escapes, and the cars parked outside.

Jimmy was still trembling. I didn't see anyone skulking in the shadows, but then, I wasn't sure who I'd be looking for. I felt at a huge disadvantage in this new town. In Memphis, I knew all the ins and outs, the smallest detail had great significance, and told me more than most people could imagine.

Here, though, I saw the details and wasn't sure how to process them. For all I knew, the faces I thought familiar might have been as new as mine. Had someone watched Jimmy and me for months without either of us realizing it?

"Smokey," he said. "We gotta—"

"I know," I said quickly. "We don't want to be late."

We hurried off the porch and headed toward the rusted blue Impala parked against the curb. It wasn't a great car, but it was the best I could do when I traded in the green Oldsmobile Jimmy and I had traveled in. We'd stopped at a discount auto dealer whose very sign looked shady, and made him a deal that he couldn't refuse.

I unlocked the passenger door and pulled it open, almost pushing Jimmy inside. Then I went to the driver's side and got in.

Jimmy's head was down. "We gotta go, don't we? They found us."

"They might have," I said, putting the key in the ignition, "but there's a lot going on in this city, especially this month, and I don't think Marvella's the most reliable source we've ever talked to."

"But Smokey, if they find me, they'll kill me." He was staring out his window, his hands clenched into fists.

He'd never said that before. I wasn't sure if he'd understood it. But he was right. He'd seen enough to implicate the Memphis police. I knew that if the police were involved, so was the Memphis city government and the FBI. The FBI had major ties with Memphis's leadership—and the Feds' involvement had been my biggest unspoken concern.

Apparently, Jimmy had picked up on it.

My silence must have startled him. He gave me a sideways look. "Right?"

"No one's going to hurt you," I said. "I promise you that."

"How can you promise?" he asked. "Stuff happens all the time."

That knot in my stomach grew harder. The kid knew more about the world than I gave him credit for. "I'll check it out. I'm not going to ignore anything."

"But what about nights when you're working? Franklin can't do nothing. He don't even notice when his family's there. All he cares about is his books and those papers—"

"I'll make sure you're protected," I said, "and not by Franklin."

My assessment of Franklin was the same as Jimmy's. I liked the man—I always had—but he wasn't a physical person. He was taking night courses, studying for a law degree, and it suited him. Franklin did his battles with words, not his fists.

I put the car into drive and pulled out, checking my mirrors for a tail. I hadn't done that since mid-June. For some reason, I'd assumed we were safely hidden.

No one pulled out behind us, but I continued to watch as we drove north through the Black Belt, heading toward the heart of Bronzeville.

Most of Bronzeville was a ghetto. Slums, broken-down buildings, gangs roaming the streets. But other parts reflected Chicago's long and proud black heritage. Stately homes lined some of the avenues—and one even housed a museum of black history in some lady's parlor. She'd been raising funds to move it into a proper building, and Franklin had been helping her.

The riots that hit Chicago after Martin Luther King died happened mostly in the black neighborhoods on the Near West Side. Buildings had been burned, looted, and destroyed. It was so bad that I no longer looked for housing there. I stayed on the South Side, having heard horror stories of what happened to blacks who ventured outside the Black Belt.

Jimmy and I had enough problems. We didn't need gangs of armed whites blocking the door to our home.

The apartment building we were going to go see was on Forty-sixth Street, just off the new Dan Ryan Expressway. Over the phone, the apartment manager had assured me that the apartment was in a good neighborhood, well kept, and clean. I'd checked the address with Franklin, who'd shrugged.

"Housing market as tight as it is, Smokey, you're gonna have to take what you can get around here."

He'd been saying that to me from the beginning, and I knew he was right. It was just that I owned my own house in Memphis—a house that had been locked and unoccupied since early April. It was in a good neighborhood where children played happily on the street.

I wasn't able to go back to it yet, but I wasn't willing to trade that sense of security for a little bit of privacy. I'd look as long as Franklin was willing to tolerate two extra presences in his small home.

Jimmy had turned around in the seat, his chin resting on his arms as he stared out the back window.

"See anyone?" I asked.

"Nope."

The apartment complex was on Forty-sixth. I scanned for the address as I drove slowly up the street; there were several apartment complexes and none with a For Rent sign in the window. I wasn't sure I liked the neighborhood—there were few trees, and the faint lingering odor of the stockyards permeated the area. I was sure the smell was exacerbated by the heat—the stockyards were no longer in use—but the old scent of manure and cows lingered all the same.

"I thought this was a good one." Jimmy sounded as disgruntled as I felt. I had had high hopes for this place. It was close to an elementary school and the price was one of the more reasonable I'd heard. Rents in Chicago were ridiculous—although I had nothing to compare them to in Memphis. I hadn't paid rent in eleven years.

I finally saw the address, metal letters on a steel-and-concrete building, about ten stories high. There was no yard to speak of, only dirt and scraggly brown grass. No trees, and a view of the houses across the street and the empty stockyards beyond.

"Maybe it'll be all right inside," I said.

"Not if it's like the last one."

He was right. We'd seen some ugly buildings in our search for a place to live. Still, I had been promised that this apartment had some amenities. It was worth the look.

"Let's check it out anyway." I got out of the car, and my feet crunched on broken glass. Several beer bottles had been shattered along the side of the street. The glass was hard to see against the gray concrete. I hoped my tires would survive.

Jimmy opened his door and got out as well. He immediately scanned the neighborhood, his eyes wide and alert. Looking for our shadow. Apparently not trusting me to see anything.

I'd been looking too and on this empty street, I knew we hadn't been followed. No cars had been behind us for the last several blocks.

I didn't like how quiet the street was, and I was glad that

my car had almost nothing to steal. Its parts were nearly as useless as it was, but my .38 was locked in the glove box. I kept the gun there because I didn't want to bring it into an apartment full of children. Taking the gun out would draw too much attention to it, and carrying it would make the wrong impression on the landlord.

"Come on," I said, and headed up the walk.

Jimmy stayed at my side, closer than he'd been in weeks. He would have clung to me if he had been a few years younger. At ten, staying close was the best he could do.

As I approached the building, I thought I saw a white face peer at me from one of the windows. A trickle of unease ran through me. There shouldn't have been a white face for miles. Bridgeport, the nearest white enclave, was at least six blocks north, and Hyde Park, one of the few areas in Chicago where the races mixed at least a little, was over five blocks south.

"What is it, Smokey?" Jimmy asked in a hushed whisper.

"Nothing," I said just as softly, even though it appeared we were one of the few people on the street. I didn't like that either.

We walked underneath the small overhang that led to the main door. It had a security lock, and an intercom at the side. The system was sophisticated enough that someone had to buzz a visitor in. There was a series of buttons that ran along the left side of the door, each labeled with an apartment number. Only a few went so far as to add the name.

I pressed the one marked "Manager."

"Yeah?" A tinny voice answered.

"I'm here to see the apartment."

In response, an electronic buzzer sounded, so loud that both Jimmy and I took a step back. Then I grabbed the door and yanked it open.

It was heavy and metal, a security door without dents, a

good sign. We stepped into a narrow interior that smelled faintly of garlic and grease. It was hot too, as if it never got any air.

The manager's apartment was directly behind the security door. There was another door, this one glass, that led into the main part of the building. That door was propped open and I could see into the first floor hallway. It was clean enough. No broken lights, no damaged doors. But it also didn't have toys on the floor or bicycles propped up against the wall or even mats in front of the doors.

Jimmy shook his head just a little as the manager's door opened.

The manager wasn't what I'd expected. I thought the white face I had seen belonged to him, but it hadn't. This man was short, bald, and had a goatee threaded with silver. He wore a clean white shirt and dark pants and was carrying keys in his left hand.

I was about to introduce myself when he turned away from me and unlocked the glass door.

"It's upstairs," he said.

I glanced at Jimmy, who shrugged. Then we followed the manager through the door and up the metal stairs.

Our footsteps echoed. That was the first real strike against the building. Any sounds in the hallways would carry. We went up all ten flights. Halfway up, I asked if there was an elevator.

"Service only," he said. "I let people use it when they move."

I didn't like that much either. Jimmy opened his eyes wide, then grimaced at me. He was ready to leave. I still wanted to see. We'd had such poor luck finding a place to live that my standards were coming down. How far, I hadn't yet figured out.

We reached the tenth floor. The manager was puffing but Jimmy and I weren't. Jimmy was in the best shape of his life. Some of that had to do with the fact he was finally getting regular meals, but the rest of it had to do with fear. He wanted to be able to run as far as he could to escape anything that came after him.

This hallway was darker. I thought I saw a movement in the shadows, but I wasn't sure. Jimmy hadn't seen anything or he would have been running for the stairs.

The faint odors of stale sweat and perfume filled the hallway. Someone had been here before us. The smells mixed with the scent of frying hamburger. Down the hall, a woman was screeching—angry shouts, followed by a slap.

Jimmy winced.

The manager didn't even seem to notice. He led us to number 1037, unlocked the door, and stood back.

The apartment was empty. It had a large living room with a stained gray carpet, a hole in one wall, and the gray remains of a leak down the other. The kitchen was to the right, its cupboards grease stained, the stove so filthy that the dirt would have to be dynamited off. I gave the bathroom a cursory glance and the bedrooms, which smelled faintly of rot, an even shorter glance.

Jimmy remained at the living room window. I joined him. The view was the only good thing about the apartment. We were high enough to see over the rows of apartment buildings and houses to the stockyards. On Halstead, just in front of the yards, sewer workers were sealing manhole covers. On the far side of the yard, I could see other workers fortifying a cyclone fence covered with barbed wire.

The International Amphitheater sat in the middle, a concrete monstrosity that seemed more like a bunker than a building. Police cars surrounded it, as did several trucks marked Andy Frain Security Services.

Apparently anyone who lived here would have a bird's-eye view of the Democratic National Convention.

To me that was the most major strike against the building. The papers had been full of the various preparations Mayor Daley had ordered to protect the city and the delegates, including blocked-off roads and searches of motorists in that area. That kind of attention was the last thing Jimmy and I wanted.

"Apartment's available September first," the manager said. It was, apparently, his only sales pitch.

"It's empty now," I said.

"Got some work."

Obviously. But I wasn't going to let him off the hook. "The ad said that the apartment was ready for immediate rental."

"That was a different apartment," the manager said, and I had the sense he was lying. "This is the only one we got and it's ready for September first."

"All right." I turned away from the window.

A tall, thin white man was standing just inside the door. The manager gave him an uneasy look. Jimmy hadn't seen the white man yet, but I knew that he would be startled. The white man looked official in his black suit, narrow tie, and polished shoes.

"You interested in this place?" the white man asked me. "Because if you are, there are security forms to fill out."

No one filled out security forms to rent an apartment. Applications, yes. Financial forms, maybe. But not security forms. This man was either police, FBI or Secret Service. A chill ran through me, and I resisted the urge to glance out the window again.

Of course. Mayor Daley's panic over some kind of black uprising during the Democratic National Convention had filled the papers all summer. The authorities would be watching sites like this, apartments that a sniper could rent, wait for the right moment, train his scope on the potential nominee and blow the election process all to hell.

I think if Martin had been the only person assassinated

this year, preparations wouldn't have been so bad. But with Bobby Kennedy's death in June, the entire country believed these political murders would continue.

"All I want," I said, making myself sound both calm and confused, "is an apartment for me and my boy."

Jimmy slipped his hand in mine. He squeezed and I felt the panic in his fingers.

I turned toward the manager. "You told me over the phone that this neighborhood was safe. Your definition of safe and mine are very different."

"It's a good neighborhood," the manager said.

"It's not what we're looking for."

"You looking for suburbia?" he asked. "Nice, clean house with a great big yard? Chicago's got lots of places like that but not for people like you and me, pal. You go outside the Black Belt and you'll learn what violence really is. Those places, they're only safe for white people."

I got the sense that speech wasn't so much for me as it was for his unwelcome white watchdog. I kept my grip on Jimmy's hand and maneuvered my way out of the apartment.

"Thanks for your time," I said to the manager, but I said nothing to the white man as I passed him. In fact, I kept my eyes averted, just in case there were pictures of me floating around some bureau office somewhere.

I hustled Jimmy to the stairs, silently cursing myself. If this had been Memphis, I would have known to avoid this neighborhood. It was only common sense that there'd be security in apartment buildings like this. With the level of paranoia the city government was exhibiting, they would do everything they could think of to guard against trouble, even if it meant trampling on some citizen's rights.

I'd allowed myself and Jimmy to be noticed—and not in a positive way. If the government assumed everyone who viewed the apartment was a sniper, then I might just have caught the attention of the very people I had tried to avoid all summer.

My abrupt departure probably hadn't helped, but I hadn't had much of a choice. I looked guilty whether I stayed or whether I left. And it was up to that official white man to determine if I was enough of a threat to be followed or investigated.

Fortunately, I hadn't given anyone our names. I'd have to make sure that I didn't drive past the building so that he could take our license number—not that it would be easy to read. I'd coated it with mud the second day I had the car, not wanting anyone to trace us easily. Some of the mud had fallen off, but not all of it.

Jimmy tried to tug me down the stairs, but I made him walk, listening for footsteps behind us. Once he started to speak, and I put my free hand over his mouth. We had walked into the exact type of place we did not want to be, and I had to get us out as unobtrusively as possible.

On the first floor, a young girl played with a doll in front of one of the apartment doors. It stood ajar, and the sounds of a television, blaring one of the noontime Chicago news and talk programs. The girl didn't even look up, for which I was vaguely relieved.

I pushed open the glass door, then the security door, and stepped out onto the brown lawn, feeling like I could breathe for the first time in an hour. Jimmy pulled me toward the car and I let him. The quicker we got out of here, the better.

I didn't glance at the building until I was behind the wheel with both doors locked. I saw no white faces in the windows. No black faces either. But I had the feeling that we were being watched.

"They knowed us, didn't they?" Jimmy asked. I'd been teaching him good grammar all summer, but when he got nervous, old habits returned.

"No, they didn't know us," I said.

"But they think we done something."

"They think we're going to do something." I put the car in reverse and went down the middle of the block until I found a place wide enough to make a U-turn without letting anyone in the apartment complex see my license. No matter how much mud was on it, it was still better to be safe than sorry.

"What'd they think we're gonna do?"

"There's going to be a big convention a few blocks from here." I checked the rearview mirror. No tail. "I'm sure they suspect we'll disrupt it."

"I don't care about no convention."

I took a side street. I was going north, although Jimmy hadn't realized it yet. I would take a number of back roads until I was absolutely positive no one was following us.

"I don't care about the convention either." I might have once. But with the way my life had changed, worrying about politics seemed like a luxury. "But everyone else around here does."

"Why?"

The next side street was blocked off. Sewer workers again. Daley's people were thinking of every single way this convention could be compromised, and were struggling to prevent it.

"It's where they're going to chose one of the two candidates for president of the United States."

"I thought they already killed that guy."

His matter-of-fact tone threw me. I glanced at him. "You mean Bobby Kennedy?"

"Yeah." He was looking out the window. His voice was calm but his expression wasn't. He was learning from me, just not the things I wanted him to.

"He was a candidate," I said. "But right now there are

several others. At these conventions, they narrow the choices to two."

"There's gonna be another?"

Sometimes the depth of his ignorance astonished me. It shouldn't have. In Memphis, I had struggled to keep him in school, but I would have been surprised if he attended more than half the time. And I sometimes forgot that for all his street smarts, he was still only ten years old.

"There was another," I said. "The Republicans met in Miami last week. They chose a guy by the name of Richard Nixon."

"What's he like?" Jimmy asked.

I thought of the charges of corruption that had followed Nixon like a stink, the petulance that culminated in the famous "You won't have Nixon to kick around anymore" speech he made to the press a few years back, the methodical coldness with which he destroyed anyone he suspected of being a Communist. Not to mention the things he said about my people, or implied, or simply failed to acknowledge.

I couldn't encase all of that into a simple sentence, so I didn't even try.

"Smokey?" Jimmy asked. "What's he like?"

"We've got two and a half months to the election," I said. "Why don't you study him and find out?"

"Sounds like school." Jimmy flounced back in his seat.

"No, Jim," I said. "I wish politics was simply something you studied in school. But it's more important than that. It's life."

"So if that's true, how come you're not gonna pay attention to this convention."

"I'll be paying attention," I said. "Just not in the ways I want to."

He frowned, then leaned forward. "Hey. We're not going home."

He caught me. But our destination was hard to miss with the downtown skyscrapers looming before us.

"Plans change," I said.

"Because of that white guy back there?"

"And because of what Marvella said."

"You think someone is following us, then?"

"Not right now." I hadn't seen a suspicious car at all. "But I can't discount it. And I promised you I wouldn't."

"So where are we going?"

I gave him a smile that I hoped was reassuring. "Someplace safe."

THREE

We picked up a tail on Division and Dearborn, near the Claridge Hotel. A police car followed at a discreet distance. Jimmy didn't see him, but I did. I had been expecting him.

We were in Chicago's Gold Coast, a neighborhood filled with mansions more than a hundred years old and exclusive apartment buildings that had been growing along Lake Shore Drive like weeds. My rusted Impala fit in no better than my skin color. Combined, they were like a neon sign advertising trouble.

Chicago police had a habit of harassing blacks who ventured into the wrong neighborhood. I always knew when I had made a wrong turn by the police car that would attach itself to my bumper.

I knew we were out of place here, but we needed to come. I was being extremely cautious, but I had to be. I had made a mistake today. Going to that apartment complex had drawn attention to us. I couldn't ignore that any more than I could ignore the fact that Marvella had seen someone follow me. If I had been on my own, I wouldn't have taken these precautions, but I couldn't protect Jimmy every moment of every day.

I had to make sure he was safe until I discovered exactly what was going on. There was only one other place I could go.

I turned on Burton and parked on the street beside a highrise apartment building that overlooked Lake Shore Drive and Lake Michigan. Jimmy was looking at me in complete surprise. He had never been here before.

I had only been here twice. Both occasions had been memorable, but not enjoyable.

As the cop pulled up behind me, I braced myself. Some things didn't change from community to community.

"Let's get out," I said. "You follow my lead."

"But Smokey—"

"Bill, for now. And do as I say, Jimmy. It'll be all right."

His face squinched into a frown so deep I could map it, but he got out of the car, just like I asked. I got out too, locked the car, and walked to stand by Jimmy on the sidewalk as if we had every right to be here.

"What's your business?" The cop had gotten out of his car and was heading toward mine. He was beefy and thick—someone I could outrun or knock down with little effort. Still, he wore his service revolver and had a nightstick attached to his belt. He wouldn't be afraid to use either.

"I've got a meeting inside," I said.

"That so?"

I knew he wouldn't believe the truth, that I knew the owner of the building personally and was going to see her.

"Yes," I said, making sure my tone was nonthreatening, my hands were visible, and my face was blank.

"What kinda meeting?"

"Job interview." It was the first thing that came to my mind.

"Then how come you brought the kid?"

"I know the doorman. He promised to watch him while I interviewed."

Jimmy stood silently beside me on the curb, his hands threaded together, his gaze pointed toward the sidewalk, as I had taught him to do whenever we were confronted by white authority. Still, I could see the tension in him. I hoped the cop couldn't.

The cop wasn't looking at him. He was frowning at me. I looked respectable enough, and I knew that Jimmy's presence weighed in my favor.

The cop nodded toward me. "Make sure that car is gone in an hour."

As if I could control a job interview like that. As if I had a job interview. "I will."

He waited. I realized that we had to head into the building, or he'd be after us again.

I took Jimmy's arm and turned him around, then led him toward the building. He was shaking. He hadn't had a day this bad since April. Maybe even since we'd left Memphis.

The service entrance was behind the trash cans, but the door was closed. I probably should have tried it to keep up the masquerade, but I pretended I didn't even see it. I went to the front.

The steel-and-glass façade would have looked expensive even without the doormen in their ridiculous red outfits, flagging cabs and opening car doors for the rich residents. I walked inside the gold ropes that led to the front door and headed forward as if I knew what I was doing.

A doorman stopped me. He was slender, white, and young. Probably not a usual doorman, but security being trained for the upcoming convention. A lot of buildings were doing that.

"State your business," he said.

"I'm here to see Laura Hathaway." I sounded confident, but no longer felt that way. I should have called ahead to see if she was home. To see if she would see me.

We had not parted on good terms the last time I was here, more than a month ago.

"Miss Hathaway isn't available," he said.

"She'll be available to me."

"I'm sure she'll call you if she needs you."

"And I'm sure you'd bar my way if she did, just as you're doing now."

He stared at me for a moment, then shrugged. "Sorry. I've had no word that anyone like you would be here."

"I'm sure Miss Hathaway confides in you about everything," I said.

"You have no right—"

"Find out if she'll see me before turning me away," I said. "I have some clout with Miss Hathaway, and if she knows how you treated me, you'll probably be out of a job."

He flushed an ugly red and went inside to the house phone. I waited. Jimmy shifted from foot to foot beside me, occasionally glancing over his shoulder, probably looking for the cop.

I prayed that Laura was in, and not just to prove my point to the young bigot barring the door. I needed her help, and I needed it now.

Ironically, it had been over her offer of help that we had our last fight. We had met in Memphis in February when she hired me to find out some things about her family, things that neither of us liked once I solved the case. Somehow, in one short month, we'd become lovers and I'd thought, for a brief shining moment, that we actually could have had something more than a single weekend.

But we didn't. Our last hope ended when Martin Luther King died. Laura flew home and I helped Jimmy escape Memphis. When I was honest with myself, I acknowledged that Laura was the reason I'd brought Jimmy to Chicago, but I hadn't contacted her for the first few weeks we were here.

When I finally did see her, I made it clear I didn't want her charity, then or now. I'd found a job, enlisted the help of the Grimshaws, and then I went to see her.

She'd been furious at me. She'd thought I was dead. She had no idea that I'd left Memphis with Jimmy—I'd sworn the one friend I'd told to silence—and she hadn't been able to reach me for nearly two months.

I'd explained the situation and she'd calmed down. That was our first meeting. It was our second—the one in which she'd offered me charity—that still stung.

Yet here I was, asking for help.

The doorman returned. His lower lip was set, his eyes narrowed. "Miss Hathaway will see you," he said. "She's on the—"

"The top floor," I said as I passed him. "I know."

Jimmy glanced at me. He'd heard the suppressed anger in my voice. The morning hadn't gone well for me either, and I was beginning to get tired of being suspect just because I was darker than the people around me.

The lobby was ridiculously ornate. A dozen families, crammed into shoddy apartments in my neighborhood, could have lived in all that wasted space. Instead, comfortable groupings of leather furniture faced Lake Shore Drive and Lake Michigan beyond. Huge plants—scheffleras, ferns, and a few potted trees—accented the furniture groupings. A shiny marble floor reflected everything on it, making the lobby seem even bigger than it was.

Two bouquets as tall as Jimmy flanked the security desk. The bouquets were made up of fresh roses, their scent filling the lobby. The desk was recessed near the elevators, as unobtrusive as possible, yet still providing all the services people in this privileged building demanded—guest screening, mail and package delivery, and whatever other whims the rich and idle might have.

I led Jimmy to the bank of elevators behind the security desk. Everyone in the lobby, from the little old lady who was digging in her purse to tip the doorman to the young executive who had come home for his lunch hour, watched us walk. I tried to ignore them, but I could feel their gazes upon me.

One of the elevator cars stood open. The elevator attendant, an elderly man, was the first black I'd seen since I entered the building.

He nodded at me as Jimmy and I boarded. I asked for the top floor and the attendant swung the lever all the way to the top. As the door closed, he said, "You got business with Miss Laura?"

Miss Laura. I'd always known she was rich. I knew more about her finances than I knew about anyone else's except my own. But her wealth hadn't come home to me until the first time I visited this building, the one her father had placed in her name when he built it shortly before he died.

"We're old friends." I watched the tiny lever above the door point out the floors as we passed them. I didn't want to discuss Laura, not even casually.

The attendant chuckled. "So you're the one."

I looked at him then. He had age spots all over his face and hair the color and texture of cotton balls. But his dark eyes were alert and wise—at least, they seemed wise to me.

"She be different since she come back from Memphis, throwin' money at causes she never thought of, askin' me if I feel 'exploited' "—he exaggerated the word, as if imitating her—"wondering if there be something she can do to integrate the buildin' without makin' the other residents mad. Some think she be just shook by the death of Dr. King, but I know it be sumthin' else. She got to see another side of life, didn't she?"

We had reached Laura's floor, but the attendant hadn't opened the door.

"Laura's expecting us," I said.

He chuckled again and pulled the lever to open the door. Behind me, I heard Jimmy gasp.

I had seen it before, this space outside of Laura's penthouse apartment. It wasn't exactly a hallway because the only door led to Laura's, and it wasn't exactly a foyer, because we weren't inside that apartment. But the space was as grand as the lobby, obviously done by the same designer—someone who favored black floors and brass trim, and a mirror to expand the space. Another large vase filled with roses stood on the table before the mirror, making an even more dramatic statement than the one downstairs.

I stepped out of the elevator as Laura's door opened. Jimmy stood slightly behind me, letting my body shield him from the woman at the door.

She looked different than she had when I first saw her in February. Then she had worn makeup and expensive clothing, her hair exquisitely styled. Now it was pulled back in a ponytail, and she wore no makeup at all. Her blue jeans were frayed at the hem and decorated with wide yellow patchwork flowers. Over it she wore a thin yellow cotton shirt and no bra.

She was more beautiful than I remembered.

"Smokey," she said softly.

Behind me, the elevator doors wheezed closed. Jimmy pressed against my side.

"May we come in, Laura? This is too important to discuss in the hall."

"I'm sorry." She flushed and moved away from the door.

I walked inside. Her apartment was huge, as large as the lobby downstairs. An oriental rug—authentic, I had no doubt—covered the black marble floor in the actual

29

foyer, and photographs, mostly black-and-white professional shots of Laura and her friends and family, covered
the wall.

Jimmy stared at it all as if he were in a dream. Laura led
us to the living room filled with leather furniture more elegant than that in the lobby. Plants draped off tables and
hung in front of doors. But Jimmy didn't look at the decor.
Instead, he was drawn to the wall of windows, revealing a
clear view of the lake.

Up here, the sun didn't seem too bright or threatening. It
was the perfect complement to the deep blue of Lake Michigan, stretching as far as the eye could see. Ships were out
on the lake, ships that looked so tiny as to be insignificant,
yet which were entire floating cities that traveled from port
to port.

The bulk of the windows faced east, but the north and
south walls had large windows as well. To the south, the city
of Chicago rose in all its dirty glory. To the north was Lincoln
Park and the suburbs beyond.

The windows were closed, but the apartment was cool,
almost frigid. I hadn't noticed the air-conditioning downstairs, although I was certain it had been on. I had simply
been too preoccupied by my encounters with the cop and
doorman. Here, though, the chill was welcome.

I hadn't been this comfortable in weeks.

"Jimmy," Laura said, facing him. "I don't know if you
remember me. I'm Laura Hathaway. We met in Memphis."

He raised his chin so that he could look her in the eyes.
"I remember you."

She smiled then, and I remembered how it felt when she
had turned that smile on me. I longed to touch her, to tuck
a loose strand of hair behind her ears, to pull her close. But
I didn't move.

"You live here?" Jimmy asked.

Laura nodded.

"All by yourself?"

"Yes." She seemed amused by the question. If she had known how we were living, she would have been appalled.

"Gosh." He shoved his hands in his pockets. "How come you don't let no one else stay here?"

She looked at me, a frown between her perfectly plucked brows. She was smart enough to understand there was more to his question than the words.

"I've lived alone for a long time," she said.

"Me and Smokey, we want to live alone, but we can't." He pressed his face against the glass, then leaned back. "It's hot!"

"The sun does that," she said, "especially when it's really hot outside. Is it really hot today?"

"Not as bad as last night." Jimmy had never been this talkative with a woman before. Either the place impressed him or the cool air did, or maybe it was the familiar face, one he'd first seen in Memphis.

Laura turned to me, suddenly all business. "Somehow I get the sense this isn't a social visit."

"No." Now that I was here, I wasn't sure how to approach her. I'd been very careful since my arrival in Chicago not to seek her out.

"Jimmy, you want some soda?" Laura asked.

"Yeah!" That got him away from the window.

"There are some cans in the kitchen. Take whichever kind you like."

"Okay." He paused, looking helplessly at the expanse of furniture, and the hallways disappearing in two different directions. "Um, where is it?"

"That way." Laura pointed down one of the hallways.

"He'll eat everything in sight," I said.

"That's all right. I take it you haven't had lunch."

"Not yet." Not that I could stomach food at the moment. I wanted to get this meeting over with.

Jimmy headed toward the kitchen. He was smiling for the first time since we'd left the Grimshaws'.

She stared at me for a moment. Her blue eyes were shadowed, her face thinner than it had been even a month before. "I missed you, Smokey."

I'd missed her too, but coming to Chicago had convinced me how insurmountable our differences were. I would never fit into a place like this. Hell, I probably couldn't even live in a place like this. Even though the housing laws had changed, Chicago hadn't. White residents had a habit of attacking black families who moved into the wrong neighborhood.

"Laura, I . . ." I took a deep breath. I almost couldn't finish the sentence. "I need your help."

The softness left her face. Suddenly she was quite serious. "What's wrong?"

"I think someone may have found us. I was wondering if Jimmy could stay with you while I look into what's going on."

Her frown deepened. "You actually think they'll go after a little boy?"

"No," I said quietly. "I think they'll kill him."

She blanched. She'd been to Memphis in those last horrible weeks. She'd seen the racism and the riots. She'd even had her life threatened by a man I knew to be an undercover FBI agent, although I couldn't remember if I had told her that.

Still, she'd seen enough to know the truth of my words, though I wondered if that truth would overcome her upbringing, in a cool glassed-in world where everyone had a private bedroom and cops protected people.

"Wouldn't he be safer with you?" she asked.

"Usually, but I can't check out this rumor and keep him beside me." I didn't mention my job, which was the only thing keeping Jimmy and I afloat these days. The money I'd brought with us from Memphis was long gone, and I hadn't been willing to endanger us further by having money wired to me.

"I don't know, Smokey. If there is someone trying to kill him, and they know he's here . . ." Her voice trailed off. She glanced toward the kitchen as if she were afraid Jimmy had overheard.

"We weren't followed," I said. "I made sure of that. And you have enough security in this building to take care of Fort Knox. No one would ever suspect Jimmy of hiding here. You can tell people whatever you like about him except the truth."

She rubbed the back of her right hand with her left, a nervous gesture that I hadn't seen before. "He can't stay inside like a prisoner."

"He wouldn't have to."

"But if someone sees him—"

"As long as you don't tell anyone who he is, he's fine. No one knows what he looks like. They only know his name and that he's with me."

She swallowed, then looked away. She was going to say no. I could feel it. I braced myself, holding back the anger and frustration that had been building all day. Of course she would say no. For all the changes Laura had professed to make, she hadn't made the deepest one, the one that would require her to make choices that were hard.

"You're expecting problems with your neighbors, aren't you?" I said. "He can't even stay here, can he? They'll protest because of the color of his skin."

"I own the building, Smokey." Her voice was cool. "What they say doesn't matter. If they get too pissy, I'll make their lives hell."

She sounded tough. I was about to speak when she continued.

"I'm more concerned about Jimmy's safety. If I take him

outside, and someone comes after him, I can't do much. You're the one with the gun and the experience."

I smiled thinly. "Most situations take ingenuity, not greater firepower. Just be aware of who is around you at all times."

She tapped her thumb against her teeth. I could see her thinking, weighing the options, trying to figure out her response. Then she let her hand drop, and looked up at me. "How long will he need to stay here, Smokey?"

"With luck only a few days. But it might be as much as a week. This town is filled with FBI and undercover cops. They're all over the Black Belt, trying to make sure that the gang leaders and the Panthers are aware of their presence so that they don't try anything before the convention starts."

"And they're following you too? What are you doing, Smokey?"

That was the kind of question I'd expected. "I'm trying to survive in this place, Laura. I haven't done anything."

"Sorry." She took a step toward. "Smokey, I'm so very sorry."

She wasn't referring to what she had just said, but everything that had gone before.

She put her hand on my arm and a tingle ran through me. At that moment, Jimmy came out of the kitchen. His mouth was smeared with peanut butter, and he held a Coke in his left hand.

"I had some stuff," he said. "Is that okay?"

"It's fine." Laura let her hand drop from my arm. The warmth of her fingers lingered on my skin.

He wasn't looking at her, though. He was looking at me.

"Come here, Jimmy," I said, ignoring his earlier question.

He came, his steps slow and tentative. He knew something was about to change. He could probably hear it in my voice.

When he reached my side, I put my arm around his shoulder. "For the next few days, I want you to stay with Laura."

"Here?" Whatever he had imagined, it was clearly nothing like this. "Are you staying too?"

"No."

"Then I'm going with you."

I had expected this argument. I knew he wouldn't want to be separated from me. I'd been his only stability for months now, maybe the only stability he'd ever had in his life. "This morning you asked me to keep you safe, remember?"

"I asked if we gotta move again. Maybe go someplace else."

"We might have to." I crouched. We had to speak on equal footing. "But I want to check out what Marvella said before we give up everything we've started here."

"We ain't started nothing."

"I don't know," I said. "It seems to me you've been making a few friends in the neighborhood."

"They're just kids," he said.

"And I've got work, and we know people here. If we go somewhere else, we won't have any of that."

"So how come I can't stay home?"

"You know the answer to that."

He did. We had discussed it earlier. Laura was watching us intently. I could feel her tension as clearly as I felt Jimmy's.

"You saw that man today, Jimmy. Men like that are all over Chicago right now and it'll just get worse when the convention starts. Some of them may be looking for a black man and a boy your age. It's better if we don't let them see that."

"I'll stick out here."

I nodded. "Yes, you will. But no one will think you're Jimmy Bailey. Would Jimmy Bailey live here?"

There was a sadness in his eyes that matched how I was feeling.

"No," he said.

Laura put her hand over her mouth. In her world, apparently, children weren't as aware of their limitations as they were in mine.

"There are guards downstairs, and locks on the doors and more security here than in any other place I could take you. I want you safe, Jim, and this is the best way to do it."

He took a deep breath. He was trying. He really was. "Can you stay too?"

I resisted the urge to look at Laura. "I'll be here every day if I can, just to see you. And if I can't—if it's too dangerous—I'll call."

"But you ain't gonna leave me here forever, are ya?"

Even though I had expected that question, it still hurt. In Memphis before Martin died, I had taken Jimmy to a foster family, and then hadn't told him I was leaving town. That action on my part, among other things, had led Jimmy to be on Mulberry Street the night of the assassination.

"I'll come back for you, I promise." I made sure I met his gaze and that my voice was firm. "If we have been discovered, I'll get us out of Chicago. We'll stay together. We're family now, Jim. We will be for the rest of our lives."

Tears filled his eyes, but he didn't move. "I don't want you to go, Smokey. Please. Don't leave me here."

"I'm not leaving you here," I said. "I'm having you stay with a friend so that you'll be safe while I take care of both of us. There's a big difference, Jim. I'll never abandon you. I'll always be with you. You know how to reach me, at work and at home, and I'll make sure Laura does too. We'll be okay, you and I. This is temporary. I promise."

He bit his lower lip, looked down at the floor, as if he were trying to gather himself. It felt as if he were moving inward, away from me, as if he were becoming the boy I'd known in Memphis, five months before.

"So I was right?" he asked. "Things are really bad?"

How to answer that? Things were really bad. They had been bad since Martin died. But were they worse? I didn't know yet.

"I'm not going to wait until things get bad," I said. "We take precautions first and then find out what's going on. You agree with that, don't you?"

"But how'll I know you're safe?"

Good question, and one without as easy an answer. "I'll stay in touch like I promised."

"What if you don't call? Does that mean you're dead?"

Most likely. But I said, "No. It means that I've found something and I don't want to lead anyone to you. For the most part, though, I'll be in touch."

He nodded, bravely, I thought. Then he leaned as close to me as he could get, his body blocking Laura's view of his face. "You really want me to stay here?"

"Yes, I do."

"But, Smokey," he was whispering now, "she's white."

Laura started, but I didn't. I should have been expecting that comment too. In Jimmy's world white people were the enemy. They had been since he was born.

"I know."

"But—"

"There are good white people in the world, Jimmy, believe it or not."

Laura winced.

He frowned, as if he didn't believe me, but he didn't say anything more.

I stood, and faced Laura.

"I'm trusting you with the most important person in the world to me," I said. She had to understand that. If she didn't, I'd find some other way to take care of him. Or I would leave, even though I didn't want to run anymore.

"I know," she said, putting her hand on his shoulder. He didn't move away. "I'll do everything I can to keep him safe."

FOUR

I gave Laura the phone numbers where she could reach me in an emergency, asked her not to keep them anywhere obvious and not to have my name on them. I told her that after midnight, I'd leave some of Jimmy's clothes at the security desk, and I asked her to warn them that I was coming. The last thing I wanted was more hassles from her building's doormen.

Then I went down to my car, which, miraculously, was still there. The cop had only been threatening, or he had found something else to take his attention away from me.

I drove south on Lake Shore, my stomach knotted in a ball. For all the reassurances I had given Jimmy, I wasn't sure I would be able to find anything out. By giving him to Laura, I may have only been delaying the inevitable.

At least he would spend the hot days of the summer in air-conditioned splendor. I went back to the Grimshaws' apartment, which seemed even hotter than it had before.

Althea was in the kitchen, making a huge bowl of macaroni salad for dinner. Usually she tried to cook before the heat of the day, but she'd had to take their youngest daughter to a swim meet at the local pool. The television was blaring, a special report about a shooting near Lincoln Park. Antiwar protectors had been gathering in the park all week, alarming the mayor and tingeing convention preparations with an air of panic.

Althea looked as wilted as I felt. Sweat dappled her face and marked the back of her cotton sundress. She was heavier than she had been when Franklin met her, but the weight gave her a solidness she had lacked in those days. If anything, she was prettier now than she had been fifteen years ago.

"Thought you had to work," she said.

"I do." I went to the refrigerator, opened it, and poured myself some of Althea's special homemade lemonade. After the morning I'd had, I deserved it.

"You want some salad? I don't think there'll be much left when you get home tonight."

I smiled. I had missed lunch. "A little would be nice."

She dished some into a bowl for me, and then went back to her preparations. Apparently the salad wasn't the only thing on the menu. She was cleaning raspberries, which either meant ice cream or pie for dessert.

I took the bowl and lemonade to the table.

"What's got you so down?" she asked.

I hadn't told Franklin much about the reasons Jimmy and I were in Chicago, and I hadn't told Althea anything at all. I didn't want them to be implicated more than they were. I knew that they suspected I wanted more than a job and a place to live and they never did question me about Jimmy, although I heard from one of the kids that they believed he was mine and I had taken him from his real mother. I let all that stand.

"Listen, Althea," I said. "Jimmy's not going to be home for a couple of nights."

"Oh?" She shut off the water in the kitchen sink, and turned to me, her hands stained red with raspberry juice.

"I have him staying with a friend."

"Is he in trouble?" She wiped off her hands on a kitchen towel, then set it on the countertop beside the empty berry bowl.

"No. But Marvella saw some suspicious characters around, and I'm not taking any chances."

Althea came to the table. She sat across from me. "Someone after that boy?"

"Why? Has someone been asking about him?"

She shook her head. "Just seems that way. You're protective of him, Smokey. I never seen you be protective before."

"He matters to me, Althea."

She chuckled. "There'd be something wrong with you if he didn't."

I dug into the salad. Mayonnaise, macaroni, peas, radishes, some dill, and a little bit of leftover chicken. The macaroni was still warm, but that didn't diminish the flavor at all.

"Have you noticed anything odd lately?" I asked her.

"There's been some people in the neighborhood who don't belong." She folded her arms together as if the conversation made her uncomfortable.

"White folks?"

"And a few black folks," she said. "But they look official, you know?"

I did know. The best undercover cops were hard to spot, but the weekenders made errors, subtle ones, but ones that said they didn't fit. "Any around me?"

"No. Why?"

I sighed and pushed away the empty bowl. I'd eaten faster than I'd expected. I'd been hungry and hadn't even realized it. "There are some things I don't want to tell you, Althea. But if there's a safe place you can take the kids, especially the boys, while the convention's on, you should probably do that."

She studied me for a moment. She didn't yell at me for bringing something dangerous into her home, and she didn't ask me why I thought she should get her children out of here, although I could see that she wanted to. She'd been around long enough to know that sometimes having information was dangerous in and of itself.

"I been planning to see my folks before school starts. They're up in Milwaukee. Think I'll give them a call." She paused, measuring me. "Don't think Franklin can get away, though."

"I'm not worried about Franklin," I said. "It's the boys. They need to get out of here for a while."

She nodded. "What about you, Smokey? You gonna be leaving us?"

"If you want me to," I said.

"You're welcome to stay here as long as you need to."

I sipped my lemonade. It was tart and good. "Even though I'm causing problems."

She put her hand on my arm. "You're a good man, Smokey Dalton, and I know things aren't always what they seem. I also know that boy seen something awful. Even if he wasn't having screaming nightmares, you can see it in his eyes. He's lucky to have you, and I know that while we're all gone, you'll take care of whatever it is in whatever way you need to do it."

I put my hand over hers. "I hope your faith in me is justified."

"It's not faith, Smokey. It's knowledge. And it's rock solid, just like you are." She slipped her hand from beneath mine, and stood, going back to the sink. "I'm making pie tonight. You and Franklin be sure to eat all the leftovers, you hear?"

"I doubt they'll be any leftovers." Then I went into the

kitchen and hugged her from behind. "Thanks, Althea. For everything."

She leaned the back of her head against my shoulder. "You make sure that boy's all right, and we'll stay square."

"I'll do my best."

"Then that's all we can ask for. The best is all we can do."

Normally, I would take the "L" to work, but that day I decided to drive. It was hard to know if you were being tailed on the "L," and besides, I wanted the freedom to investigate when my shift was over. I also had to take Jimmy's clothes to Laura's. There was no way I was going to walk in that neighborhood at night.

I'd been working at the Conrad Hilton Hotel as a security guard for more than two months now. I needed a regular paycheck. I'd worked as an unlicensed detective in Memphis—describing my work as odd jobs to the occasional white person who asked—and I had a regular stable of customers, most of whom were probably quite angry at me for disappearing.

Moving that sort of business to a town where I knew almost no one and understood less than the greenest local was impossible. Not to mention the fact that I wasn't sure how long we'd be here.

Which meant I needed a paycheck. I applied for jobs. I probably wouldn't have gotten anything if it weren't for Franklin and a few of his friends. They'd offered to be listed as references. I wanted to work in the black community, but most of the jobs there were patronage jobs, just like they were everywhere else in Chicago. Only in the community itself, the patron wasn't Mayor Daley, it was the head of the neighborhood, whoever that might be. And I didn't know anyone well enough to qualify for those jobs.

So I had to look elsewhere. Most of the detective agencies

in town were white owned, and all required a license. Security guard positions paid well, and often hired based on size, always an advantage for me. On Franklin's suggestion, I used his last name and the recommendations from his friends ensured that no one checked my identification.

Thanks to all that patronage, I got the Hilton job on my first interview. I kept it because of my detecting skills.

The hotel employed only a handful of black security guards. Mostly we had the invisible shifts, from late evening to early morning. I had been moved to afternoons and evenings after I'd solved some thefts that had been plaguing the hotel for more than six months.

A white guard would have been promoted, maybe given a raise, and certainly would have gotten some sort of public recognition. Me, all I got was respect. And considering how much that had been lacking earlier, respect was a considerable reward.

I also got a parking voucher, to be used sparingly, and I got taken off job probation, which meant I was entitled to company benefits, such as they were for a first-year employee. Mostly, it amounted to a few sick days and paid holidays. No vacation time. I wouldn't get that for five years.

The idea of staying at a job for five years terrified me. In the space of a summer, I had become someone I didn't recognize, someone who cared about the respect of white people, who wanted a parking voucher, and who looked forward to the day when he got a week's paid vacation.

I parked the car in the underground lot, in the far back section reserved for low-level Hilton employees. The garage was humid and damp, smelling of gasoline and mold. My footsteps echoed as I walked toward the stairs.

I was completely alone. So far as I could tell, no one was following me. But I'd give it another day or two, just to make sure.

I was getting to my job nearly an hour early. The staff had called a meeting. Anyone who missed it would be fired, no exceptions.

It annoyed me that I couldn't come and go as I pleased. I was itching to do some investigating, and instead, I had to sit in a stuffy room, listening to someone talk about procedures that seemed to be designed to irritate instead of accomplish something worthwhile.

I entered the hotel through the employee entrance. Employee areas of hotels, I'd learned, were not decorated. The concrete walls remained their ugly gray; the floor was covered in ancient linoleum. The employees had their own cafeteria, where we got leftover food from the dining rooms as well as some unpleasant casserole mixed up especially for us; a break room, which was the only place employee smoking was allowed; and locker rooms, so that we wouldn't be seen on the street in our all-important uniforms.

The men's locker room was near the laundry, so the air smelled of dryers and lint, and was even more humid than it was anywhere else in Chicago. The floor shuddered from the vibration of dozens of industrial-strength dryers rotating all at once, and the walls were wet with condensation. The very unpleasantness of the area made it impossible to linger, even if I had been inclined, which I wasn't.

Every guard was assigned two uniforms. The uniforms had numbers on them and were hung in rows near the locker room doors. After completing a shift, we were supposed to give our uniforms to laundry and dry cleaning where they'd be cleaned and pressed and hung for the new day. The only thing we were responsible for was our shoes—expensive shoes that had to be polished perfectly or we'd be fired.

There were many firing offenses at this job. So far, I'd managed to dodge all of them.

I changed out of my street clothes, and went to the staff

lounge—usually off limits for such lowly employees as me—for the meeting.

The room was smaller than I expected it to be. Metal folding chairs, lined up in rows, didn't help the impression of size. Someone had placed a portable chalkboard up front along with a podium that seemed too big for the room. Most of the chairs were full. I slipped into one in the back, crossed my arms, and waited.

It didn't take long. Promptly at three o'clock a group of men in suits entered. They all wore gold Hilton name badges, like I did. I sighed and settled in, and then froze.

Following the Hilton employees were more men in suits, only these guys looked like official government employees, probably FBI. Althea was right—white or black, there was a look to these men that wasn't quite the same as the rest of us, as if they wore armor under their clothes. Something in their faces brooked no questions, and their eyes seemed dead.

Behind them were four Chicago cops in uniform. They were laughing and joking with each other, which didn't make me any calmer.

"This is a final formal training session for the Democratic National Convention," said Walt Kotlarz. He was my overall supervisor, solid, decent in a midwestern sort of way. He'd insulted me half a dozen times while I'd been working for him, but all of the insults were unintentional. In fact, if I had pointed them out to him, he would have been appalled.

He was clinging to the podium as if it were his lifeline. Apparently Kotlarz wasn't used to speaking before a group.

"In previous meetings, we established behavior for the upcoming convention. Those plans will remain in place. However, due to the growing number of young people and agitators in Lincoln Park, the city has asked us to make other changes. And we've received some involvement from the federal government as well."

I stiffened.

"Since many of the delegates and all of the candidates will be staying here, we've been assigned an extra contingent of Chicago police officers who will help with security—"

I cursed silently.

"—but we have expectations of the rest of you as well." He glanced over his shoulder. "Let me let turn this over to Roy Gaines. He's with the United States Secret Service."

Murmurs ran through the group. We had been warned that there would be Secret Service in the hotel, but we had been told that they would handle the candidates. We would be responsible for the rest of the guests.

Apparently that plan had changed.

Gaines, a slender, balding man, stepped up to the podium, but didn't touch it. He wore a loose suit coat that probably hid a weapon and his dark gaze missed nothing. It met mine for a moment, and I had to will myself not to look away.

"After the assassination of Dr. Martin Luther King, Jr., the president asked Congress to authorize Secret Service protection for all presidential and vice-presidential candidates." Gaines paused. "Congress did not take action until after Senator Robert F. Kennedy was assassinated in June. Senator Kennedy, if you'll recall, was shot in the kitchen of Ambassador Hotel, an upscale establishment not unlike this one."

He had our attention. No one fidgeted, and the room was silent.

"The kitchen was an unsecured area. A dozen kitchen employees stood around, waiting to see the famous man. Hotels are places where strangers gather. Not even hotel employees know each other. Sirhan Sirhan stood in that kitchen along with everyone else. No one knew him. No one checked him for weapons. And when he pulled a gun, everyone was surprised."

A chill ran through me.

"The candidate went down instantly, and even though the gunman was subdued at the scene, the damage was done. Kennedy died the next day."

"Jeez," murmured the guy next to me. Apparently he was having the same thought I was. We'd known how Kennedy died. We'd seen the photos, heard the recordings. We followed the press coverage in shock like everyone else.

And while we knew it had happened in a hotel, we hadn't understood what that meant for us. I hadn't thought about it at all. I knew the Democrats were coming to Chicago, but I hadn't been paying a lot of attention. I had other things on my mind.

"The highest level of security will run through us," Gaines said. "Most of your dealings will be with the Chicago Police Department. We are expecting a lot of trouble. There have been plans to disrupt this convention since December. Groups like the Yippies have made a national crusade of coming to Chicago at the end of August."

The man in front of me shifted in his chair, hands clenching. Two of the official men in suits stared at him. No one else seemed to notice the movement.

"A young man was shot this afternoon near Lincoln Park. He was identified as a Yippie. He fired at police with a thirty-two. They returned fire. He died at the scene."

Gaines spoke of this as dispassionately as he spoke of Kennedy's death. Behind me, someone exhaled loudly.

"We do not expect more shootings, but we must be prepared for them. We've heard reports from various intelligence-gathering sources that weapons have been sent to Chicago to be used to assassinate presidential candidates.

We've also heard that black militants plan to lay siege to the city. Hundreds of thousands of protestors are expected. They've been applying for marching permits, which have been and will continue to be denied by the city."

My own tension grew. I knew we were only hearing a miniscule amount of the information that the Secret Service had.

"As I said, hotels are particularly vulnerable. We do not want to invade the privacy of guests, but we will need to keep a close watch on anyone suspicious, especially in the employee sections of the hotel, the out-of-the way byways, and the service elevators."

Finally he leaned on the podium as if he were trying to draw us closer to him.

"Your job as hotel security will be to report anything out of the ordinary, escort unwelcome individuals out of the hotel, and to keep an eye out for things that seem abnormal."

I suppressed a sigh. In my short two months here, I'd noted nothing normal about day-to-day operations. Life at the hotel constantly shifted in response to the stream of guests that came through it.

"We've already gone through your ranks and cleared out the questionable employees," Gaines said.

I felt another chill. I'd been investigated and I hadn't even known it. Apparently they hadn't investigated too deeply. Probably just double-checked references and addresses. And then they probably fired the troublemakers. It was a good thing I had lain low, and a good thing the management liked me. Otherwise I would have been one of the people dismissed.

"The rest of you," he said, "will be placed on twelve-hour shifts starting Sunday. In the interim, those of you who have not gone to the riot-training sessions must report tomorrow afternoon. We do expect crowd-control problems, and we will need your help handling that if it extends inside the hotel."

I let that last sentence reverberate through my brain. In other words, he expected protestors to charge the hotel and perhaps get inside. Now I was more relieved than ever that Jimmy was out of the apartment. I wouldn't have been able to spend time with him even if I wanted to—not and keep my precious job.

At least I'd already gone to the riot-training session. It had been ridiculous. I could have done a better job. In fact, I *had* done better in Memphis—and even that hadn't prevented surprises.

One of the guards raised his hand. Gaines nodded at him.

"Will we be assigned weapons?" he asked.

A cop rolled his eyes, but Gaines didn't seem surprised. "For the most part, you'll follow standard hotel procedure, which means you will not have weapons. There are ways to subdue violent offenders quickly and efficiently. That's part of what you'll learn in your riot-training session."

Maybe it wouldn't be as bad as Gaines was making it sound. After all, it was his job to prepare us. There had been riots at the Republican convention in Miami, but they had been restricted to Libertyville, the black area. They never got closer than a mile away from the convention hall and never hit the hotels.

Chicago was doing everything it could to prevent riots in the Black Belt. And I didn't really see the same kind of black unrest focused at the Democrats. The Republicans were perceived as not only lily white but as unsympathetic to civil rights. The Party of Lincoln had stopped caring about the black man more than fifty years ago.

The Democrats had become our party, and while we did need to make them aware of the problems within our communities, there didn't seem to be the same sort of agitation about it as there was with the Republicans.

No, Gaines and his companions were more afraid of the Yippies and the hippies, people who could get into this hotel easily because they were white and looked like they belonged—if, of course, they dressed the part.

The problem was, because of my skin color, I'd have trouble stopping them. But I wasn't about to say that to anyone.

"We have a new work schedule posted in the break room," Gaines said. "Anyone who has questions should see his immediate supervisor. Any questions?"

The questions mostly reiterated the points Gaines had made earlier. If he had thought us the weak links in his little army before he came into the room, he had to be convinced of it now.

For the first half of my shift, I was assigned lobby detail. It consisted of standing in one spot and watching the arrivals. The hotel was beginning to take on its convention persona. The advance men had arrived a few days ago, but the rest of each candidate's staff stood in line waiting to check in, their boxes of posters, buttons, and campaign hats kept near their feet.

People greeted each other noisily, shook hands, and made false-sounding jibes about their opposition's chances. The media had started to arrive as well—mostly the television support staff, gofers, research assistants, electricians. Daley had made it impossible for the TV crews to do live coverage throughout the city, so the three networks brought in vans, trailers, and large teams to coordinate coverage. Most stayed at the hotel, and most checked in that day.

At the end of our meeting, we'd been briefed on the various kinds of passes—everyone from press to the delegates had to wear passes at all times—and we were assigned passes of our own. The garages and doors would be guarded. In order to enter, we had show that we had official reason. Since our uniforms were inside, the pass provided access.

I hated the rules almost as much as I hated standing in one spot. The entrance to the hotel was grand and ornate—columns that went up three stories, stairs winding in two different directions, ballrooms off each, and a ten-foot-tall marble clock in the middle of the floor.

But the lobby, which was inside double doors on the first floor, was square and low ceilinged. A bank of elevators stood on the west wall, and people gathered in front of them, carrying on long conversations before heading to the Haymarket Lounge, the hotel bar. By the end of my shift, the cigarette smoke was so thick, I could barely see the registration desk.

I was happier to leave than I usually was. I grabbed a box with a Hilton label as I walked out the employee exit, and placed Jimmy's clothes in it when I reached the car. If anyone looked, it would seem like I was making a late-night delivery for the hotel.

No one followed me to Laura's. I left the clothes at the security desk as I had promised, acting as if it were a delivery too. Until I knew what was going on, the less I stopped here, the safer Jimmy would be.

And Laura as well.

I returned to the apartment at one-thirty. Franklin was still awake. He wore a loose cotton robe over a pair of shorts, the robe open, revealing his no-longer-firm stomach. His hair was thinning on top. We were all getting older. Sometimes I didn't notice it in myself, just in my friends.

He sat at the kitchen table, law books open before him, a legal pad underneath the lamp he had moved from one of the end tables. A plate covered with the remains of raspberry pie teetered precariously off a three-ring binder.

Being in air-conditioning all evening made the apartment

seem even hotter than it was. The two big fans the Grimshaws owned were in the living room, one blowing the inside hot air out through the fire escape window, and the other trained on Franklin. They didn't seem to be making much of a difference.

"You shook up Althea real good," Franklin said.

I opened the refrigerator and took out the last of the lemonade. "I didn't mean to."

"I've never seen her pack and leave so fast."

There was no ice left in the trays. I took them out of the freezer and poured water on them, then put them back inside.

"You want to tell me what this is all about?" Franklin asked.

"No," I said.

"Smokey, I knew you and the boy were in trouble. That was obvious when you called me from Wilmette. It would take a threat of death to get you out of Memphis. Which is what this is all about, right? Someone's after you?"

There was one piece of pie left, and even though I was hungry, I didn't feel entitled to it. I sat down at the table.

"This isn't something you want to know, Franklin."

"I want to know why my family's spending the next two weeks in Milwaukee."

I sipped. The lemonade was sweeter toward the bottom, where the sugar had settled in the pitcher. "If you want me to move, I will. I was just afraid that even if I vacated your apartment, you might still have problems."

"I'm not asking you to move, Smokey. I'm asking you to talk to me."

I sighed.

"I'll keep my own counsel," he said. "I won't tell Althea or anyone else if that's what's bothering you. And you know you can trust me."

Yes, I did. If I hadn't known that, I wouldn't have come to him in the first place.

I got up and took that last piece of pie. Then I told him the entire story.

The night Martin died, I had been in my offices on Beale Street, cleaning up client files, doing final billings, and tending to work I had neglected the previous few weeks. Laura had just left, although I didn't tell Franklin that. Jimmy was living with a foster family. His foster mother called to tell me that he was missing. He'd been disappearing a lot, searching for his older brother, who was mixed up in troubles of his own.

I had a hunch I knew where Jimmy was—or at least the places he might be. I had made the mistake of telling him where I had last seen his brother. Jimmy had been known to trail after Joe. I told Jimmy's foster mother I'd do what I could, when I heard shouts from the street below.

The shouts had a strange quality to them. I told Jimmy's foster mother I'd get back to her, then I hung up and went to the window.

The street was full of people. It had been empty when I watched Laura cross. Now crowds covered the sidewalks. Some people had run into the middle of the road. They were crying and shouting and holding each other.

Something was very wrong.

I hurried out of my office to the street below. I had to push my way through the crowd. When I asked what was going on, a woman said, "They say Dr. King was shot down at the Lorraine."

"Who says?"

"Everybody. They been running through the street, shouting it."

The Lorraine Motel was only a few blocks away, but I

hadn't heard anything. I had been preoccupied with my phone call.

While Martin was being shot.

I didn't even thank her. I ran toward the Lorraine Motel. I wasn't the only one running. Others were heading in the same direction, as if they were drawn by the news or as if their disbelief had forced them to see if what they had heard was true.

Sirens filled the neighborhood and the closer I got the more police officers I saw. When I reached Mulberry Street, where the motel was, I was shocked to find it already blocked off.

The ambulance was just leaving the motel as I arrived, yet there were dozens of police officers on the street. Firemen from the nearby station were hauling barricades and placing them on side roads.

Cops were all over the hotel's balcony, and I recognized some of Martin's lieutenants, talking to them, looking stunned.

That was when a white cop grabbed my arm.

"This area's restricted," he said.

I couldn't believe what I had heard and there was too much chaos around me. I wanted to confirm the story.

"Who was shot?" I asked.

"King." The cop said Martin's name as if he'd found it offensive.

"Did you get the shooter?"

"You have to leave," the officer said, his grip tightening.

More cops had arrived. A lot of them were standing around. A few were removing bystanders.

Two cops had hold of a little boy and were trying to force him into a squad car.

The boy was black. He looked familiar.

It was Jimmy.

He was screaming and struggling as if he was afraid he was going to be killed. The cops were having trouble holding him. They called for backup.

I had to get to him, but I couldn't let the cop who was holding me know what I was doing.

"Just let go of me and I'll walk out of here," I said to the cop.

I must have said it with enough force because he dropped my arm. I started to turn to throw him off, make him believe I was leaving the restricted area. Then I switched directions and ran toward Jimmy.

Cops tried to stop me, but I managed to dodge them. I reached Jimmy fast, and pulled the cops off him, elbowing one cop in the stomach and pushing the other away.

A third came toward me, and I kicked him before he could get close. The driver of the squad started to get out of the car, but by then, I had Jimmy's arm.

With the help of the crowd, I got him out of there and to my house. I made sure we weren't followed. After we got inside, he told me what happened.

He had gone to the Canipe Amusement Company because I had seen his brother there a few days before. Jimmy's brother wasn't in Canipe, so Jimmy had gone to a nearby vacant lot to wait. The lot was across from the Lorraine Motel. Some vagrants sitting on a cardboard box beneath a low-rent apartment complex pointed out Martin Luther King standing on the hotel balcony. Jimmy looked, curious to see such a famous man.

Then Jimmy heard a shot behind him, and Martin collapsed. A moment later, a man carrying a rifle ran past Jimmy, taking his gun apart. He threw part of the gun under a bush and put the rest in his jacket. Then he jumped onto the street and started to walk as if nothing had happened.

Jimmy understood what he saw and for the first time in his life, he went to the authorities for help. Once he got inside the nearby fire station, he told some cops that he had seen the shooter.

They pulled Jimmy into a corner and asked him what he saw, where he lived, and who he was. He answered all their questions, but wondered why no one was going after the guy with the gun. Eventually, more cops came into the building. He heard one of the firemen tell them that Jimmy had seen something he shouldn't have. Before Jimmy could run, the cops grabbed him, and tried to force him into a squad car.

That was when I had arrived.

His story had startled me but didn't surprise me. There had been too many cops on the scene too soon after the shooting and most of the cops hadn't seemed upset. The hell of it was that I didn't think the Memphis cops were acting alone. The Memphis chief of police had once worked for the FBI and had maintained his ties. He had removed Martin's usual security detail, and replaced it with a detail of his own, a detail that had disappeared just before the shooting. There were other discrepancies—including the fact that the description of the shooter—James Earl Ray, not the man Jimmy had seen—was released to the news media minutes before Martin was shot.

Even if I hadn't believed Jimmy when he told me the story, I would have believed him soon after. Not an hour after we escaped Mulberry Street, the police showed up at Jimmy's foster home. They spent the night searching for Jimmy more vigorously than they searched for James Earl Ray—or any other shooter.

We'd barely gotten out of Memphis in time.

"There's FBI all over town," Franklin said when I was done. He wasn't surprised by the story. Not many black folks would be. We'd all had our run-ins with white authority. We knew how it could be.

"I know there's FBI," I said. "And Marvella saw someone tailing me."

Franklin leaned back in his chair. "They got pictures of Jimmy?"

"No. Jimmy didn't have much of a family. His mother abandoned them in December, and he and his brother got evicted in March. Jimmy was able to salvage a few things, but I doubt there were any pictures in the belongings." I got up, rinsed out my lemonade glass, and filled it with water. "I don't think the authorities know much more than the fact that he's with me."

"They don't know he's in Chicago?"

"I was as careful as I can be. Cash only, fake names at motels. We switched cars before we left, and then I bought that Impala with cash, using a false name. I'm not on your lease here, everyone who doesn't know me calls me Bill, and they all think Jimmy's last name is Grimshaw. Besides, he blends in with your family. Not too many people know he's mine."

"Seems to me you did all you can."

"I don't know." I drank the water down, but it wasn't enough to cool me off. "I probably should have changed our names and gone far away, like L.A. or San Francisco. Started all over. This is the halfway measure, Franklin. I was hoping we could go back to Memphis someday."

He folded his hands on top of his law books. I had no idea if he'd make a good lawyer, but he'd be a good judge. "After all this?"

"At first, I thought the truth would come out. There's too many people involved to keep it hidden. And maybe it would have, if Bobby hadn't died. But with that shiny Kennedy name, and the fact he was an anointed white man, well, no one seems to think of Martin much anymore— except as a martyr and a political tool."

"Cynic."

"Don't you agree?"

Franklin's smile was rueful. "I didn't say you were wrong. Just a cynic."

"So you understand why I wanted the kids out of here."

"I appreciate precautions, Smokey." His gaze met mine. "So, now what do we do to find out who's following you?"

"I have a few ideas," I said. "It won't be easy."

"I know that," Franklin said. "But white guys stand out down here and—"

"We're not looking for a white man, Franklin. We're looking for a black man."

His eyes narrowed. "Come on, Smoke. None of our people would be involved in Dr. King's assassination."

I stared at him for a long moment.

His frown deepened. "You believe this."

"Ask Marvella. The man she saw tailing me was black."

Franklin pushed his chair away from the table. "Why would anyone do this?"

I shrugged. I didn't entirely understand it either. "A lot of blacks worked undercover for the FBI in Mississippi in '64."

"I'm sure they had to," Franklin said. "When a person's family is threatened—"

"No, Franklin." My voice was soft. "A lot of black people came in from the North as undercover operators. The practice hasn't stopped. I ran into a guy in Memphis who was pretending to be a Panther. He got the street gangs to incite the riot during Martin's last march."

"How do you know he was undercover? The Panthers don't believe in Martin's teachings. Maybe he—"

"I'd known him for a long time," I said. "He was with army intelligence when I saw him last."

That made Franklin stop. "Army intelligence?"

I nodded. "He enjoyed that work too. He wasn't the kind of man who'd give it up."

Franklin stared at me.

"The army gave these guys a place to belong. They continued to work for the government after they retired. They felt that they had pulled themselves up by their bootstraps, so everyone else should too. They call fighting for equal rights whining."

Franklin shook his head. "I can't picture it, Smokey. I mean, they live it. They should know."

"Come on, Franklin," I said. "You've met men like that. I'm sure Mayor Daley has a few black toadies on the payroll."

"Yeah," Franklin said after a moment. "Oreos."

I grinned. I hadn't heard the term before, but it fit. Black on the outside, white on the inside.

"Well, we got one after me," I said. "And we have to find a way to stop him."

FIVE

Franklin and I stayed up for several more hours, raiding the refrigerator and talking. It was possible, even likely, that the shadow Marvella had seen hadn't been mine. Franklin believed she thought the tail was after me because I was new in the neighborhood, and an unknown factor.

I wondered if Marvella's cop cousin had asked her to lie to me about the shadow, just to make sure I wasn't some kind of unknown trouble. Franklin admitted that might be a possibility as well.

We made a list of the people in the building that the shadow might actually be tailing. At least one member of the Blackstone Rangers, the largest street gang in the city, lived here. His grandmother had an apartment a floor above ours. I'd seen him a few times and he looked surprisingly harmless.

Franklin said that the man in the attic apartment, a teacher at the local high school, was becoming active in the Black Panthers, the California Black Power group that had spread nationwide in the last year. Chicago had only recently established a branch and, Franklin said, it hadn't been on very fertile soul. There were other Black Power advocates in the neighborhood, most of them Black Muslims who had followed Elijah Muhammad or were devotees of Malcolm X, who had been assassinated three years before.

We decided, as dawn inched closer, that Franklin would discreetly canvass the neighbors—most of whom were his friends—to see if any of them had seen anything out of the ordinary. I would talk to Marvella and find out exactly what she had seen.

And then we would go from there.

It was daylight when Franklin went to his room. I put new sheets on one of the twin beds in the boys' room, and lay down there, the first real bed I'd been on in months. But I couldn't shut off my mind.

I worried about Jimmy and Laura, and Franklin's entire family. Maybe the next best step for me was exactly what I had told Franklin: get a new name and a new life, start over far away, with Jimmy posing as my son.

I supposed it might even be logical for me to send Jimmy to a real family, and me to a city I'd never been in before. But I couldn't do that.

The main reason, of course, was Jimmy. He'd never known his father, been abandoned by his mother and brother, and then lost his best hope for a real family when he saw Martin's killers. I was the only constant in his life, and I felt guilty for leaving him with Laura. The boy needed someone to be there for him. I had to be that someone.

But there was more to it than that. When I was a boy, my parents had been lynched. I was sent to my uncle's family, who couldn't deal with me, and then adopted by a couple I barely knew. They changed my name from Billy Taylor to Billy Dalton, then nicknamed me Smokey. They rarely referred to my past.

I knew how devastating it was to be cut off from everyone

and everything familiar, how difficult it was to go through life without acknowledging the events that formed you. I didn't want any of that for Jimmy. I'd do everything I could to prevent it.

I had to find a solution that allowed us to remain together and that kept us both safe. I wasn't sure that was possible in Chicago, but I had to try. I had to give it my best.

Marvella lived alone in a small one-bedroom apartment across the hall from ours. Apparently she had lived there through two husbands and several jobs. She was as much a part of the building as the walls.

I had never been inside before. The living room had a high ceiling—a feature of most of the apartments in this part of the city, and a huge bay window that overlooked the backyard. A window seat, covered with plants that trailed to the hardwood floor, circled around the window.

The kitchen was small, an add-on like Franklin's. Marvella kept it clean. The entire apartment was decorated in oranges, browns, and reds, with striking wooden sculptures of faces that looked vaguely familiar to me. As I studied them from the couch, I realized that most of them looked like Marvella.

She pulled over one of her kitchen chairs, and sat on it backward, resting her chin on the chair's metal back. She wore tight red shorts that accented her legs, no shoes, and a white tube top that set off her skin. On her left arm, she wore thick wooden bracelets that also had an African look to them.

She had just given me a root beer in a brown glass that matched the rest of the room. "You sure I can't make you some lunch?"

I shook my head. I wanted to be out of the apartment as quickly as I could. "I'm meeting a friend." Franklin. We were going to prepare notes.

Marvella tilted her head. Her dark eyes missed nothing. "This isn't social, is it?"

"No," I said. "I wanted to talk with you about what you saw."

"That man?"

"You've seen him again?"

She shook her head. Strands of hair clung to the nape of her neck. Her apartment was cooler than the Grimshaws' but it was still hot.

"What did you see?"

She frowned. "He was about a block away. That day you talked with the boys playing in the water pouring out of the fire hydrants, he watched the entire time. Arms crossed, leaning back, just staring, like that was the most interesting thing he'd ever seen."

I glanced at her bay window, with its view of the backyard. The yard wasn't much, mostly brown dirt and sickly trees due to the heat of the summer. The hydrants were in front. Not even her bedroom window would have a view of the street.

She saw my glance, and flushed. "I was coming back from the store when I saw him. I remembered what my cousin told me. I wanted to see who this guy was looking at. He was looking at you."

"You're sure of it?"

She nodded.

"Have you seen him since?"

She shook her head. Her eyes seemed wider than before, as if she were finally realizing that I took this entire matter very seriously.

"Can you describe him?"

"Tall as you. Thinner, maybe. Had a 'fro, which threw me. I didn't think cops had 'fros."

Most of them didn't, but undercover cops often looked different from the others. "What about his face?"

"Couldn't see that real clear."

"Then what was it about him that made you notice him?"

A frown creased her brow. She closed her eyes for a moment, as she tried to remember. I studied her. She was certainly the most beautiful woman I had seen in years. Maybe ever. And I felt no attraction to her. If anything, I found myself thinking of Laura, and wondering how she and Jimmy were faring. I'd have to call them when I was through here.

"He didn't move." She opened her eyes and found me staring at her. A faint smile touched her lips. "I thought he was some kind of statue at first."

"How'd you know he wasn't?"

"A statue? He nodded to me."

"I thought you watched him."

"That was after. I was going to the store when I first saw him. He was still there when I got out. I just stood back for a while. He didn't see me. He was concentrating on you."

"You're sure it was me? Not the building? Not one of the boys?" I made sure that last question sounded no different from the others. I didn't want her to know that Jimmy was a possible target.

"No," she said. "You went to your car and got a bag out of it. He was looking at you."

I finally remembered which day she meant. Tuesday, just a few days before. I had bought squirt guns for Jimmy and the boys. I gave them out while they were playing in the water. When I went to the car to get them, I had a feeling that I wasn't alone. But I had canvassed the neighborhood and seen nothing.

Yet Marvella and this man had been watching me. It worried me that I missed both of them.

"Where was he exactly?"

"You know that building they're rehabbing at the end of the block?"

I did. There were a number of abandoned buildings near here. Only one was being restored kitty-corner from the apartment. Anyone standing there would have had a good view of our front lawn.

"He was in the doorway, just under the awning. In the shade. If I hadn't seen him on the way there, I wouldn't've known he was there."

I'd looked directly at him and I hadn't seen him. A shiver ran down my back. He was good.

"Where were you?"

"About a half a block east. I sat on one of the stoops and ate some strawberries while I kept an eye on him."

I had seen her. She had smiled at me. I had waved a hand in greeting, and had assumed that she had been the one watching me. Then I had turned my back on the person who really had been.

She peered at me. "It bothers you, don't it, that you didn't see him?"

"Yeah." I took a sip from the root beer. It was warm.

She got up and came over to the couch. She sat so close to me that I could smell her faint floral perfume. "What're you running from, Bill?"

I rolled the root beer glass in my hands. I supposed it was obvious that I didn't belong, that things made me uneasy. But I didn't like that she had seen me clearly.

"That's not your real name, is it?" she asked.

"It's my name," I said softly.

"You don't like it, though." She was too perceptive by half. "You wince whenever I say it."

I set the root beer down. "I feel like I'm suddenly talking to your cousin the cop."

She was silent. I looked up at her. A chill ran down my back.

"He asked you to question me, didn't he?"

She shrugged, a careless female gesture that implied she was talking of unimportant things. "In June."

"You've been spying on me since June?"

She laughed, that open throaty sound that I had always admired about her. "Of course I have, Bill. A good-looking single man across the hall? I've watched you from the moment you moved in."

"That's not what I meant, Marvella."

Her gaze was steady. I could see her pulse beat a small rhythm in a vein in her throat. "He heard me talk about you and your boy and that you were from Tennessee. He said the station got some weird wanted notice from the FBI for a man and a boy just after Dr. King died. He said I was to ask you a few things."

The muscles in my back and shoulder were rigid. "Did you ask those things?"

"Not till now." She opened her hands. "My grandmother lives in Mississippi. My parents moved here after the war. I seen what it's like down there. If the FBI wants a black man and his son, I gotta be suspicious—of the government."

"But your cousin is a cop."

She nodded. "He's a good one, too. He's proud of what he does. But it's what he does, Bill, not what I do."

"So why ask at all?"

She put her hands on her knees. I could sense her discomfort. She clearly wasn't in situations like this often. "Because that man was watching you. My cousin said that outside agitators got followed, but this looked like something else. Then there was that wanted information." She took a deep breath, as if she were steeling herself. "I like you, Bill. I don't want to be part of something that happens to you. I thought it would be better if I warned you."

"So that I'd come and have a root beer with you?" I said

as lightly as I could. I had already made this too big a deal, I could see that now. I had to change it, if possible.

She licked her lower lip, and then her gaze fell on mine. "Or kiss me."

I reached out and cupped my right hand against her cheek. Her skin was warm and soft. "You don't know me, Marvella."

She leaned into me. "Since when do you need to know someone to kiss them?"

The odd thing was that I wasn't really tempted. I thought of kissing her the way I weighed other options—the political benefits, the risks, the possibilities. Attraction didn't seem to be part of the package. Friendship did, though.

I leaned in, meaning to kiss her the way I hadn't kissed a woman since Laura in Memphis. Instead, my lips found Marvella's cheek. Even that felt like a betrayal.

She bowed her head. "You're married, aren't you?"

If only it were that simple. "Involved." I wasn't sure if it was a lie or not.

"She's not here, though."

"No."

"What kind of woman leaves a man alone for months?"

The trustworthy kind. The one who was, even as we spoke, guarding a child with her life.

"Marvella," I said softly, "you're probably the most beautiful woman I've ever seen."

She glanced at the sculptures. Obviously their creator had told her the same thing. "But?"

"No buts. You've done me a great kindness. I owe you."

"I gave you a way to pay me."

"I don't pay like that." I paused, my hand still on her warm skin. "But I do return favors. And I never forget one."

She took my hand away from her cheek. She ran her fingers over mine, stopping at the calluses and scars as if each held special interest for her.

"Maybe there is something you can do for me," she said. I resisted the urge to pull my hand back. "What's that?"

"I heard you caught some thieves at the Hilton."

"Really?"

She nodded. "It was in the *Defender*, did you know that?"

The *Chicago Defender* was the premier black newspaper. I'd even read copies of it when I lived in Memphis.

"No," I said, stifling my annoyance. No matter how hard I tried, I always seemed to get noticed. "I hadn't known that."

"A friend of mine needs some help. Her son is missing."

I let out a small sigh. Maybe Marvella was helping out her cousin the cop. Maybe she was investigating me.

This time, I did pull my hand away—gently, trying to make the movement seem natural. "She should go to the police."

"She has," Marvella said. "They don't care."

"She should go to your cousin."

"She did. He's doing what he can, but he's on a twelve-hour shift for the next two weeks. He won't have time to help her."

"I don't have much time either, Marvella." As the words came out, I regretted them. I wanted to close the door to any possibility at all that I could do detective work. "Besides, I'm a security guard, not a police officer."

"The *Defender* said you did so well that the Hilton staff praised you to the police. A lot of people said you were better than the pros."

I smiled at her. "Don't believe everything you read, Marvella."

"The boys were talking about it the other day. I heard them. Your son says you're some kind of hero."

I'd heard Jimmy fighting with the Grimshaw boys over me once. They thought I was a deadbeat because I didn't have a home or, at that time, a job. Jimmy had used strong language then too. Just because I hadn't heard him defend me since didn't mean the teasing had stopped.

"I was in Korea. That's probably what he means."

"It sounded more serious than that," Marvella said. "He said you saved his life."

"I got him away from a bad home situation, Marvella. That's all."

Her lips thinned. She rubbed her hands over her knees. "You said you owed me a favor, and I'm asking. I have a friend who's frantic because her son is missing. She needs help and she's not getting it. I don't know where else to go."

"There's got to be detectives around here—"

"White ones."

"People in the community, Marvella. I'm going to be on long shifts this week as well. I won't have time—"

"Talk to her, Bill. Please? Or help her find someone to look for her son. She's going crazy."

Missing persons were the worst kind of cases. Most of the missing had disappeared on purpose. The rest were either dead or wanted to die. This one was even worse because I didn't entirely trust Marvella. Her cousin may have set this up so that he could find out if I was one Smokey Dalton, odd-jobs man and sometime detective.

"How old is the boy?" I asked, knowing I was hooked.

"Fourteen," she said. "But he looks older."

"Has he been in trouble before?"

"Not that I know of, but I'm not there all the time. All I know is that she's really worried."

I sighed. "Does she live here?"

"Down the block. Can you see her?"

If I was going to find the boy, I would have to start soon. I only had two free days.

"I suppose," I said.

Marvella smiled at me. "Good," she said. "Let's go."

As I walked with Marvella down the block, I realized this wasn't how I planned to spend my afternoon. I had to check in with Laura, and I was going to have lunch with Franklin. Instead, I was starting on a case, a case I didn't know how to get out of.

Marvella led me into an apartment building much like the one we'd left. Only this one wasn't as well cared for. It hadn't been painted in a long time, and the front stoop sagged. The main door hung crookedly. Any determined thief could have opened it with a crowbar, no matter how many locks were on it. The fact that no one had tried told me how impoverished the residents were.

The door had been left open. I didn't know if that was because it always stood like this or if it were an accident. Marvella opened it as if she came here often.

I followed her inside. The hallway was stiflingly hot. The overhead lights were out, and it was dim even though it was the middle of the day. There were no windows here. I hadn't realized that places this depressing existed only a block away from ours. It showed me again how little I knew about the city.

Marvella went to the end of the hall and knocked on a closed door. She rocked back and forth as she waited, then glanced at me. No one answered.

She knocked again, and finally called, "Grace? I brought some help."

Still no answer. She held up a hand, then disappeared out the back door of the building. I could hear her knocking on windows and calling for her friend.

After a moment, she returned. "I bet she's out looking for him. Can you wait?"

I shook my head. "I have things to do this afternoon."

"I'll see if I can track her down," Marvella said. "I have to work tonight, but I'll leave you a note."

"All right," I said, feeling as awkward as I had earlier. "Maybe she's found him."

"We can only hope," Marvella said.

I left her outside our apartment building, and drove toward Washington Park. I was supposed to meet Franklin at a diner there for lunch. I wanted to arrive early so that I could find a phone and call Laura.

I kept my eyes open for a tail, going down side streets, watching for familiar cars, but I saw nothing. I stopped at one of those shopping centers with a grocery store, a liquor store, a small restaurant, and some insurance offices, parking toward the rear of the lot as if I wanted to protect my car. The shopping center had a pay phone beside the liquor store.

I went inside the booth and sat, dialing Laura's number from memory as I surveyed the parking lot.

No strange cars. No half-familiar faces.

The phone was ringing.

No one drove in, saw me, and turned around. I didn't feel watched.

The ringing continued.

People left the store pushing carts. A man exited the liquor store with a large brown bag under his arm. No one looked at me.

I was beginning to wonder if Laura wasn't home when she picked up.

"Laura?"

"Smokey. Thank God." She sounded relieved.

"Is everything all right?"

"I didn't want to leave the apartment until I'd heard from you. This is all so strange."

"Is Jimmy all right?"

"Let me switch phones."

She set the receiver down. I heard her footsteps fading

away on the hardwood floor, then a click as she picked up another phone. Then that receiver went down, and I heard footsteps again. She hung up the first phone before speaking to me.

"Still there?"

"Wondering why all the subterfuge."

She sighed softly. "He's in his room."

He already had a room. I thought that sad, considering the Grimshaws had him share a room with the boys and his foster mother had had to divide an attic space for him. Laura, who hadn't been expecting him, had enough space to give him a room of his own.

"But it's too close to the phone."

"So what's the problem?" I didn't want problems, not with this arrangement. I had no backup and I was more uneasy than ever after my discussion with Marvella.

"He's quiet, Smokey. He misses you and he's afraid for you." Then she lowered her voice. "We both are."

My heart leaped, and I didn't want it too. Laura and I had moved away from the relationship we had in Memphis—if moved away was the proper term. We seem to have mutually decided not to get involved again.

And we both seemed to be having trouble with that.

"I'm all right," I said.

"But not all right enough to come here?"

"I haven't found anyone yet," I said. "But after the conversations I've had today, I'm pretty convinced someone was watching me. I'm just not sure why. I have to know that before I see him."

"He doesn't want to be here."

"I know."

"He's going to need to see you."

"Can you deal with him? Because if you can't, I'll find somewhere else for him to stay."

The words came out harsher than I expected. There was

a pause before she replied. "He thinks you're never coming back, Smokey."

"He said that?"

"No. He asked me how long I'd keep him here before dumping him on the street."

"Jesus, Laura. What did you say?"

"Two or three days." Her voice was laced with anger. "What did you think I'd say? I'll keep him here forever if I have to. I've never seen a sadder, more frightened child. He's afraid to touch anything. He's afraid of *me*, Smokey, and I haven't done more than feed him, provide a bed, and try to have a conversation."

"He's not used to white people."

"I've gathered that," she said. "He asked me if we all live like this. And I told him that I was one of the lucky ones. Most people, whether they're white, black, or purple, live differently from me."

In spite of myself, I smiled. She probably wouldn't have said that six months ago. Hell, six months ago, she probably wouldn't have understood why I wanted her to take Jimmy in.

"Do you have a problem with that?" Her defensiveness was back. Apparently she took my silence for disapproval.

"No. I think it was the appropriate answer."

"Smokey," she said, "I'm afraid he's going to sneak out. I'm afraid he'll try to find his way back to you."

"All right," I said. "Let's see what we can figure out."

"I've been thinking about this all night," she said. "Why don't you meet us at my father's office tomorrow? It's Saturday. No one should be there. We'll arrive a little after noon, and you can come around three. No one will even know we were in the same office, let alone seeing each other."

I was surprised by the level of planning she'd put into this. "You'd have to wait until long after I left."

"I know."

"What would you do there all afternoon?"

She sighed, "You told me to look into Dad's business, and I haven't done it. I should start."

"And Jimmy?"

"He can read, can't he?"

"Yes."

"Well, then, he'll help me."

"Laura, he's just a boy. An afternoon of—"

"Smokey, please. I'm doing this for him, not for me. I've needed to go to Dad's office all summer and I haven't gone. This is the best solution, I think. Better than a restaurant where we'd be noticed, better than some park or something that's hard to watch."

She was getting good at this. It surprised me, pleased me, and alarmed me all at the same time. But I also felt great relief. She was working hard to keep Jimmy safe.

"Sorry," I said. "You're right. I'll be there around three."

"Good."

"Now, may I speak to him?"

"Sure." She set the phone down before I was able to add anything. I had planned to thank her for all that she was doing, but she didn't give me the chance. Or I hadn't taken the chance.

Everything with her had become so awkward. And I had the odd sense that it was mostly my fault.

After a moment, Jimmy picked up the line. "Smokey?"

"Hey, Jim. Told you I'd call."

"You said you'd come."

"I said I'd come if I could. I still haven't found the guy, but I talked with Marvella this morning. I'm convinced he's real and watching me. I just have to find out why."

"You think it's because of me?"

"I'm hoping that there's another reason."

"But you don't think so?"

"I don't know, Jimmy." A car backfired as it pulled out of the parking lot. I jumped.

"Smokey?" Jimmy sounded panicked.

"It's okay. It was just a car. I'm at a pay phone." I didn't want to tell him that I was afraid that someone might be tapping the Grimshaws' line. I didn't want him to know the extent of my concern.

"Laura and I arranged a way for me to see you tomorrow. I'll make sure I'm not followed."

"I can come home then?"

"Not yet," I said.

"But Smokey, what if something happens to you? Then what will I do?"

Excellent question, and one I hadn't dealt with. "In the short term, at least, Laura will care for you. We'll discuss it tomorrow, the three of us, and make some decisions. Is that fair?"

"Yeah." His voice was very soft.

"Jimmy." I scanned the parking lot. No cars that looked familiar. No familiar faces. A woman was pushing a grocery cart and struggling with a toddler in the seat. The toddler was trying to pick food out of one of the brown bags. "Finding people and taking care of myself are the two things I'm the best at in the world. I'll be fine."

"You promise?"

"I can't promise that. No one can make promises like that. But I can guarantee you that you'll be safe for the rest of your life. That much I can do."

"I don't want to stay here, Smokey." His voice was almost inaudible.

"Is she mean to you?"

"No."

"Are you eating?"

"Yes."

"Are you finding things to do?"

"She wants to play stupid games."

Poor Laura. Probably trying to entertain Jimmy the way she was entertained as a child. Their lives couldn't have been more different. "Well, help her out a little. She's not used to young boys."

"Yeah, I know."

I smiled again. Two elderly men passed me on their way to the liquor store. They frowned at me. I glanced to see if there was a line behind the booth door, but saw nothing. I squared my shoulders, feeling odd that so much as a frown could make me wary.

"I'll get you out of there as soon as I can," I said.

"Promise?"

"Yes, I can promise that."

"Good," Jimmy said. "I'll see you tomorrow?"

So much hope in his voice. So much worry. I closed my eyes. I wasn't used to having a dependent. The changes it brought startled me. I couldn't just pick up and hunt anymore.

"Yes," I said. "I'll be there."

Then we hung up. I sat for a moment longer in that booth, feeling uncomfortable. I hadn't expected to worry about Jimmy and his unpredictability. He knew the importance of staying where he was, but he was also a ten-year-old boy whose world had been destroyed.

He had shown in the past that he would take matters into his own hands.

I had to make sure that didn't happen.

I went to my meal with Franklin feeling very discouraged. And the news Franklin gave me didn't make me feel better.

The neighbors had seen a number of strangers in the area, a lot of them cops. The strangers' presence was obvious and they weren't trying to hide in any way. Most of them were following the avowed Black Panther from the attic apartment, taking turns keeping close watch on him. Others were stalking the Blackstone Rangers and the kids who belonged to the less active gangs.

We were in one of the area's better diners, and it was packed with Friday afternoon customers. The diner had air-conditioning that was struggling to keep up with the sweating bodies, the ovens, and the grill, but it was still cooler in here than it was outside. The waitresses were having to hustle customers out of their booths when they were done eating, just to keep the line at the door to a minimum.

"Anyone watching me or Jimmy?" I had ordered a cheeseburger, which came on a kaiser roll. The burger was so thick, I had trouble biting through the sandwich.

"I didn't know how to ask that specifically. So I asked about my family and friends. No one saw anything, Smokey."

I set the hamburger aside. It was good, but too much food for a hot afternoon. "What do you think?"

"I think if you are being followed, it's because of something different." He finished the last of his corned beef.

I nodded. "I'm thinking that too."

We stared at each other for a moment. Then he said, "I've got an idea. Why don't I follow you and see if I can see this guy?"

"If he's as good as he sounds, he'll notice you." I sipped my iced tea. "But we might be able to flush him out."

"How?"

"I think he lost me on the way here. If so, he'll be waiting for me at the building. We'll set up a route here, beforehand. You won't follow me. You'll be stationed. When I walk by, you'll be able to tell if I'm being tailed."

Franklin smiled. "I like that, Smokey."

"We won't catch him this first time, Franklin."

"I know," he said.

"But we have a couple of days. We'll recognize him soon enough."

We drove back separately, our plan mapped out. I parked in front of the apartment and went inside to give Franklin time to get into place, and to give my shadow a chance to notice me.

The inside of the apartment was stiflingly hot. We hadn't closed the windows or the curtains the way that Althea did. It was only the middle of the afternoon. The heat of the day hadn't passed yet. Sleeping would be impossible that night.

I poured myself the last of the lemonade and drank it in one long gulp. Then I grabbed a glass pitcher, filled it with water, and dunked the tea bags inside it. I planned to take the entire thing outside. If someone stole it, I'd replace it. But my hesitation in the front of the building had to look normal or our watcher would know he was being watched.

I took the pitcher downstairs. To set it in the sun, I had to wedge it beside the stairs leading up to the building. A young boy, too young to be the missing child, watched from the sidewalk. I'd seen him before. He lived in the building.

He was frowning at me. "Whatcha doin'?"

"Making sun tea."

"What's that?"

"Another way to make iced tea."

He came up the sidewalk, his frown deepening as if I were doing an arcane magic trick. "Never seen nothing like that before."

"You may not see it again if someone takes this pitcher. Are you going to be around?"

"For a while."

"Keep an eye on it for me, will you?"

He nodded.

I stood all the way up. The sun was still high enough to

hit the tea. I scanned the area as if I were looking for something he had just mentioned. Franklin sat on the stoop almost two blocks over. I couldn't see his face from this
distance, but his body language was not relaxed. I wondered
how long it had been since he'd done something like this. I
hoped the skills involved were the kind a man never forgot.

"You live with the Grimshaws?"

I started, and glanced at the boy. He was not looking at
Franklin, as I thought he would be. He was looking at me.
He shoved his hands in the pockets of his cutoffs, trying to
look unconcerned. But the question had an edge to it.

"Yeah. Why?"

"Where's Keith gone?"

Keith was Franklin's ten-year-old son.

"His mother took the family to visit their grandparents."

"Did Jim go too?"

It took me a moment to realize he meant Jimmy. I'd taken
to calling him Jim on occasion, but I hadn't realized anyone
else had. "Yeah. He's gone for the next few weeks."

The boy kicked at the sidewalk with his bare foot. His
shoulders hunched forward. "That stinks."

"Why? Were you planning something?"

He shrugged.

"I'll be talking to them. I can tell them you were here."

"My name is Brian. I live here," he said in a tone that
implied I was stupid.

"Then I'm not quite understanding what the problem is."

"Everybody's gone, okay?" he said, raising his head. His
almond-shaped dark eyes flashed. "They're gone. David's
gone. Even my dad's gone. Everybody's going away but me."

I didn't know who his dad was. "I'm sorry," I said.
"They'll be back soon."

"And summer'll be over. This just stinks." He pushed
past me and went into the building. I watched him go, wishing I could have said something to make him feel better. I

had a hunch the outburst had nothing to do with Keith and Jimmy and everything to do with his father.

I sighed, glanced at the pitcher a final time, then started down the sidewalk, making sure I looked nonchalant as I headed to the store.

There were a lot of people outside. Some kids were playing kickball in the street. Several adults were sitting on stoops, like Franklin was. One woman waved a paper fan in front of her face. She looked as hot as I felt.

I tried not to act any differently than usual. I nodded at people if our gazes met, otherwise I continued forward, feeling like the stranger on the block. I knew that I was being watched—I could sense it—but I wasn't sure if I had that feeling because of Franklin or because of someone else, the someone we'd been looking for.

Some faces looked familiar to me: an elderly man standing in the doorway to one of the neighborhood's few single-story houses. A middle-aged man sat on a lawn chair in the middle of the brown grass between two apartment buildings. He was reading the *Chicago Daily Defender*, but he looked up as I passed. His expression was cold and unwelcoming.

As I got closer to Franklin, four boys in their late teens turned their heads toward me in unison. They deliberately stared at me, trying to unnerve me. I smiled at them, and they looked away.

I did not walk up the street where Franklin was sitting. That would have been too obvious. Instead, I went a block past. I was about to cut across the street when I heard shouting behind me.

I whirled. Franklin and another man were grappling on the corner. The man was yelling as if Franklin were hurting him. Franklin was using all of his bulk to shove the man toward the brick building on the corner.

I hurried back. Franklin had managed to get the man's

arms behind him and was pressing his face against the building. The entire neighborhood was watching. I could feel the mixture of amusement and alarm.

"What the hell are you doing?" the man was yelling. I wondered the same thing. We'd agreed that Franklin would note the face and then let me take care of it.

"Franklin," I said when I reached his side. "What's going on?"

"This is the one," he said. "He followed you all the way up the block."

"Really?" I leaned against the building, arms crossed. His description was similar to the one Marvella gave me—he was tall and rangy, and he had an afro. But he seemed younger than I expected—eighteen at the most. I had expected someone in his thirties or older. "Have you been following me?"

"I didn't mean nothing," he said, his face squished against the brick.

So he had been.

"You want to tell me why?"

"Because you're a cop, man."

I grinned. My gaze met Franklin's. He was frowning. He shoved the boy hard against the building.

"Don't make shit up," Franklin said.

"I'm not." The boy struggled against him. "You're hurting me."

"I'll do a lot more if you're not honest with us."

"I am being honest." The boy's voice rose. "There's been a lot of cops here and he's one. He even smells like a cop."

The boy had a good nose. Detectives and cops weren't that far off, and since I'd moved here, I'd been uneasy and on alert. I could see how that would be interpreted as cop behavior.

"And how did you get to be such an expert on the police?" I asked.

He closed his eyes. Franklin shoved him again.

"He's not going to stop until we have some answers," I said.

"Son of a bitch," the boy said, but he wasn't cursing us. He was cursing the situation. "You are a cop."

"Actually, no," I said. "I'm a security guard. That's probably what you saw."

The boy looked up at me, his expression sullen. "You stare at stuff."

"Is that a crime?"

"Cops do that."

"So, apparently, do you. Now, do you want to tell me what this is about or should I have my friend use that brick wall to scrape the skin off your face?"

"I wasn't doing nothing, man. I was just supposed to follow a cop to see if I could find out what they were doing."

Franklin shoved him harder. The boy's face was pushed so hard against the wall that his features were mushed together. I glanced sideways at the street. None of his friends were coming toward us, although the four young men I'd passed earlier had come closer. People on their stoops were acting as if they weren't seeing anything. And the kids had stopped playing in the street.

"That's all, man," the boy said. "I wasn't doing nothing else. Honest."

"What's your name?" I asked him.

The boy grimaced.

Franklin pushed him harder. "He asked you a question."

"Malcolm."

"Malcolm what?" I asked.

"Malcolm Reyner." The last name was too unusual to be made up, at least by this kid.

"I'll be keeping an eye on you, Mr. Reyner." I looked at Franklin. "Let him go."

Franklin didn't move.

"Let him go," I said again.

Franklin dropped his arms. The boy staggered forward, leaning his face on the wall for support. He probably would have fallen if he hadn't been pressed so hard against the building.

He stood up. He was taller than I was, but rail thin, and as young as I had initially thought. His left cheek was scraped by the brick's uneven surface, and his left eye was swelling shut. Franklin was better in a fight than I thought he would be.

"The cops," I said, "are trying to scare you. Mayor Daley's afraid the city will burn next week and he thinks we're going to start it. Your behavior isn't reassuring me. Could he be right?"

"No way." Malcolm touched his damaged cheek, then checked his fingers for blood. "We're not doing nothing. Most of the guys have skipped. A few are going to Lincoln Park, but that's for the war, man. The rest of us are lying low. We just don't like the Man in our neighborhood."

"I don't either," I said.

He looked surprised. Then he glanced at Franklin and back at me. "Shit. You thought I . . . ?"

Franklin nodded. I didn't.

"Je-zus. He looks more like a cop than I do." He nodded toward me.

"That's the point," Franklin said.

The boy's eyebrows went up. He seemed comical, suddenly, and very young. "You think they're that undercover? But I seen white guys and guys in suits—"

"You've seen cops," I said, confirming his suspicions. "Stay away from them. Don't follow them. They're not going to be in the best mood."

The boy swallowed.

"Now get the hell out of here."

He didn't need a second invitation. He ran down the street toward the Grimshaws' building.

I moved closer to Franklin, so close that the people who were watching us—and that included most of the neighborhood now—couldn't hear me.

"What the hell was that?"

"He was following you."

"And you were supposed to make a note of it so that I could take care of it."

"I stopped him."

"Thank you very much. I could have handled a kid."

"But you didn't."

I let out a long sigh. "You think he's the one Marvella mentioned?"

"He fits the description and he was after you."

"Franklin, whoever's after me is a pro. This kid saw me walking down the street and decided to check me out. I'd have stopped him when I got to the store."

Franklin shook his head as if he didn't believe me.

"You just let everyone in the neighborhood know that I believe someone's following me," I said.

"Or that we've had a problem with this kid."

"Maybe they'll believe that, but I doubt it. If I'm being followed for the reasons I think, then they'll know who I am. And they'll know I don't handle punk kids this way."

Franklin ran a hand over his face. "I knew I'd get in the way. I just thought it would be because I couldn't fight anymore."

"I think that kid will disagree."

Franklin looked at me over his thumb and forefinger. "Really?"

"He's got a black eye and more bruises than I could count. Plus you got him to that wall in less than sixty seconds. Yeah, I think he'd disagree."

"Wow." Franklin's hand dropped. He seemed bemused

by his own physical prowess. Then his expression changed. "Seriously. I thought my brains would help us, not get us in trouble."

"You haven't done anything like this in a long time."

"I've never done anything like this. Maybe that's the problem."

It was. He was too enthusiastic. But he knew that now. I'd have to be a lot more careful when I took his help.

"Head on home, Franklin. I'll go to the store and finish this."

"You don't want me to keep an eye out?"

I shook my head.

"I blew that for us, didn't I?"

"Yeah," I said. "Let's just hope our friend wasn't watching."

"I didn't see anything unusual."

"If he's as good as I think he is, you wouldn't have seen anything at all this first time."

Franklin nodded. He sighed and nodded again. "I'll meet you at home."

"All right." And then I left him. I clenched and unclenched my left fist as I walked, working out the anger, the adrenaline from the moment.

Things had just gotten a lot harder. I didn't like that at all.

SIX

That night, my dream chill was even worse. It mingled with the scrape-scrape-scrape of shovels on the icy earth, the hushed voices of the men trying to stay awake in the cold Korean night. The moon was full, sending an eerie silver light across the snow. I clutched my rifle in my hands, leaned against the edge of the trench and stared at the empty hills.

Someone was coming. Someone—

Then I woke up. The chill lingered for a moment, and it took me a while to realize I was covered in sweat. The apartment hadn't cooled down much, despite the fan we'd put in the window. We had faced it outward so that it would suck the hot air from inside and theoretically fill the place with cooler air. The theory hadn't worked. There was no cooler air to be found.

I only dreamed about Korea in times of extreme stress. Usually the dreams were not about the end of my service but the beginning, when I realized that being in an integrated unit not only meant that the whites had to put up with me but that I had to put up with them.

I rinsed off my face, just like I had after the first dream, then went back to bed. But it took a long time for sleep to claim me again.

Marvella's note had said that she had been unable to reach her friend. She asked that I see her in the morning and that we try again.

I went to her apartment, wishing I had never agreed to this. But somehow I always got hooked into cases I didn't want.

In Memphis, I would have been most content working for black insurance companies, banks, and lawyers, doing work in the black community that private detectives did in the white one. But somehow my caseload filled with troublesome cases: missing persons, stolen money, divorces.

The man who trained me, Loyce Kirby, always said I had to be firm, to say no to anything I didn't want, but I couldn't. My imagination was too powerful and my conscience too strong. If I later learned that a fourteen-year-old boy met with trouble, I would have wondered if it were this boy and I would have regretted not doing all I could to find him.

But I didn't do this kind of work in Chicago, and admitting that I did made both Jimmy and me vulnerable. Our lives held against someone else's. Mine didn't matter that much, but Jimmy's did.

Apparently this was the week to test that theory. And if something happened to me, I'd have to trust Laura.

I'd tell her when I saw her this afternoon. She had to know I was relying on her to make the right decisions.

Marvella gave me a strange look as she joined me. "I know you don't want to do this, but I appreciate it."

"I'm not the right person for this job," I said.

"I think you can help," she said. "Don't you want to help?"

"I'll listen. That's all I can do." I wasn't going to make any promises. I didn't dare.

We left our building and went down the block. The complex's door was open as it had been before. This time when Marvella went down the hall, she pushed open the apartment door.

I followed slowly, trying to imagine being a fourteen-year-old boy growing up in this place. For all the difficulties of my youth, being raised in poverty was not one of them. My adoptive parents were comfortably middle class, living in a black neighborhood where racism touched us only when we ventured outside of it.

Then I stepped into the apartment and was amazed at the amount of light that greeted me. The narrow entry opened to a bank of windows overlooking a lush garden, one that had been walled off. The furniture was comfortable and not at all shabby. Flowers rested on an end table, and the apartment was clean.

In the middle of it stood a woman, her hands clutching Marvella's. Marvella leaned into her, talking softly.

I took my time, trying not to be noticed. I wanted to absorb the environment first, to see if the child had a reason to run away.

I didn't see any obvious one. There were photographs on the walls—two boys playing basketball; two boys posing side by side; school pictures, ending with one that had a tassel hanging from it, a tassel that had a gold '67 hanging from it, and another that said "With Honors."

Marvella had joined me. "That's Daniel. He's at Yale now."

"Yale?" I couldn't keep the surprise out of my voice.

"My boys are smart." The woman in the center of the room spoke with pride. "Daniel got a full scholarship based on his grades and his SAT scores, not his color."

I looked at her for the first time. She was about my age, slender to the point of gauntness. Her skin was very dark, but in the full light it had turned gray with exhaustion and worry.

"I'm sorry," I said.

She shrugged. "You look at this place and you expect something else."

I was ashamed to admit that I had.

"But there's just me and my sons, and I do what I can." She twined her fingers and rubbed her thumbs together, a nervous gesture I wasn't even sure she knew she was making.

"You see why I asked you?" Marvella said.

I didn't look at her. Instead, I kept my gaze on her friend. "I work as a security guard at the Conrad Hilton Hotel."

"I don't care how you make your money. You're a friend of Franklin Grimshaw's and Marvella said you can help. That's good enough for me." Her voice trembled just a little, despite the bravado of her words. She was keeping herself together by will alone.

"How long has he been gone?"

"Two days." She swallowed hard. "He usually doesn't leave without telling me. I came home from work Friday and he wasn't here. He hasn't come back and hasn't called. I don't know what happened."

I touched Marvella's shoulder. "Would you mind waiting for me outside?" I asked.

She frowned slightly as if she were assessing me. I hadn't told her that I wanted to be alone here. It was important for two reasons: I wanted to have all of her friend's attention, and I didn't want Marvella to know how competent— and used to this—I was.

Marvella seemed to be thinking things through. Finally she said, "I'll just go home. You don't need to worry about me. Just help Grace."

90

Then she left us.

I put out my hand. "I'm Bill."

"Grace Kirkland." She put her hand in mine. Her fingers were small and fragile, but the skin was covered with calluses. This was a woman who worked hard for this little patch of privacy. "Please, sit down."

She led me to the living room. The couch had been her domain—the dent in the cushions, the bits of Kleenex wadded up near the armrest. I took the armchair off to the side. From there I had a view of the garden, lush despite the heat.

Grace sat down across from me, in the very spot I had avoided.

"Marvella says you went to the police."

Grace looked toward the garden. Tears welled in her eyes, and she blinked them back. "They told me boys his age usually joined gangs. They'd arrest him soon enough."

Son of a bitch. "I thought Chicago had black officers on the force."

"That's why I went to Marvella next. She sent me to her cousin. He said he'd do what he can." She paused, swallowed hard, and took a deep breath.

"But you didn't feel confident that he'd help?"

"He said . . ." Her voice shook. Her back straightened. "He said that there was going to be trouble this week, and that there'd be a lot of strangers in town, and that he couldn't guarantee anything."

"The police never can."

"If it had been a month ago, he wouldn't have been as worried. But, he said, that right now was one of the most dangerous times for a young man to be on his own."

"That was comforting," I said.

"He wanted to scare me." She apparently didn't hear the sarcasm or she ignored it. "He told me I should get my friends to help and to call all my relatives. He said we'd have better luck than he would this week. And he warned me to be careful. He said there'd be a lot of strangers in town, and most of them not nice ones."

I wondered what provoked that kind of comment. Did he think the boy was dead? Or having gang troubles? Or was there something else that I was missing?

"Tell me about your boy."

"Elijah," she said.

"Tell me about Elijah."

"He's my baby." Her voice broke again. She had been alone with this too long. She looked at me and made a helpless movement with her hand.

"Take your time," I said.

She took a deep shuddery breath and grabbed some Kleenex from the table. Holding the thin tissue seemed to calm her. "He's a straight-A student, top of his class, just like his brother. He's going to be a lawyer, he says. He did a report on Thurgood Marshall last year. It won an award."

"Has anything changed this summer?"

She shook her head. "Truman asked that too."

I assumed Truman was Marvella's cousin.

"It could be something small?"

She shook her head even harder. "He was volunteering at the library, doing the reading program for the really little kids. And he was trying to find some work to help me, but he's too young to do anything legally and he didn't want to work under the table. I wouldn't let him, even though he looks old enough."

"How old is he?"

"Fourteen," she said, confirming what Marvella told me. "But he got his growth this year. He's nearly six feet, and his voice changed. He's been tripping all over everything. . . ."

Her eyes filled again and her voice dropped off.

"All right." I made sure I sounded as gentle as I could.

"You said he's interested in the law. Is he interested in politics?"

"He wouldn't do that." She glared at me.

Finally, we were getting somewhere. "Do what?"

"Join those people. He knows better."

"What people, Grace?"

"Those hippies."

"Did you talk about it?"

"He knows how I feel."

"How does he feel?"

She closed her eyes and leaned back against the couch. "He said all the boys who're dying in Vietnam are black. He says the white boys can get away from it. He says Daniel's lucky because he got a deferment, but if there wasn't the pass for students, Daniel would be dead now."

"He's not worried about his own possible involvement?"

"I told him the war would be over by then."

"What does he say?"

Her entire face hardened. She wasn't a woman I would want to cross. Her eyes remained closed. Obviously, she didn't like to discuss this subject.

"He says that it doesn't matter what'll happen in four years. Boys are dying now and it's not right and the war has to stop."

"Maybe he's at Lincoln Park, then," I said.

Her eyes flew open. "He would have called me."

"Are you sure?"

"He knows how I worry. He would have called."

"Then what would you have done?"

"I'd've gone to get him." She stopped, as if the realization hit her. He was a fourteen-year-old boy. The last thing he would want was his mother taking him away from something he felt was important.

"He knows that, doesn't he?" I said. "That you'll come for him."

She put a hand over her mouth and then stood. She went to the window and looked at her garden.

I let her stand there for a moment, waited until she straightened her shoulders and looked as if she had gained some strength. Then I stood too, and joined her.

The garden was as lush up close as it had seemed from across the room. Tomato vines climbed the fence and fat green tomatoes hung off them. Broccoli grew close to the ground next to some nearly ripe cauliflower. Ripening beans grew on the far end of the garden, and marigolds lined the edges of the entire plot.

The garden looked like it was usually well tended. But a handful of ripe tomatoes, the ripe beans, and the broccoli told me it had been neglected since Elijah disappeared.

"I'll find him," I said. "I'll make sure he comes home."

"You don't think he's really there, do you?" She had wrapped her arms around herself.

"I think it's possible."

"He's only fourteen. There's drugs up there and criminals and people with no respect for human beings. They're going to get in trouble, and that's what the mayor is waiting for. Then he'll attack us, our people. Someone already died up there, and no one cares because he was an Indian boy. What'll happen when things get really bad? They'll go after us, our people, and my Elijah will be in the middle of it. He doesn't understand this. He doesn't understand."

"I know."

"He would have called me," she said. "He wouldn't have gone there. He would have called me."

That litany had probably gone through her head from the moment he disappeared. I wasn't so sure. Fourteen was an age of change, and this was a politically charged summer. He might have gone.

"I'll need a photo of him," I said, "as well as a physical description."

"You're going to look for him?"

I nodded. "I have time today, but starting tomorrow, I'm also working overtime."

"I'd appreciate whatever you can do," she said.

"I have some errands to run, and then I'll go up to Lincoln Park. While I'm gone, I want you to make a list of all his friends—with phone numbers and addresses if you have them."

"I've called everybody."

I bet she had. "Well, let me give it a shot. And give me the names of any relatives that he might go to."

"It's just us."

"Where's his brother?"

"Summer school," she said. "We couldn't afford to send him back and forth."

"There are buses that run between Chicago and the East Coast. Call your son and see if his brother went out there."

"He wouldn't—"

"We have to check everything," I said, "no matter how far-fetched."

She seemed to accept that, and nodded.

I could feel the time ticking away. I wanted to look at Elijah's room, but I needed to start making my way toward the meeting with Laura.

"I'll be back later tonight. Please have it all ready for me then, plus anything else you can think of."

"All right." Then she turned to me. "I'd like to pay you for your time."

I shook my head. "I'm just helping out a friend."

"You've done this before," she said softly.

"I have a lot of friends."

The meeting had taken an hour. As I left the apartment, I felt an irritation at myself. I didn't have the time to look for a boy who wanted to protest the war, but I was doing it anyway because Marvella asked, because Grace was trying so hard to be strong, because I didn't like the way the entire city was beginning to feel like a war zone.

That thought reminded me I needed to be cautious. I scanned for my shadow, seeing no one. I had originally planned to spend the afternoon on the "L" crisscrossing the city several times before I went to the Loop. Driving was too conspicuous, and I'd already risked enough by going to Laura's apartment twice.

I wouldn't be able to follow my original plan, but I still had time to take the train.

I figured the "L" would be the safest and easiest way to travel. Since it was Saturday, there wouldn't be as many passengers on the trains heading into the Loop. I modified my route, and boarded the Jackson Line, staring at the subway map as I rode all the way north to Addison.

As I rode, I watched the faces. Most of them I saw reflected in the grimy windows or only in passing. The rest of the time, I held on to the steel bar in the middle of the car, kept my head down and looked out of the corner of my eye.

My route was long on purpose. I went from the Black Belt beyond the Loop to Wrigleyville, figuring that black faces wouldn't be that unusual on the way to a baseball game. I had no idea if the Cubs were playing or not and had forgotten to check, but it didn't matter. My presence wouldn't be unusual on that train.

And it wasn't. There were others, many of them college age, wearing stylishly ripped clothes and with afros. They had peace symbols sewn onto their clothing and were talking about the upcoming convention. Most everyone on the train seemed to be in Chicago to protest. I found that some of them chose the moment to be tourists as well seemed at odds with their political commitment.

I compared their faces to the pictures I'd seen of Elijah.

He didn't seem to be here. And, Grace had assured me, his hair was cropped short.

The Addison Street station was one of the aboveground stations that made Chicago's public transportation system so unusual. I had to take the stairs down, cross the street, and climb the other side to catch the train heading south.

I liked that. I crossed the street, stopped in front of some dilapidated buildings housing stores that specialized in Cubs merchandise, cheap food, and tickets, then doubled back as if I were confused about where I was going.

All of the black faces I'd seen were trundling toward the stadium, which rose incongruously in the middle of an ancient neighborhood. It was cooler here—the wind was off Lake Michigan—and I stopped for just a moment to enjoy the breeze.

Then I turned around again and climbed to the platform. The train that arrived was nearly empty. I shared it with an elderly white woman who sat as far from me as she could. She clutched her purse to her chest and looked at me nervously. When she got off at Fullerton, she nearly ran from the train.

I got off at Fullerton as well, and transferred to the Ravenswood Line, heading south. I watched for others getting off, tried to see if I were being followed. It didn't appear that I was.

A few hippies whose long stringy hair and ripe body odor made it clear they hadn't bathed in weeks, and some white college students wearing Clean for Gene buttons sat in opposite parts of the car, as if they made each other as nervous as I had made the elderly woman. None of them seemed to notice me.

This train took me south of the Loop. At State and Dearborn I made my final transfer, to the Milwaukee Line, and took it north and west. As I did, I watched the other cars. There were windows in the doors that linked the cars. A good tail would get onto the next car over and watch through the door, disembarking at the same station as his prey.

The population of this train was mostly black. No one even looked at me and I felt as if I could blend in. I sat down and stared at the ads above my head, trying to be casual as I examined the other passengers. I saw no afros, no people with that look of wrongness that Marvella had mentioned.

Between Western and California, I got up and walked through the door that linked the cars. That car was nearly empty. I walked through it to the car beyond. I stayed out of sight in the last car, counted two stops, and got off at the very last minute.

No one else got off the train.

I breathed a small sigh of relief. I went down the stairs, crossed underneath the platform and climbed up the other side. Trains didn't run as often on Saturday, and I had to wait nearly fifteen minutes before another arrived.

By that time, three white men in uniforms I'd never seen before joined me. They were clearly on their way to a late shift somewhere in the city. They didn't look directly at me. They stood on the far side of the stop, conversing softly, occasionally glancing at me over their shoulders.

I continued to scan the platform. No one else joined us. We were at the edge of an old neighborhood, although the brick houses were far away. A nearby billboard caught my eye:

MAYOR DALEY, A FAMILY MAN, WELCOMES YOU
TO A FAMILY TOWN.

Finally a train stopped. It was jammed with passengers. This was another moment when I had to be careful. If my shadow realized where I had lost him, he would be on this train, coming to this stop, hoping I hadn't caught anything else.

There was no crowd on the platform for me to hide in. Anyone inside the passing cars would see me. I had one more trick, and then I would feel safe.

The pneumatic doors opened, and no one got out. The taxi-cab strike was making everyone equal, and cramming them all onto the "L." I climbed onto one car, the three uniformed men onto another.

The next stop came quickly. I got off at the last minute, just as I had the stop before. A dozen people milled on the platform, most of them having just left the same train. I made a show of heading for the stairs, so that it looked like I was crossing to the other side, to catch the "L" back north.

If my shadow was on that train, he would believe he had lost me for good.

I waited until the train left the platform before climbing the stairs again. This time, the train arrived more quickly. It was just as full as the other one. As I boarded, I noted a greater number of black faces, and for a moment felt some relief. Then I realized most of the men had afros. I scanned them quickly. They were too young to be my shadow. Besides, they all had duffel bags or backpacks and they all appeared to be traveling in a group.

One young man had a recorder and he was playing music that sounded vaguely Indian—snake-charming music. I wondered if he meant it that way, or if he was simply amusing himself.

The music irritated me. When the train reached the Washington Street Station, I was happy to get off.

By this point, we were underground. I hurried to the exit, then slipped into the shadows, loitering there. I watched the other passengers hurry past me, some of them giving me uneasy glances. I did not meet their gazes. I continued to look past them as if I were waiting for someone. I guess, in a sense, I was.

Finally the group from my train had gone up the stairs. The next group was disembarking. I waited until they passed before heading up the stairs into the sunlight.

All Laura had given me was the address of her father's office. Her father had been dead for eight years, but his corporation lived on. Laura had shares, but her father, believing that a girl could not run a company, made sure she had no real power.

She still had keys to the building and, as a major stockholder, no one dared ask her to turn them in. I wondered how she would be faring after an afternoon in that building, sifting through old memories and discovering more of her father's secrets.

I doubted she'd be happy.

I'd emerged just south of the Civic Center Plaza. There were a lot more people in the Loop than I would have expected on a weekend. Some were sight-seeing. Others seemed to be on their way to or from work. There were some young people, many of them with their Clean for Gene buttons prominently displayed. And in the middle of the intersection was a policeman, wearing a helmet, a nightstick at his side and a whistle in his hand. Behind him was a motorcycle cop who seemed to be watching everyone who passed with great intensity.

The massive city-county building, a stone edifice that dominated part of the Loop, looked neglected. The Plaza itself was pretty empty. Very few people were heading north. Most of them were heading toward the shops farther down in the Loop.

I walked up Dearborn to Randolph. There, at the corner, was a stone building with a rounded front, nearly dwarfed by the skyscraper beside it. In its day, the eight-story building had probably seemed huge. It looked incongruous now, the remnant of a forgotten age.

I stopped in front of the building and double-checked the address. It was the one Laura had given me. She had never said that it was right across the street from the Civic Center Plaza, in the very heart of Chicago's downtown.

Her father, who had worked his way up from a small-time crook to one of the richest men in Chicago, had a lot of balls. Just the location of his offices told me that much.

I crossed to the east side of Dearborn and reached the building. The bottom two floors were made of cast iron and were a different color from the rest of the building. Shops nestled on the lower floors, their windows dark. Apparently this far north in the Loop, no one believed in catering to Saturday business.

The entrance was on the Randolph Street side. I went through the iron doors into an atrium that had once been magnificent. Now it was dingy and dark, the Victorian scrollwork covered in almost a century of grime. Still, I felt out of place and uncomfortable. My work—my life—rarely brought me to places like this.

The office that Laura wanted me to go to was on the seventh floor. The elevators were old and had no attendant. I worked the lever myself, feeling more than slightly disconcerted by the action. I had yet to see a white elevator attendant in Chicago. Most of them were black and elderly and all of them seemed to have had their jobs forever.

The elevator lurched to a stop on the seventh floor and for a moment, I thought I wouldn't be able to get the doors open. Then they eased open and I found myself staring at a modern office suite, done in pale blues and blond wood, with oddly shaped postmodern furniture, the kind usually displayed in expensive magazines.

As I exited my elevator, I wished it were newer, so that I could send it up to the top floor. Having it stuck here was like an arrow pointing to us. I checked the other elevators. Two were on the fifth floor and one was on the fourth floor. The rest waited on the ground floor.

At least the sign wouldn't be that obvious.

Someone had propped the main glass door open. I walked into the empty reception area. The rounded couch matched the blue carpet and looked very uncomfortable. On the oversized blond coffee table rested a pile of magazines and Friday's newspapers. The reception desk, also blond, had nothing on its surface except a blotter. Behind the desk was a gold sign that clearly predated this remodel: Sturdy Investments, Inc.

When I had first seen the name of the company, I had thought Sturdy was someone's last name. But there had never been anyone named Sturdy connected with the business. Laura's father, Earl Hathaway, had been shrewd. He'd initially called the company Sturdy and Sons Construction and had built it from there. Eventually the "and Sons" got dropped, and all that was left was a name that spoke for reliability and strength.

The man's ability to reinvent himself constantly amazed me.

I turned right, as Laura had instructed me to, and walked down a narrow hallway. Doors flanked me on either side. The end of the hallway opened into a large sitting area filled with plants, more blond furniture and uncomfortable couches, and a glass conference table that filled the center of it.

Jimmy sat at the far end of the conference table, cards spread before him. He was playing solitaire.

"You winning?" I asked.

"Smokey!" He launched himself from the table and wrapped himself around me so hard that I had to take a step backward. I put my arms around him, holding him close. It felt like we'd been separated for weeks, not days.

Finally I eased him back. I slipped my arm around his shoulder and led him to one of the couches. It was as uncomfortable as it looked.

"How're you holding up?" I asked.

"Today was better," he said. "We had some goofy lunch-breakfast thing."

"Brunch?"

He nodded. "At this fancy restaurant. She made me dress up for it like we was looking for apartments. And they called me sir and everything."

I smiled.

"You ever have eggs with sauce?"

"Hollandaise sauce?"

"I guess."

"Once or twice."

"It's weird, but good. Laura says there's lots of weird but good things in the world."

"She's probably right about that."

His animation relieved me where his hug had not. Maybe he would be all right. Or maybe he was animated because I had come back to him.

"You found the guy?" he asked.

"Not yet," I said.

"You said you couldn't see us if you didn't find the guy."

"I told you yesterday I'd be here. I spent most of the afternoon making sure I wasn't followed."

"Oh." Jimmy's shoulders sagged. "I guess you want to see Laura."

"I don't mind staying with you."

"It's okay." He slid off the couch. "Come on."

He led me across the conference area to an office that overlooked the Plaza. The office was rounded. It had light and warmth, and the decor was different here. There were flowers on the tables, just like there were in Laura's apartment. I didn't have to look at the name on the door to realize this was her office.

Half of the room was filled with comfortable wooden chairs with upholstered seats—and the other half housed a mahogany desk. The windows were to the desk's right. The placement made the windows the focus of the room, a feature in and of themselves.

Laura sat behind the desk, her head in her hands. Her lips were pinched, her skin pale. Before her, old files scattered like leaves.

"Smokey's here." Jimmy couldn't contain the enthusiasm in his voice.

Laura raised her head. She looked a little dazed and somewhat tired. For a moment, I thought she'd stand and extend her hand as if she didn't know me at all.

"I'm glad you're here," she said, and that sense of unfamiliarity disappeared.

"What are you doing?" I asked.

"Learning stuff I didn't want to know." Her voice was husky, but whether she was holding back tears or anger, I couldn't tell.

"Laura said she'd get us an apartment."

Laura's lips got even tighter. I glanced at Jimmy. He didn't seem to notice the tension.

"Oh?" I had to remain neutral. Jimmy sounded excited about it. Laura seemed strained, and I didn't know how I felt. I certainly didn't want anyone's charity.

"The corporation has a lot of real estate holdings," she said. "It's where we—it—we—they make most of their money."

Laura usually wasn't tongue-tied. She'd discovered something in the files while trying to help us out.

"She thinks maybe one of the buildings has room for us."

Or she had thought that. What Jimmy didn't seem to notice was that something had changed while he was playing solitaire.

"That would be nice," I said. "Maybe after the convention—"

"Smokey," Jimmy said, "if we move now, this guy won't be able to find us. We'll be all right."

So that was why he was excited. Laura's gaze met mine. There was sadness in her eyes.

"I wish it worked like that, Jim," I said.

"It'll be okay," he said. "You'll see. If we go—"

"If we move now, we go to a place where we're the strangers. We only know about this man because a neighbor warned us. Otherwise we would have no idea at all."

"But you want privacy."

"So do you," I said.

"Jimmy, we don't have anything that's immediately available." Laura's voice still had that husky quality.

"You didn't say that." He sounded betrayed. I could feel his building anger. I put a hand on his shoulder, holding him back.

"Is that why you look so sad?" I asked.

She shook her head so slightly that I doubted Jim noticed. "I was hoping we'd have something that was open now. All we have are places that rent on September first."

"Well," I said, "that's better than nothing."

She didn't answer. Instead she came around the desk and leaned on it, as close to me as she could get. All it would take was a movement of my hand, and I could pull her into my arms.

I couldn't step back—Jimmy would notice—so I made sure my tone was cool. "Can you give us a minute, Jim?"

His frown was quick. "I thought you came to see me."

"I did, but—"

"You got grown-up talk."

"Yeah." I was more grateful than I wanted to be for the understanding.

"So's you can figure out what to do with me." He sounded adult and bitter.

"No." I reached for him, but he stepped away. "I just need to talk to Laura alone for a minute, that's all."

His lips formed a thin line, but he didn't say anything more. Instead, he left the room, slamming the door behind him.

I raised my gaze to hers. Her look was steady and even, and very sad. "What's going on?" I asked.

The sadness left her face. She opened her mouth to answer, then shook her head.

"What do you care?" she said. "You don't work for me anymore."

The harshness of the words took my breath away. "I thought—"

"You thought? What did you think, Smokey? You certainly don't think about me."

I didn't know what was causing this, if it was a delayed reaction to my request for help or if it had to do with something she had read. "If Jimmy's a problem—"

"I'm not talking about Jimmy." She kept her voice down, but I could hear the anger in it. "He's a great kid, and I'm happy to help him."

Help him. Not me. "But?"

"You and I are another matter."

"There is no you and I, Laura." The words escaped before I could stop them. She turned away from me, but not before I saw that all the color had left her face.

"Look," I said, "I'll find another place for Jimmy. It may take me a day or two, but I will. And then we won't bother you anymore."

"You don't understand, do you?" She sighed, and closed

her eyes. Then her mouth formed into a bow, like it sometimes did when she had made a decision. Her gaze met mine
and it was clear. I didn't even see anger in it anymore.

She took a step toward me and put her hands on my
arms. Her fingers were warm, her touch gentle. I couldn't
have pulled away if I wanted to.

"I thought you'd been killed, Smokey," she said. "Then
you come here, and tell me you'd been in hiding, and you
didn't call me. Not once. As if I didn't matter. I offer to
help you find a home, a job, and you scream at me, and
then I don't see you again."

"Until I need your help." I kept my voice soft.

"No," she said. "Until Jimmy needs my help. If it had
been you, you wouldn't have come at all."

She was right. She knew me better than I gave her credit
for.

I didn't want her to know me that well.

I touched her face. Her skin was as soft as I remembered.
She leaned into my hand and closed her eyes.

I caressed her cheek, let my thumb linger on her chin. I
wanted to kiss her. Instead, I moved my hand away. "It's
not possible, Laura."

"Why not?" She opened her eyes. "Let's start over, de-
clare the past dead, and see what happens. Chicago isn't
Memphis, Smokey. It's a new place—"

"It's your place, Laura. And I don't belong."

"But you can," she said.

"What are you going to do? Tell all your high-society
friends to piss off if they don't like me?"

She stared at me for a moment.

"You gonna fight every cop who pulls us over because he
thinks I'm taking advantage of you? You gonna fire every
doorman who tries to keep me out of your building?"

"Smokey, I—"

"This isn't the time, Laura. I don't even know how long I'll stay in this town. I've got Jimmy to consider. He has to come first."

She bit her lower lip, then nodded once. After a moment, she nodded again. Then she let go of me and backed away, walking to the desk. She took the files, stacked them, and set them aside.

"I guess," she said slowly, "we need to decide how best to protect him."

"I'll find somewhere new—"

"No." She raised her head. Her gaze was strong. "You were right. He's safest with me. No one will suspect. For reasons we just discussed."

"Laura," I started, but I didn't know how I was going to finish. I let her name hang between us for a moment.

"Why don't you get him?" she asked. "We have a lot to talk about."

That cool, abrupt tone was the one she always used when she was uncomfortable. The imperial tone that used to grate on me so much. This time, it made me want to soothe her, even though I was the one who had upset her.

But I didn't reach for her. Instead I went to the door, and called Jimmy.

It took him a moment to join us. I closed the door after him. He looked at Laura, then at me, clearly feeling the tension in the room.

"Let's find a place to sit down," I said.

Laura grabbed one of the wooden chairs, turning it around. Jimmy climbed into another nearby and I took a third.

I took a deep breath, forcing myself to think about Jimmy and the threats, not Laura and the feelings she raised. I couldn't afford to think about that now.

"I told you both I believe this threat is very real," I said.

"I'm searching for someone now, where before I was just trying to confirm the entire rumor."

"Are they after you or Jimmy?" Laura asked.

"I don't know," I said. "But there's no real reason to look for me, except to find Jimmy."

Jimmy's lower lip trembled.

"I know you're afraid," I said to him. "It's normal."

"I want to be with you," he said.

"I know," I said. "But we decided to keep you safe, remember?"

He nodded.

"Remember the last time you went out on your own?"

His entire face turned gray. The last time he went out on his own, he had seen Martin die. "That's not fair, Smokey."

"It's true," I said. "You have to stay. This city is full of cops and FBI and undercover officers. You come home now and you may hurt us both."

Laura frowned at me over Jimmy's head.

"You mean kill us both," Jimmy said.

I studied him for a minute. "Maybe I do."

Laura's frown grew deeper.

"What happens if he gets you?" Jimmy asked. "What happens if you die?"

He had asked that on the phone the day before. Apparently he'd been turning that possibility over and over in his mind.

"You think that could happen?" Laura sounded shocked.

I shrugged one shoulder. "Not really."

What I didn't say was that if Jimmy was gone, I wasn't a threat. I wouldn't go after the entire Memphis Police Department just to get revenge for Martin's death. I couldn't. All that left was mainstream channels—reporters, lawsuits— solutions that usually didn't work for men like me. They certainly wouldn't work without Jimmy. If he were gone, there would be nothing I could do or say to have anyone believe me. I'd be dismissed as a crank and nothing more.

"But," I continued, "Jimmy's worried about it, and I think as a practical matter, we have to address it."

Laura folded her hands together. Jimmy looked down as if I were embarrassing him.

"If we don't," I said, "and something does happen . . ."

I let my voice trail off. I didn't want to finish that sentence. Neither of them seemed to want to finish it for me.

"Here's what I want to do." I stood up. I needed to move around. "I'm going to call in every day. If you don't hear from me for forty-eight hours, I want you to leave Chicago."

"Call?" Jimmy straightened. "You gotta see us."

"It's too risky. I left the apartment at twelve to make sure I wasn't followed. Even then, I wasn't certain until about a half hour before I came here. This guy is a pro."

"Police?" Laura asked.

I was thinking FBI, but I didn't say that. "Maybe."

"What if you find this man before the convention's over?" Laura asked.

"I'm going to assume he's not working alone," I said. "I want to wait until the strangers leave town."

She sighed and ran her hand through her hair. The long blond strands fell about her face, messy and attractive.

She caught me staring at her. I looked away.

"Why do we have to leave town?" Laura asked.

"I want Jimmy out of here," I said. "If they find me, then they'll know he's here."

"But they won't know he's at my place."

"We have to assume they'd find out."

Laura's gaze met mine, and in it, for the first time, I saw real fear. "Where should we go?"

I shrugged. "I don't know and I don't want to know."

"But how will you find me?" Jimmy's voice rose. His

hands were trembling and he grabbed on to his knees to steady them.

"I thought of that already," I said. "Laura, when you're safely out of town, you'll find a pay phone miles from where you're staying. Then you'll call the two phone numbers I left you. You will not stay on the line longer than thirty seconds. You will not leave a message or give your name. If I'm not there, you'll promise to call back later."

"Thirty seconds?" she asked.

"Phone calls can be traced in about a minute, sometimes less. Thirty seconds is safe."

She nodded.

Jimmy's eyes grew wide. His Adam's apple bobbed. He was swallowing compulsively.

I wanted to go to him, to put my hand on his shoulder and calm him. But I didn't dare. He needed to be uneasy. He needed to understand the stakes.

"If I don't sound like myself," I said, "or if I sound funny, as if my voice is strained or slightly unfamiliar, hang up."

"You think someone else could impersonate you?" Laura asked. "I'd know your voice anywhere."

Those words hung between us for a moment. Slowly color built in her cheeks.

"We're being cautious here," I said. "That's the key. If you can't reach me in two more days or you're not satisfied with the way I sound, find some place to hole up for a month. Then contact my friend Roscoe Miller in Memphis. You met him at the Peabody. Pick a place to have him meet me. Make sure it's far away from you. Don't let him know where you are. Leave a message with the doorman of your building, so that I know where I'm supposed to meet Roscoe and when. Roscoe will know me, and he'll know if something's wrong. If he has a doubt, any doubt, make sure he tells you. If he has none, then set up a place, through him, where the three of us can be reunited."

"This sounds so convoluted," Laura said.

"It is," I said.

"You're really scared of these people, aren't you?"

"I'm not scared," I said, and it was true. I was focused and maybe even a little angry. "I know who we're dealing with. I just worry that we're not being cautious enough."

SEVEN

When I left Laura's office, I walked to the "L" station. It was time to head north, to look for Elijah. I hoped I would find him with the hippies. Otherwise the search might take longer than I expected.

The midafternoon heat was grueling, made worse by the tall buildings around me. The humidity got trapped in the city's canyons, making it hard to breathe.

The oppressiveness had a weight to it; the air so thick that I glanced at the sky, hoping for a storm. The storm would come, I knew, but probably not the kind I wanted. And the oppressiveness would only get worse.

The news had been trumpeted for days that the antiwar protestors were meeting in Lincoln Park. The bulk of them were in town that day for a "Festival of Life," which the Yippies had been promoting since January. The Yippies called themselves the Youth International Party, but from all I'd seen in the various media, they'd mostly devoted themselves to street theater.

They didn't seem to be serious. Just the day before, they'd announced their presidential candidate in the Civic Center Plaza. They called the candidate Pigasus, whose platform was garbage, and they brought an actual pig into Chicago's downtown. That got the attention of the media, caused an uproar in the middle of the business day, and got poor Pigasus a new home at Chicago's Humane Society.

The serious ones were the Students for a Democratic Society, who were also gathering in the park. They had been planning some kind of protest against the Democratic convention since December. Their agenda seemed a lot more professional—assemblies at the various parks, speakers, and eventually a march on the Amphitheater.

So far, the city had been able to stonewall the protestors on the issues of permits and marches, and seemed to think that would be enough. Up until this point, all I had cared about was the way these demonstrations would affect the Hilton. I hadn't expected to go to Lincoln Park. It wasn't a place I usually frequented.

The "L" train going north from the Loop was mostly empty. I took a seat near a grimy window and waited for the darkness to go by. Finally we surfaced from the underground station and I could see the hazy sunshine spreading over the city like a cloud.

I got off at Sedgewick. My side of the island platform was empty. On the other side, two girls wearing headbands, love beads, and ankle-length dresses leaned together, laughing. They swayed slightly as they did so. I wasn't even sure they noticed me.

I took the metal steps down to the street level. The Sedgewick Station huddled underneath the tracks. It was an old brick building with new windows, crosshatched with steel to protect them from destruction. The door was closed and the blinds were pulled. The entire place looked like a fortress, locked against an impending attack.

I walked east on North Street, heading toward the park. I hadn't been to the Old Town section before. It was dingy and run-down, a remnant of an age gone by. The air smelled faintly of marijuana and regular cigarettes. Down a side street, I heard a guitar being played badly. The stores I passed were businesses that thrived on cheap rent: a psychic with her own storefront boasted tarot readings; a head shop displayed drug paraphernalia in the window; and a record store positioned a bin on the sidewalk, the album covers faded and frayed.

In the distance, I heard chanting, too faint to make out, and more music. There were also ripples of laughter that floated toward me and seemed to come from nowhere.

Most of the people on the streets were young, and most of them wore casual clothes—blue jeans, shorts, or T-shirts. A few of them raised the index and middle fingers of their right hand as they passed me—they had co-opted the old V for Victory sign and made it into something they called the Peace Sign. I still wasn't used to it.

Instead of making the sign in response, I nodded my head and continued walking. The atmosphere seemed festive, but what disturbed me—and what the kids didn't seem to see— were the huge number of police cars on the streets. In less than a block, I had passed three police cars, and seen five officers conversing in a small group. They watched me pass, and I felt the hair on the back of my neck rise.

As I got closer to the park, a girl-woman with dreamy, unfocused eyes and bad skin gave me a flyer. On the top, it said: *Daring Expose—Top Secret Yippie Plans for Lincoln Park*. I scanned down the sheet. The next two days would be devoted to "training in snake dancing, karate, and non-violent self-defense." After the convention started, there would be a music festival, a beach party that included "folksinging, barbecues, swimming, lovemaking." One day would be set aside for the Yippie Olympics, the Miss Yippie Contest, "catch the candidate, pin the tail on the donkey, pin the rubber on the Pope, and other normal, healthy games."

I began to wonder how anyone could take these kids seriously, until I saw two other notations. On August 28, there would be a march to the convention itself. That one didn't worry me as much as the one scheduled for Sunday. It read:

August 25 (P.M.): Welcoming of the Democratic Delegates—Downtown hotels (to be announced).

I sighed. Amid the fun and games there would be some serious protesting after all.

I folded up the paper and stuck it in my pocket. The girl who had given it to me was handing out the sheets to anyone who passed. But beside her, a young man watched everyone she gave them to. His gaze met mine and I felt the coldness in his eyes.

Finding Elijah, if he were here, wasn't going to be as easy as I'd thought.

When I reached the edge of the park, I saw activity on Clark Street, just beyond the Moody Church. Some young men with short hair and serious expressions were tacking up signs made from poster board and Magic Marker.

Welcome to Chicago, U.S.A., one read, and instead of an *S*, there was a swastika. A woman was dragging a chair toward them. She seemed trim and competent, moving with purpose.

The chanting had grown louder. It was clearly coming from the park. The guitar music had faded, but nearby someone was playing a flute. I thought I heard the beat of drums as well, but I couldn't quite tell. The chanting had a rhythm all its own.

I crossed Clark and went into the park. It felt slightly cooler here. The lake wasn't that far away. I couldn't see it, but I could smell it, vaguely fishy. A seagull circled overhead, reminding me that Chicagoans preferred to think of Lake Michigan as an inland sea.

The grass was green and well tended. Obviously, in this hot summer, the park had been getting more than its fair share of water. The park was huge—I'd seen it on the city's maps—and this section was an open expanse.

Between the park and the lake, cars passed, their movement almost hypnotic, white against a sea of blue. The colors were brighter here than they were inside the city, the sunlight clearer, as if the haze that settled over the rest of the city was being blown away by the fresh lake breeze.

A long line of people, six across and at least twenty deep, linked arms and were bouncing from foot to foot as they moved forward. They were the ones chanting, something that sounded like "Wah-Choy."

Reporters surrounded them, photographing them, and a man trailed after them, holding a television camera above his head. Crowds had assembled in the center of the park, most of them sitting and talking, many of them smoking or eating or waving their hands at each other.

Near the trees, one of the few black men—more a skinny boy—led a group of doughy white kids in basic karate moves. As I watched, a blond girl tried to stand on one leg, lost her footing and fell. Others fell beside her, laughing.

This didn't seem like the big crisis the city had been preparing for. It would have felt like a party if it weren't for all of the police lining the park's pathways, hovering near the park entrances and driving by on large police motorcycles.

I wandered through the crowd, looking for black faces. I found some, most of them male, and most of them college age. I asked a few about Elijah, but got no response. One white student, who overheard my questioning, laughed.

"This isn't a place for kids," he said.

I agreed. If I did find Elijah here, I would get him back to Grace Kirkland as quickly as possible.

Near the field house, a group of twenty-five people sat on

the ground. There were no love beads here. It looked like a college class meeting on a lawn. Young women, their hair pulled back by bands, sat in the front. A few young men were sprawled on their stomachs, resting their chin on their hands as they listened.

The speaker was a woman wearing jeans and a tight T-shirt. Her close-cropped hair was boyish, her attitude all business. She held a sheet of paper in her hands and she was reviewing it with them. Her voice was strident and firm. As I got closer, I could just barely make out the words.

". . . help them avoid arrest by forming small groups, breaking out of the park, and heading toward the Loop." As she said that last, she gestured behind her, pointing vaguely in the direction of downtown.

A rail-thin young man stood beside her. I hadn't noticed him at first. He took a step toward the crowd, and said, "It's an awesome responsibility. You're going to have heavy tasks. You have to make these demonstrations work."

I saw only one black face in the group, a serious man in his midtwenties, wearing a white button-down shirt and a pair of black pants. He had a notebook on his lap and was taking notes. Whenever someone whispered near him, he glared.

He was not Elijah Kirkland.

Two men stood toward the back of the group. They had taken off their shirts in the heat, and their stomachs were so white that they were startling. One of the men had long frizzy hair. The other wore a duffel bag over his shoulder, its strap cutting into his bare skin. Even though they were casually dressed, they seemed important, and they both noticed me at the same time.

Frizzy hair spoke to his neighbor and then nodded toward me. I felt that same coldness I had felt earlier, the assessment, the way they all watched me.

And then I recognized it. They thought I was undercover. They thought I was spying on them.

I toyed with explaining myself and then realized how it would play. A middle-aged man asking them if they had seen a young boy, in a place where young boys were clearly not welcome. It would sound like an excuse, a made-up reason for eavesdropping on their meeting.

I wandered down a park path, trying to look inconspicuous. But I was conspicuous partly because of my age and dress, and partly because of my color. I did not belong here. Despite the occasional black face, this was a white man's movement and a white man's cause. And I felt hopelessly out of place.

If I felt that way, then Elijah Kirkland would have felt it even more. Perhaps my instincts were wrong. Just because he opposed the war didn't mean that he would come here. Perhaps Grace didn't know as much about him as she thought she did. Maybe Elijah Kirkland had joined the Blackstone Rangers after all.

I walked back to North street, intending to return to the "L" stop. As I stood there, I looked down the row of stone buildings, with their rounded faces, speaking of an era long gone. People flowed into a building not far from me. Outside it, women in long skirts sat on the sidewalk, Indian blankets in front of them, displaying some kind of wares. The girl I had gotten my flyer from had worked her way to the corner. She still swayed to music only she could hear.

I crossed to that side of North Street and walked down the sidewalk, pretending to be interested in the stuff on the blankets. Most of it was cheap jewelry, made from beads and thread. One blanket was covered in books, thick textbooks that had dented corners and ruined spines. Another held a variety of spoons, and it took me a minute to realize they weren't for food.

I reached the building. The door was propped open. The sickly sweet odor of marijuana was stronger here. I was surprised that the cops hadn't done anything about it, but they didn't seem that interested in this section of the street. They didn't seem interested in much of anything. It made me wonder how many undercover officers they had inside.

As I approached the door, two people came out. They were laughing and holding each other up. They both had long stringy hair and their clothing reeked of pot. I had trouble figuring out what gender they were. They saw me watching, laughed harder, and staggered away from me.

I slipped inside.

The air was a gray-green with smoke, marijuana mixed with clove cigarettes. A tinny radio blared Jefferson Airplane but the murmur of voices nearly drowned it out. I had expected to see people lying around in a drugged fog. Instead, this place was a hive of activity.

Piles of paper were crowded in boxes. Three women were sorting through them, giving piles to the teenagers leaning against the wall. They were folding the papers into flyers. In the center of the room, poster board covered the floor. A man bent over one of the boards. With a pencil, he was carefully outlining letters. They were too faint to make out.

My eyes stung in the smoke-filled air, and I could feel myself getting light-headed. There was enough pot in this enclosed space to make anyone high. What a great way to go home, smelling like this. I hoped I avoided cops as I went.

Here I was not the only black face. I saw at least a half dozen, maybe more, most of them male, but none of them were young, or at least, young enough to be Elijah Kirkland—even if he did look older than he was.

As I stepped away from the door, a heavy-set man with black glasses and a thick black beard barred my way. My gaze met his. He held out his hand, fanning Magic Markers like they were a bouquet of flowers.

"You here to work?"

"Actually, I—"

"Because we need signs, man. We got to have ways to let people know what's happening, you know what I mean?"

I didn't, but I took a marker.

"You can help Josh." My instructor pointed to the young man sprawled on the floor. "He needs a colorer."

I walked toward Josh, wondering at how easily I was accepted. I sat down beside him. I still couldn't make out the words. "What are you writing?"

He sat up, squinted at me as if I had just appeared before him—which, judging by his level of concentration, I probably had. "It's for Pigasus, man."

I looked at the poster board. In big loopy letters he had written The Pig in '68.

"I thought Pigasus had been arrested." Arrested had been the Yippie term on the news.

He chuckled. "Well, you know. When one pig disappears, there's always another to take his place."

I leaned closer to him so that I could speak without being overheard. "Listen, I'm looking for a fourteen-year-old boy named Elijah."

"Oh, shit, man." The pencil artist slapped his hands against the poster board. "And I thought you were on the level."

"I am on the level," I said.

"No, you're not. You're a fucking square." That last word was so loud that it rose over the din of the radio. Several other people looked at me. A few took up a chant: *Square, square, square.* It grew louder.

I stood. "I'm looking for Elijah Kirkland. Anyone know where he is?"

The chant got louder: *Square, square, square.* The bearded man who gave me the marker scurried toward me and plucked it out of my hand.

"You shouldn't go pretending you're someone you're not."

"I wasn't pretending anything," I said. "I was searching for Elijah—"

"There's no Elijah here," a girl said. She had long blond hair and clear eyes. When I looked at her, she raised her chin slightly. Her words were forceful and also unnecessary. For the first time since I'd come to Old Town, I got the sense that my original hunch was right.

"If you see him, tell him to call home."

"We don't believe in home," the girl said.

"You believe in love, don't you?" I asked.

"Love and peace." The girl crossed her arms.

"Elijah's mother loves him. She's worried about him."

"It's none of her business if he's doing his own thing," the girl said.

I was getting tired of the rhetoric and the stench in the large room. My eyes felt swollen and dry.

"Well," I said, "he's underage, and if he gets caught in here, you all get into trouble."

"Age is relative, man," said the pencil artist.

"Not under the law," I said.

"The law has nothing to do with us." The bearded man spoke. "All it does is send us off to die."

"You should understand that, man," the pencil artist said. "The law hasn't done your people any favors either."

"My people," I said, enunciating each word clearly, "are missing a fourteen-year-old boy and we're afraid something bad has happened to him. A little cooperation would be nice."

The artist tucked his pencil behind his ear. "How do we know you're not a pig?"

"I'm not a cop. I'm just looking for a boy who may have gotten himself into some trouble."

The girl was still watching me, her gaze steely.

"Anyone?" I asked.

They were silent. The radio had moved onto playing "Eve of Destruction." It was the only sound in the large room. Somehow, in the space of a few minutes, I had gone from a potential volunteer to the enemy. I understood their hostility: this generation's dislike of anyone over thirty had been well publicized. What astounded me was that they had initially accepted me. It was either due to the color of my skin and the fake openness of their politics or it was due to the smoky haze in the room, and the fact that no one realized how old I was until I started asking questions.

I reached into my pocket and removed a dime. I balanced it on my right thumbnail. "All right. You don't have to answer me. But if any of you know Elijah Kirkland, have him call home. He doesn't have to say where he is or what he's doing. Just that he's all right. I'll even pay for the call."

I flicked the dime into the air. It flipped several times, a tiny missile barely visible in the smoke, and then clattered against the wooden floor. No one had moved. I turned my back on them, and left.

The sunlight seemed too bright after the darkness in that room. I breathed deeply several times to clear my lungs and possibly my head. I knew my eyes were red, and my clothing stank of pot and cloves.

Before I went back to the "L," I wandered the streets and alleys, looking at people as I passed. Maybe I would pass Elijah Kirkland on the street. If I was lucky—which, of course, I wasn't.

I saw a lot of stoned kids, though, sitting on porch steps, passed out in alleys. The other young people didn't seem to notice. They were all busy with their own thing, as that girl had so quaintly put it, selling junk on the sidewalk or making signs or handing out flyers.

The cops watched it all, not making a move, a solid blue presence that seemed to have grown since I went inside.

They looked out of place in this environment, like soldiers in a foreign land.

I remembered that feeling. I'd been on both sides of it, as a soldier in Korea and a black child raised in the South.

I showered before I went to see Grace Kirkland. I put the water on lukewarm and I spent extra time scrubbing, getting the smell off of me. I was a little hungry and a little woozy—signs I had probably gotten high in there—but I knew the feeling would wear off shortly. Besides, the lukewarm shower cooled me off. For the first time that day, I didn't feel as if I were melting in the heat.

But I had a new problem. I was going to look through the material Grace had gathered for me, but I still trusted my original hunch. The hostility of the girl in the room and the way she had looked confirmed that hunch.

I wanted to investigate further. But no one in that group would talk to me and we all knew it. That was why, in Memphis, I never worked outside of my own community. I needed the contacts, the networking, and the ability to walk in and out of various venues. I lacked all of that here. I was starting over, and I didn't like it.

I got dressed, grabbed the last of the salad that Althea had prepared, and then left the apartment.

Heat shimmered on the concrete. It was a little after six, but it still felt like afternoon. Barefoot children stayed on the small patch of grass, playing a game in which they turned each other into statues. Adults sat outside, fanning themselves and conversing or watching the children. From somewhere nearby, I smelled the odor of lit charcoal and grilled hamburgers. A simple summer evening. I hadn't had one of those all year.

As I walked toward Grace's, I scanned the block, looking for my shadow. Any good tracker would have come back to the apartment after losing me on the "L." I had a hunch he was watching, but I didn't see him. He was that good.

The door to Grace's building stood open, just like it had that morning. A child's shrieking laughter echoed from the back of the building. I stepped inside, overwhelmed by the odor of frying onions. The hallway was hotter than it had been that morning—the heat of the day had been trapped inside—and now there were toys scattered on the scarred floor like booby traps for unwary adults.

I picked my way around them and knocked on Grace's door. There was a moment of silence, then a clatter as if something had fallen over, and footsteps running toward the door. I debated entering—thinking there might be a problem—and then the door was flung open.

Grace stood there. She crossed her hands above her left breast and sighed heavily when she recognized me. "Oh, Bill. I'm so glad to see you."

"Did something happen?"

"Come inside." She grabbed my arm and pulled me into the apartment. It was hot too, but a breeze came from the patio doors. A single lawn chair stood in the middle of the small garden, a glass filled with soda and melting ice on the ground by its side.

The end table near the couch had fallen over. Grace righted it as she led me into the living room.

"What happened?" I asked.

"I had the strangest phone call." She went to the garden and picked up her glass. Then she carried it to the sink and poured out its contents. The movements were by rote, as if she needed something to do, as if she were too restless to sit still.

Maybe my visit to Old Town had borne fruit after all. "When?"

"Just a little while ago. It was Daniel."

It took me a moment to place the name. Her eldest son. Curious. "Oh?"

She nodded, then opened the refrigerator. "Can I get you anything?"

I hadn't realized how thirsty I was. It had been a long, strange day. "I'd love a glass of ice water."

She took down another glass, put ice in it, and filled it from the tap. Then she opened a can of Hires root beer and poured some into her glass. She brought the water glass to me.

"What was strange about the call?" I asked.

"He said he'd heard that Elijah was missing. He wanted me to tell him how that could happen."

"I thought Daniel was at Yale."

"He *is*," she said. "That's what so strange."

I suppressed a sigh. Obviously Daniel wasn't at Yale. He had come home to Chicago without telling his mother. Probably for the protests. Considering how opposed she was to this type of political action, I could understand his need for independence.

"What did he say, exactly?"

"He'd heard from some friends in Chicago that Elijah was missing. He wanted to know if it was true."

"When did he hear?"

"Just before he called."

"Had you told anyone besides me?"

"All our friends," she said. "But not anyone who would call Daniel."

"Do me a favor," I said. "Call him back."

"I can't afford—"

"Call him back, Grace."

She licked her lips and went to the green phone hanging on the wall near the refrigerator. Before she started to dial, she consulted a piece of paper attached to the refrigerator door by a magnet.

I peered over her shoulder. The slip of paper listed three numbers for Daniel: One for his dorm, one for his hall monitor, and one for his job.

Grace dialed and then clung to the receiver with both hands. I could hear a faint ringing, and then a click.

"Hi," she said. "I'm calling for Daniel Kirkland."

I sipped the water. It had the metallic taste common to Chicago tap water. After three months, I still wasn't used to it.

"No." She glanced at me. "That's not possible."

I held my breath.

"When?"

I knew what the person on the other end was telling her. Daniel was in Chicago, and he hadn't called her.

"Is there someone else I can talk to?" Her small face grew even narrower. "This is his mother."

There was a longer pause. She turned her back to me, and I could see her shoulders shake.

"Hi," she said again in a different, more businesslike tone. "This is Mrs. Grace Kirkland. I'm calling for my son Daniel. . . . I thought the term had one more week. . . . No, that's not possible. He would have told me. Besides, he can't afford it. . . . A protest bus?"

She said this last weakly as if she didn't want to hear it.

"When do you expect him back?" She leaned her head against the wall, her entire body hunched away from me. "No, no. That's all right. I'll call then. Thank you."

Then she hung up.

She didn't move for more than a minute, as if the news had wounded her somehow, given her one more blow than she could deal with. I waited, not quite sure how to comfort her, or if comforting her was the right thing to do.

Then she squared her shoulders and stood, facing me. "They say he's in Chicago."

I nodded.

"But you knew that already."

"I knew it when you said he called. I left a message that Elijah should call me. Apparently Daniel got the message."

"Why would he come home and not tell me?"

I set my glass down. "I don't think he's here for a social visit."

"He sounded so worried about Elijah. What's going on, Bill?"

"I'm not sure," I said. "If Daniel calls back, tell him I want to talk with him. Tell him I'm the one looking for his brother, and I may need his help."

She nodded.

"In the meantime, did you get those names and phone numbers I asked for?"

"Yeah." She sounded distracted. Her entire world had changed—or maybe just her perception of it. Which meant that I couldn't trust most of what she had told me that morning. I would have to find Elijah on my own.

She went back into the living room and grabbed a sheet of notepaper. Names, phone numbers, and addresses were scrawled all over it. Beside them were the letters *D, E,* or *G.* She pointed to them. "I marked whose friend this was. I thought it would be easier."

It was, although, I noted, there were very few Es on the list. I didn't like that either.

She said, "Is Daniel in trouble?"

I looked up from the list. "They said he took a protest bus?"

She nodded.

The white Chicago papers had said groups of students were coming from all over the country for the convention. The *Defender* had said a lot of the buses were canceled because people were expecting trouble at the convention. But if Daniel was already here, he had come as a leader, not as a follower. The main group of protestors wasn't expected until tomorrow.

"He's exercising his rights as an adult, Mrs. Kirkland," I said, "even though you and I may not think of him that way."

She put a hand over her mouth. "I wanted him out of here."

I nodded. "He'll go back."

"Why is he worried about Elijah?"

Why indeed? "You're worried about him."

"But this was different. He sounded scared."

And that was my biggest clue. "I'll see what I can find," I said, and let myself out.

In a normal investigation, I would have returned to Old Town and looked for Daniel Kirkland. He hadn't been in that room; I would have recognized him from the photographs in the apartment. I hadn't seen him in the park or in the streets either. Someone had told him about my visit, someone who hadn't been willing to tell me about him.

I doubted those kids would talk to me. I was too old and, in their words, too straight. They had already confused me with the police once. I was sure they would do it again.

So I had to come up with something else, and because of my limited resources, I had to take a risk.

I retraced my steps from the day before when Franklin and I were trying to flush out the shadow. Halfway up my block, I saw the same group of teenagers, huddled together.

Malcolm Reyner leaned against the wall, his arms crossed and his head down, pretending that he was asleep. He had apparently been standing like that when I passed him the day before. Then he had peeled off that wall and followed me.

This time I went to him.

The other boys grew silent. They glared at me. I was getting very tired of being stared at, and the heat wasn't helping my mood.

I grabbed Malcolm's arm, nearly pulling him off balance. "You're coming with me."

"I didn't do nothing!" he said.

"I know. You're still coming with me."

His friends were milling now. They had seen the fight yesterday and had probably heard about it in even greater detail from Malcolm. They didn't want to take me on. Malcolm wasn't a big enough member of their little gang to make it worthwhile.

I led him to an abandoned building nearby. No one sat on the stoop. No one stood across the street, either. His friends remained on the corner, watching, but they weren't going to do anything.

"Sit down," I said.

"Why?"

"Just sit."

"Fuck this, man."

I cuffed him lightly on the side of the head. "Be polite. And remember that I'm older and stronger than you."

"Older maybe," he said, but he sat down.

The stoop had a brick-and-stone railing. I leaned against it. "You know a kid named Elijah Kirkland?"

"No." Sullen. He didn't even meet my gaze.

"Sure you do. He lived down the block. You probably knew his brother better. Daniel Kirkland."

Malcolm shrugged. He glanced around me. His friends still hadn't taken a step toward him. He was on his own and he knew it.

"What do you want?" he asked.

"I want you to answer my questions."

He lifted his head. His left cheek was badly scraped, and

he had a black eye. "You don't got me shoved against no building today."

"Not yet."

"And your fat friend isn't here to defend you."

"I don't need him to defend me," I said. "I need you."

Malcolm snorted. "Sure you do."

"How committed are you to those Rangers over there?"

"They're not Rangers," he said.

"Well, they're either Blackstone Rangers, baby Black Panthers, or the Devil's Disciples."

"You don't know nothing."

"Well, I know if they're none of the above, they're part of that little wannabe organization, the Black Machine."

His lips thinned.

"You think they care about you?" I asked. "They watched while you got beat up yesterday. They're watching now, and they know what kind of threat I am. You're just an errand boy for them, and that means you're dispensable."

He looked down at his hands. Apparently that thought had crossed his mind in the last twenty-four hours. He was as smart as I thought he was.

"So," I said, "you want to help me out?"

"I don't even know who you are, man." He kept his head down. The tone was sullen again, like an unprepared student in an oversized classroom.

"No, you don't."

"Then why would I want to help you?" The rest of the question was implied. At the expense of his relationship with the boys who were watching us now. At the expense of all he knew.

"I'll bet they treated you differently last night, didn't they?" I looked over my shoulder at the three of them and smiled. "Teasing, with a nasty edge to it. No one helped you with your eye or your scrape. No one cared when you

131

tried to talk about it. Someone told you that you just didn't get the job done."

A flush started at the base of his neck and rose.

"Maybe someone even said you were worthless or suggested that they had put too much time in you when you clearly weren't Machine material."

This time, he didn't correct my guess. His flush had moved to his cheeks. I was hitting home.

"Has anyone spoken to you yet today?"

"What the hell do you want, man?" He didn't raise his voice, but he spoke with such intensity that it felt like he had shouted.

I suppressed a smile. I had gotten through. "I told you. I want your help."

"And what," he asked, with that same intensity, "can a loser like me do for an old fart like you?"

"Talk to me."

"Shit. You are a cop."

"Nope. But I am helping out a friend."

He hadn't moved. It was clear he was listening now. I had his attention. I wasn't sure how long I could hold it.

"Daniel Kirkland?"

"His mother, actually. Elijah is missing."

"Shit."

"Do you know him?"

"Elijah? Who doesn't?"

"Is he a Ranger—I mean, part of the Machine?"

"He's a baby," Malcolm said.

"What about Daniel? Was he in any of the neighborhood gangs?"

"He's gone. Some high and mighty school." There was resentment in Malcolm's voice, resentment I recognized.

I ran a hand over the railing's stone surface. It was cool to the touch. "When did Daniel stop being your friend?"

Malcolm raised his head and his one-eyed gaze met mine. The movement was involuntary, his surprise obvious and impossible to hide. "We're not friends."

"Anymore. But you used to be."

"He tell you that?"

"You did."

"When?"

"Just now. The way you talked about him."

"What kind of game is this?"

"It's no game." I folded my hands. "Grace Kirkland went to the cops for help finding Elijah. They told her that she shouldn't worry—he was probably in a neighborhood gang and they'd arrest him soon enough."

"Elijah? No way."

"So she went to some black cops, friends of a friend. They said they couldn't do much, not with all the things happening in Chicago right now."

"Yeah?"

"Then she came to me."

"What're you, God?"

I smiled. "I'm a guy who gets things done. I got close today. I managed to sniff out Daniel."

"That's easy. He's at Yale." Another giveaway to the old friendship. Along with that deep bitterness.

"Actually, no. He's in Lincoln Park."

"Shit. What a dumb-ass."

"Yeah." I spoke softly. "My problem is that I can't talk to him. I had one chance to get into that community and I blew it."

"They let you in?"

"Not really." I paused for effect. "They thought I was a cop."

"No shit."

"So, I was wondering if you could arrange a meeting with me and Daniel."

"What do you want to meet with him for? You said he was surprised that Elijah's missing."

Interesting lead-in. "Are you surprised?"

Malcolm turned his head toward the other end of the block, away from me, away from his so-called friends. "Yeah. Elijah's different, you know? Keeps to himself."

"His mother says he's a good student."

"Sure. Him and Daniel. They're smarter than everyone else." That resentment again.

"How do you know that?"

"Grades. Daniel got some scholarship. He did good on that test too, the one they give to let you into college."

"Did you take it?"

"Shit, no."

I let the words hang between us for a moment. I recognized his attitude. If I had left Jimmy alone in Memphis, he would have become like Malcolm. Bright, but unable to translate his intelligence into a viable skill, because his life got in the way of his opportunities. If something happened to me, his life might still get in the way.

I made myself concentrate on Malcolm.

"So you have no idea how you could have done on that test."

"Don't patronize me, man."

"I'm not," I said. "I'm asking you to help me."

"If I do this, what do I get out of it?"

Satisfaction wasn't something a teenager wanted. Doing the right thing might get him in trouble. I sighed and said the only thing I could think of. "Money."

"How much?"

I had no idea. I hadn't asked for money from Grace Kirkland. I didn't dare. I didn't want people to know I had done this before. Any money was going to have to come out of my own pocket.

"Let's do it by the hour," I said. "You got a job?"

"Nope."

"You do now."

"How much an hour?"

"I'll give you a dollar over minimum."

"That all?"

"It's all I can afford."

"Fuck, man, I'm worth more than that."

I smiled. "Yes, you are. But I'm paying you more than those guys are. They're just using you and not very nicely either."

"I go with you, and I can't go back there." He inclined his head toward the group who had moved away from the corner. They were back in their usual spot, and they didn't seem to be paying attention anymore. Although, on occasion, one of them would sneak a look toward us.

"I know," I said. He couldn't go back anyway. Yesterday, Franklin and I had made him look weak. It would only be a matter of time before the gang turned on him completely.

"That's gotta be worth something too."

"Your life, maybe."

He bowed his head, then shook it once as if he were arguing with himself. Trying to get his help was a long shot—kids his age were usually pretty established on their course—but he was clearly the new man in his group, and he was taking orders at an age when he should have been giving them. Either he'd lacked power for a long time, or he had finally given up and joined the gang.

I was gambling that he had joined because he didn't know what else to do.

"So you pay me a handful of dollars, and I gotta move out of the neighborhood."

"Maybe," I said. "Or maybe you do a good enough job that when something else comes up, I hire you again."

He clearly hadn't expected that offer. I hadn't expected to give it. But it was out now, and couldn't be taken back.

"You're shitting me."

"No," I said. "I believe in being paid for good work."

"What if you don't got no more work?"

"Then maybe you can find a regular job."

He laughed. "Yeah, right. Like they'd hire someone like me."

"What's wrong with you?"

He held out his hands, then turned them over, indicating his dark skin. "That, and I don't got my diploma. So they figure I'm no good, you know?"

"And you were setting out to prove them right?"

"Hey, man, you don't know—"

"No, I don't know." Clearly it was a sore spot for him. Which meant it was important. I had guessed correctly. "But I do know that Bronzeville's like the rest of Chicago. Who you know is important."

"And who do you know?"

I smiled, thinking of Franklin. "I have a fat friend who seems to know everyone."

Malcolm gazed at me in disbelief. "Why would he help me?"

"Because I asked him to."

"He live in your pocket?"

"No. At the moment, I live in his. But we have an understanding, and he trusts me."

Malcolm threaded his fingers together, then turned his hands inside out, stretching his arms and cracking his knuckles. "Your promises are vague, man."

"Not the money."

"It's not enough."

I sighed. Time to end the conversation. I wasn't going to get any further here. "It's all I got."

I stood up. My elbows were sore from leaning on the stone. I started to walk away.

"Hey! Wait!"

I stopped. Malcolm caught up to me. As he did, he shot a nervous glance at the boys near the corner. They were all watching now.

He had made his choice, and all of us knew it.

"Yeah?" I asked, pretending a disinterest that I didn't feel.

"I'll do it."

"Good," I said, and kept walking. Malcolm had to hurry to keep up with me. He averted his eyes as we approached the group on the corner. He hadn't been part of them long, and he wasn't good at hiding his emotions. I'd have to remember that if I used him on anything else.

"Whatcha doin', nigger?" one of the kids asked. "Doncha know that's the Man?"

I felt Malcolm stiffen beside me. I didn't say anything. This had to be his choice, all the way.

"Hey, idiot," said another. "You know what happens to people who go with the Man?"

"You ain't part of us no more."

"Where you gonna sleep, bro? Huh? You think you can just walk out?"

That last almost caught me. But I didn't look at them, nor did I say anything else. I kept walking and, to his credit, Malcolm kept up with me.

We went down the block to my car. I opened the driver's door and indicated the other side. Malcolm got in quickly, then slid down as if he could hide from his former friends.

I got in, closed the door, and turned the key in the ignition, but I didn't put the car in gear. "Last chance."

"Just go."

I shifted to drive and pulled out, glancing in my rearview mirror as I did. No tail yet. The boys were still watching us.

"You staying with them?" I asked.

"Ain't none of your business, man."

It felt like it was. I didn't want to be responsible for making someone homeless, no matter how wretched his home was. But I wasn't going to push it.

"So tell me what you know about Daniel?"

"Besides the fact he's a fucking prick?"

"Yeah."

"You got the basics. Brains, luck. He got out, man."

"And that makes him a prick?"

"No." Malcolm looked out the passenger window. He didn't seem ready to tell that story yet.

We were going east. I wanted to take Lake Shore. It was the quickest.

I checked the rearview. There were two possible tails: a beat-up white Ford that seemed to have too much horsepower for a car that decrepit, and a dark blue Oldsmobile that was trying too hard to seem inconspicuous. My money was on the Ford. It was nearly a block back. The Olds was two cars behind me, and occasionally it moved toward the left as if it were going to pass.

"What's behind us?" Malcolm asked. Observant too.

"Don't know yet," I said.

"There's a lot you don't know."

I nodded, and turned north on Lake Shore Drive. Night was falling and most of the cars had already turned their lights on. Bugs committed suicide on the windshield, leaving green goo as a reminder of their sacrifice.

The lake was deceptively smooth. Motorboats dotted the surface, their lights on. The sailboats had already returned to port.

Traffic was thin. The Olds and the Ford were still behind me. Neither seemed anxious to pass.

"Tell me about Elijah," I said.

"He's a little kid."

"He's fourteen, tall for his age. Straight-A student who works at the library, at least according to his mother."

"How come you say it like that?"

"Like what?"

" 'At least according to his mother.' " His imitation of me was excellent. He even caught the accent.

"I don't know Elijah," I said. "I never met him, and I've only talked with you and his mother about him. Mothers usually don't know their children real well—especially teenagers—so I hedge my bets a little. I figure she may be right and she may be wrong. I won't decide until I've gotten more information."

Malcolm leaned his head against the seat back. The darkness was growing. I had to wait until we passed under a streetlight before I could see his face. He appeared to be thinking about what I'd said.

"Elijah," he said after a moment, "lived for Daniel."

The past tense surprised me. "Lived?"

Malcolm shrugged. "Daniel moved."

Leaving Elijah and Malcolm behind. I glanced in the rearview. The white Ford and blue Olds were side by side in the double lane, five cars back. We had nearly reached the Loop. I expected one of them to turn off soon.

"His mother said he was interested in the antiwar movement?"

"Yeah, Daniel's always been political."

"No, Elijah."

Malcolm frowned. "He parroted whatever Daniel said. I didn't think he cared much otherwise, you know?"

I did know and I thought it fascinating that Malcolm knew as well. Maybe his decision to join me had less to do with my powers of persuasion than the fact that Elijah was the one who was missing.

"So, if you were Elijah, where would you go?"

"If I was Elijah, I'd be home, reading." Surprisingly there was no bitterness in Malcolm's voice. Reading was what he expected Elijah to do.

"What about drugs?"

Malcolm stiffened. He thought I was asking about him. I pretended not to notice. "What about them?"

"Do you think Elijah uses or maybe runs them for one of the neighborhood gangs?"

"Elijah?"

"Yes."

"Hell, no."

"Why not?"

"He doesn't want to mess up his mind."

"Are you sure?"

"Yes." The word was emphatic. There had clearly been more than one conversation on this topic.

We'd gone over the Chicago River and were heading toward the Gold Coast. I resisted the urge to glance at Laura's building as we passed, to see if there were lights on her floor.

Instead, I looked in the rearview mirror again. Only the white Ford remained, nearly ten cars back now. I looked ahead of me to see if the blue Olds had passed me and I had somehow missed it. That was an old tailing trick that sometimes worked.

There was no Olds immediately in front of me, but it could have been lost in the sea of taillights farther up. Although, if it was, it would have a hard time knowing when I turned.

I slipped behind a large gray Cadillac just to be safe.

I nearly missed the LaSalle Drive exit. I took a quick right past the beach and then a left under Lake Shore. I was driving too fast. I eased off the accelerator and let the car move through the south part of Lincoln Park on its own momentum.

Cars were parked on either side of the road, some haphazardly. Many were vans covered in stickers and bumper stickers, most of them big yellow flowers or with pithy phrases like "Make Love Not War."

The large afternoon crowd had left the park. Those who remained were clustered around two bonfires. Smoke trailed through my open window, along with voices singing "Blowing in the Wind." The faint sounds of flute and bongo drums floated after it.

Malcolm stared as if he had never seen anything like it. His gaze also caught the cop cars parked haphazardly on Clark Street. The cops still guarded the entrance to the park, watching the people inside.

Behind me, the white Ford appeared. It had no other car to hide behind now. Finally, I had my man.

I took LaSalle to Clark and Clark to North, two rapid turns that the Ford had to follow or lose me. Then I turned into an alley just off North Street and parked beneath a fire escape. The white Ford drove by slowly, as if he were looking for me.

Malcolm had turned toward me. "Now what?"

I told him about my visit earlier, and the fact that Daniel had called shortly there after. "Find him," I said, "and bring him to the car."

"Find him? He could be anywhere."

"He's around here. I probably got real close this afternoon. The building I went into is over there." I pointed.

"You're not going to do anything to him, are you?"

I smiled. Malcolm was just as involved as I thought he was. "I'm going to talk to him. You can stay with him, if you're worried about it, and he doesn't have to get into the car."

"What are you going to do while I look?"

"Wait," I said. "There's not much more I can do."

"I'll hurry," Malcolm said.

"It's better if you take your time."

He frowned at me.

"You'll have more of a chance of finding him."

Malcolm nodded and let himself out. I waited until he'd

been gone for five minutes before I got out of the car. I locked it, stuck my keys in my pocket, and headed toward North Street. I knew I'd be back before he was.

The street was mostly empty. A longhaired person—I couldn't tell if it was a boy or a girl—was sleeping on the sidewalk in front of the building I had been in that afternoon. Someone sang an old Beach Boys song loudly and off-key. In one of the apartments above the street, a pale light streamed through an orange-and-red tie-dye curtain.

More police gathered near the church, apparently making plans to patrol the park. A group of motorcycles rode by—twenty-five or more—their engines loud in the quiet night.

The white Ford was parked in front of a brownstone across the street. At first glance, the car seemed empty, but the windows were down and there was still a bit of fog on the windshield.

I crossed the street, careful to walk as quietly as I could. The motorcycle engines covered me. As I got closer to the white Ford, I could see something in the front seat. I walked up alongside it.

A man was slumped in the seat, a hat pulled down over his face. He was slouched too awkwardly to be sleeping. He had seen me and was hiding.

With one hand, I yanked open the driver's door. The man reached under the seat, probably for a gun.

"I wouldn't do that if I were you," I said. "There are police all over this neighborhood and they're nervous to-night. You know what nervous police officers do, don't you?"

The man looked up at me then. The streetlight illuminated his face.

I took a step back.

He was white.

EIGHT

W hat do you want?" He did a credible job of sounding scared. I might have bought it, too, if he hadn't reached under the seat for a weapon before he confronted me.

"You were following me. You want to tell me why?"

"I wasn't following anyone. I live here."

"Really?" I kept my voice low. "Is that why you drove around North Street twice, slowing the last time as you looked into the alleys?"

"I—"

"Yeah, that's right. Only a person who lived here would hunker down in his car for more than five minutes after he got home, hiding from everyone around him."

"Look, I'll give you what I have." he said. "It's not worth much, but you can have it."

"Even the gun under the seat?"

His eyes hardened. He looked younger than he was. I pegged him for twenty-five, even thirty, although he still had that thinness that went with youth.

"You wanted me to see you," I said. "No one tails people in a white car. Why are you after me?"

"I live here," he said again.

I leaned in, grabbed him by his collar, and yanked him toward me, hoping he'd pull the gun on me. His right hand still trailed down the side of the seat.

I kept one hand around his collar, choking him. His fingers gripped my wrist, tugging furiously. With my other hand I reached down, pawed the dirty floor, and found the gun. It was a service revolver.

"You're a cop." I loosened my grip on his collar.

All the pretense fell away from his face. "I wasn't tailing you."

"Oh, really?" I held on to the gun. "You're after big, bad teenage boys now?"

"If they run with a gang."

"You think that boy is with a gang?"

"Did you take a close look at his friends?"

I didn't answer directly. "You picked the wrong fish. He's a minnow and he just jumped out of the pond."

The man laughed. "What are you, his father, his dealer, or his priest?"

That was new. No one had accused me of being a priest before. I guess I sort of fit the stereotype of an urban minister, out to save the lost. But no urban minister would take a lost child and bring him to Old Town.

I pushed the man away from me. I used enough force to send an average man sprawling across the seat. He barely moved. "You're done for the night."

"You don't give me orders."

I stared at him for a minute. Then I opened the chamber and removed the bullets. "Your trouble isn't coming out of Bronzeville, and you know it."

"The mayor thinks it is."

"The mayor is a bigot and a fascist, and with these strong-arm tactics, he's only going to make matters worse." I handed the gun back to him.

144

The cop took it, looking surprised. "You say that as if I can make a difference."

"Maybe you can." I pocketed the bullets and walked away. He didn't move. He didn't even close the car door. I didn't know if he was ignoring what I had just said to him or if he was waiting to see if I'd do anything else.

I walked back to my car and slipped into the driver's side. No Malcolm, although I didn't expect him yet. I settled into the seat and rolled down all the windows, just like my cop friend had. The night was warm—too warm to spend inside a car.

Down the alley, kids spilled out of a side door. Most of them staggered, laughing, holding each other up. Gray smoke followed them out and wisped into the night. I kept glancing into the rearview mirror. My cop friend didn't follow me. He hadn't even gotten out of his car. He just sat there, as if he were waiting.

Along North Street, an occasional patrol car moved slowly. The singing continued, sounding far away. There was laughter and the occasional shout. People walked toward the park, some of them my age. The cops didn't bother them. In fact, if it weren't for all the police, it would have seemed like a normal Saturday night.

It was nearly eleven when Malcolm reappeared. He came from the north end of the alley and he wasn't alone. He avoided the revelers, stepping over those who had sprawled on the concrete as if they disgusted him.

His companion was tall and thin. As he came into the light, I recognized Daniel Kirkland, only he didn't look like his photos. He had a large afro, and he wore a red headband tied around his forehead. His dashiki was rumpled, and strings trailed from his cutoffs. He wore sandals on his feet and a large class ring on the third finger of his left hand.

I stayed in the car. Getting out at this moment might be perceived as threatening.

Malcolm came to the window. "He won't get in."

"I figured," I said. "Bring him on over."

Malcolm looked at Daniel and beckoned with his fingers. Daniel glanced over his shoulder, then came toward me. He stood outside the window, hands in the back pockets of his cutoffs. He swayed slightly, but his eyes were clear.

"Your mother asked me to find your brother," I said. "It seems I found you instead."

"You didn't tell her I was here, did you?"

"No," I said. "One of your roomies at Harvard did that."

"Yale." He bristled. His voice was deep, the most adult thing about him.

"She's wondering why you didn't come see her."

"This isn't about her," he said.

"No, it's about Elijah. He's been gone for two days. Did you tell him you were coming here?"

Daniel shook his head.

"Did you say anything to him about the convention?"

Daniel let out a small sigh. "Last winter, maybe."

"Last winter?"

He nodded. "Yeah, when Gregory—you know, Dick Gregory?—when he said that thing."

"What thing?"

"He said he was going to lead a protest during the convention. I said that would be worth coming home for."

"So you were home for Christmas."

"I thought it was going to be the last time." His voice was cold.

"You wanted out of Chicago."

"I wanted out of Bronzeville, man. You've seen it. Is that any way to live?"

His words echoed my thoughts of that morning too closely. "Your mom made you a home."

"Yeah, as best she could. I'm going to do better."

"Well, then," I said, "maybe instead of calling her to yell

at her for letting your little brother slip out of her grasp, you should help us look for him."

"I wouldn't know where to start."

"But I do," I said. "You're not a new activist, are you? Your mom hated what you were doing and forbid you to participate. She was probably afraid you'd get shot. Am I right?"

Daniel glanced at Malcolm. "What'd you tell him?"

"Nothing," Malcolm said.

"Elijah knew about it, and he knew if you came home one more time, it wouldn't be for your family, it would be for your cause, am I right?"

"So?"

"So I'm willing to place money that he's waiting for you somewhere, not realizing that you're up here, making trouble near the park."

"I'm not making trouble. This is a legitimate action. The war is wrong, man, and people like you are the problem. You don't get it—"

I held up a hand to stop him. "I get it. I just have other concerns at the moment. One of them is your little brother. He's not involved in the Rangers, is he?"

"Elijah? Hell, no." Daniel sounded offended that I even thought it. Malcolm looked down at his shoes. He seemed to melt into the background. Was his friendship with the gang a rebellion against Daniel? Or was he just out to prove he was as worthless as his old friend thought he was?

"There've been a lot of strangers around," I said. "There's concern that the entire South Side is going to erupt."

Daniel nodded. "It will. We got stuff planned for the Amphitheater."

I remembered the barbed wire and the crews working the roads. Daniel's friends would be lucky if they got near the Amphitheater.

"What happens next week doesn't matter," I said. "It's right now I'm worried about. With all those unfamiliar faces about, it's hard to know who is who. If someone wanted to snatch a kid, it wouldn't be that hard."

Finally, I had Daniel's attention. "What are you saying?"

"I'm saying that if we don't find Elijah with your friends, he's in very real trouble and he's been in that kind of trouble for days."

The blood drained for Daniel's face.

"So," I said. "Do you want to help me or not?"

He glanced at Malcolm. "You swear he's legit?"

Malcolm shrugged. "He's done what he said he'd do so far."

"Call your mother if you're concerned," I said. "I'll wait."

He hesitated. Then he rubbed his face. "Why don't you walk with me?"

I got out of the car. Malcolm watched, rocking back on his heels. "Where are we going?"

"This way." Daniel led me toward North Street. The singing had stopped and I couldn't hear the drums anymore. The squad cars had moved as well.

I felt a prickle at the back of my neck. Something had changed.

"There's a white Ford parked half a block up," I said. "The man inside is an undercover cop. He's following Malcolm."

"Me?" Malcolm's voice rose.

"How do you know that?" Now Daniel sounded nervous.

"It was pretty obvious."

"What does he want with me?" Malcolm asked.

"He thinks some of your friends may cause trouble."

Daniel stiffened. He thought the reference was to him.

"Will it be a problem if he knows where we're going?" I asked.

Daniel shook his head. "The cops have every place staked out. It's pig heaven up here."

"All right, then."

We left the alley.

"I don't like this," Malcolm whispered. "Why's he after me?"

"We'll talk later," I said.

"How do you know it's not you he wants?"

"I asked him."

"What?"

We passed several brownstones. A middle-aged white man wearing a T-shirt and shorts waited while his small terrier sniffed a light pole. The man cringed as we went by.

"I asked him," I said, "while you were looking for Mr. Kirkland here."

"Why?"

I glanced at Malcolm. He seemed terrified. "I figured if he was after me, I'd give him the same treatment you got yesterday."

"Fuck," Malcolm said. "You're crazy, man."

I didn't answer that. The white Ford was still parked in its spot. The cop had finally closed the driver's door. He was sitting upright now—no need to hide, I guess—and seemed to be watching us.

"That him?" Malcolm asked.

"In the flesh. Want to talk to him?"

"No. Jesus. What are you thinking?"

Only that I didn't like all the undercover work going on around me and the attendant intimidation. "The best way to get someone to stop intimidating you is to take control from him."

"I don't mess with cops," Malcolm said.

"That's good news."

As we crossed Wells Street, two men and a woman left a white building with frescoes on its side. They were arguing, hands gesticulating wildly.

We continued past them. I listened for the sound of a car door.

"You're not afraid of cops?" Daniel asked.

"Should I be?"

He shrugged. We turned left, crossing the street a few blocks from the Ford. I watched out of the corner of my eye. The car door opened, but didn't close. The cop stood, stretching, as if he were stiff from sitting too long.

"He's out of the car," Malcolm said.

"Yep."

"Aren't you going to do anything?"

"There's nothing to do. He and I already had a little talk."

Daniel stopped. "I don't like this."

"You have a choice," I said. "Give me the addresses where you think I might be able to find Elijah or come with us."

"You can't get into those places."

"No, but I'll wager Malcolm can."

Daniel looked at Malcolm. They were sizing each other up. "Something happens, man, this is on your shoulders."

"No," I said. "It's on mine."

We passed an outdoor flower market and a vegetarian restaurant that, even though it was closed, smelled strongly of patchouli. Daniel started down a flight of stairs that led to a door beneath the building.

The cop was a block back. Not that it mattered. A patrol car was parked directly across the street. We were going somewhere that was already under obvious surveillance.

The door's window was covered with a ripped poster that

said Yippie in chunky purple letters. Over the poster, someone had taped another poster of a longhair wearing a hard
hat and saluting. Across the top, it said, If You're Going to
Chicago, Be Sure to Wear Some Armor in Your Hair.

I glanced at Daniel, wondering if he had even seen the
warning before. But he ignored it and tried the door. It was
locked.

He pounded on the glass, hitting the poster with his fist.
It looked like he was punching the hard hat.

"Leave us the fuck alone," someone shouted from inside.

"It's Dan Kirkland," he said.

There was a moment of silence. The upper corner of the
Yippie poster was pulled back, ripping it even farther.

Then the lock clicked and the door swung open.

Daniel stepped inside. Malcolm and I followed. We were
in a narrow room filled with ancient desks, old typewriters,
and beanbag furniture. Posters of Che Guevera and old rock
concerts covered the wall. Sleeping bags were unfurled on
the floor. Empty beer bottles filled a box in the corner, and
the remains of a pizza cooled on a metal table.

Beyond the main room, a hallway trailed into the back.
The man who opened the door, white with a full red beard
and long red hair, eyed me suspiciously. I ignored him.

"Nice poster," Daniel said, and there was sarcasm in his
voice. He didn't approve of the message.

"It's going to be a war, Dan. You know it."

Daniel shrugged. "I'm looking for Elijah. My mom says
he hasn't been home for days."

The redhead was silent. Malcolm walked toward the hallway, peering down it. I waited.

"Come on, Angus," Daniel said. "He's only fourteen."

Angus shrugged. "A couple of days ago, he was at *Ramparts.*"

Nice, smooth. Not quite a lie. There was a bit of truth
to it.

Malcolm had disappeared down the hall.

"Where is he now?" I asked.

The redhead didn't look at me. "What's this all about?"

"He's missing," Daniel said, and for the first time I heard both panic and fear in his voice.

"No, he's not." Malcolm came out of the back room, Elijah at his side. Elijah was as tall as his brother, his hair cut short and matted against his head. He was rubbing his eyes with fingers stained with blue mimeograph ink.

When he saw Daniel, his face lit up.

"What the hell are you doing?" Daniel asked.

The joy left Elijah's face, followed by bewilderment. "Working."

"You didn't call Mom."

"You never did either."

Daniel walked toward his brother and grabbed his shoulders. For a moment, it looked like he was going to shake the boy, and then he pulled him into a hug.

Elijah held on as if he had been drowning.

Malcolm started for the door, but I caught his wrist. None of us were leaving until this was over.

Finally Daniel let his brother go. "What the hell were you thinking?"

"You said this sounded like a good idea."

Daniel rolled his eyes. "In December."

"You're here."

"It's different for me."

"Yeah," Elijah said. "You lied to Mom and took her money."

Daniel flinched. Malcolm poked at a loose beer bottle with his toe. A handful of people appeared at the entrance to the hallway. They all looked like they had just woken up.

"Mom's worried about you," Daniel said.

"So?"

152

"So she had to hire some guy to find you. You could have called her."

"You never did," he said again.

Daniel shook his head. He started for the door. I stopped him too.

"Elijah," I said, "My name is Bill, and I'm taking you home."

"No," Elijah said and crossed his arms.

"He's free to stay here," Angus said.

"No, he's not. I'm taking him and Daniel back to their mother. They seem to have some family issues to sort out."

"In this place, people can do what they want."

"Really?" I kept my tone dry. "Is this a church?"

"No."

"Then the laws of sanctuary don't apply."

Angus frowned at me. "I won't let you take him against his will."

"Did he find this place on his own or did you kidnap him and bring him here?"

The group in the hallway just watched. Elijah looked alarmed. Neither Malcolm nor Daniel moved.

"He came on his own," Angus said.

"Then I think he can find his way back if he wants to." I looked at Elijah. "Your mom has been crying for two days. She thought something had happened to you. You owe her an explanation."

He said, "Daniel—"

"Daniel will face his mother as well. You both owe her an apology." I looked at Daniel. "You especially."

"Shit, I don't owe her."

I stared at him. He met my gaze for only an instant, and then he had to look away. After a moment, he walked toward his brother.

"Come on, Elijah," he said. "Let's go home."

As we stepped outside, the air was filled with shouting.

Pigs!

Peace Now! Peace Now! Peace Now!

Stop the Democratic Convention!

Horns honked from just a few blocks away. When we reached North Street, kids ran past us, the smells of incense and pot trailing after them. Police cars filled the street, and cops stood at intersections, arms crossed.

"What the hell?" Malcolm asked.

"They must've cleared the park," Daniel said.

A bearded man with dark eyes was leading a group toward us. They were all chanting "Om" and staring at their hands. Another group of kids clutching rocks ran toward Clark Street.

"We've got to get out of here," I said.

We hurried down the block. A group of protestors were carrying a Vietnamese flag and clapping their hands. Another group followed them, shouting, *Ho, Ho, Ho Chi Minh.*

Television cameras followed them. I ducked out of the way, pulling Malcolm and Elijah with me. We crossed the street, threading our way through the marchers.

The cops were setting up barricades at the intersection of Clark and North.

"Something's going down," Daniel said.

"And we're not staying for it." I ducked into the alley. To my surprise, all three boys followed me. We got into the car, and I backed out. I had to stop at the sidewalk and then inch my way through the crowd.

Instead of turning east, I went all the way to Sedgewick before turning south. I wanted to take Lake Shore home but that wouldn't be possible. I didn't think driving through the Gold Coast with a rusted Impala full of black males was a good idea.

As we drove, squad cars passed us going the other way, their sirens on, lights flashing.

"Shit," Daniel said.

"You knew this was going to happen," I said.

"Not yet. We haven't done anything yet."

I glanced at him. He was in the backseat with Elijah.

"You came here. In Chicago, I think that's enough."

The white Ford followed us south. I was surprised. I would have thought the undercover cop would have stayed to help fight the demonstrators. Apparently, though, he was following orders like a good soldier. I didn't mind. It was a welcome distraction to the tension in the car.

Daniel was whispering angrily at his brother, demanding to know what Elijah had been thinking, and Elijah was whispering back, defending himself using his brother's past behavior.

I wished I were still in Memphis. I would have taken them to my friend the Reverend Henry Davis. He was a compassionate man with a gift for counseling. He would have found a way to make this family work.

The Ford didn't even try to hide. Not that it could have easily. It was nearly 1:00 A.M. and there weren't many cars on the road. For long stretches, we were the only ones.

Malcolm occasionally leaned over so that he could look in the rearview mirror. The idea of the cop tailing him disturbed him. I thought it might be a good object lesson about his future.

I did think it strange, though, that my shadow wasn't tailing me. I wondered if that blue Olds I had seen earlier in the evening had been following me, and it decided to veer off when it realized another officer was following as well.

Or maybe the cop had lied to me, although I doubted that. He was one of the many who had been trying to intimidate the leaders of the black community. There was no reason to lie to me.

The neighborhood was silent as I turned onto our street. Two streetlights were out, not that that was new. They had been out since I had moved in. My usual spot was open, and I parked there. I planned to walk the boys home, and then talk to Malcolm.

But as I stepped out of the car, all thought of that left my mind.

There was a dark shape against the stoop, huddled like a bum sleeping off some Wild Turkey. I held up my hand, signaling the boys to wait, and then I walked down the sidewalk.

As I got closer, I realized the shape was too small to be an adult.

My throat clenched shut, and I took short, shallow breaths, my eyes seeing what my mind did not want to.

An arm, sprawled on the brown grass. A sneaker half off a small foot.

Jimmy, I thought, and hurried to his side.

NINE

When I reached him, I realized his face was wrong. The nose was too short, the jaw too square. I recognized this face too, but it wasn't Jimmy's and to my shame, I felt a profound relief.

I touched the boy's cheek. It was cool.

Someone came up behind me.

"What's going on?" Malcolm.

I felt the boy's neck for a pulse. I didn't find one.

"You know Marvella?" I kept my voice calm, my head bent.

"Yeah."

"You know where she lives?"

"Yeah."

"Send those two home. Then go upstairs to her apartment. You got that?"

"Yes, but—"

"Tell Marvella to call her cousin the cop."

"But—"

"Do it, Malcolm," I said. "Do it before your friend the undercover cop pulls up. Hurry."

He hovered for a moment, then backed away. I wished

for more light. The silver threads that came from the street-lights weren't quite enough. I recognized that face, but couldn't place it. And I couldn't see what had killed him.

Daniel's voice rose just enough for me to hear it. "I've got first-aid training. I've been planning all summer for something just like this."

"Bill said to go home."

"Well, he's not doing anything." Daniel's voice grew closer. I heard all three sets of footsteps: Daniel's easy stride, Malcolm's frantic one, and Elijah's soft one. Then I heard a car door slam.

In a moment, Daniel was over me. "Move."

"Back off," I said. "Malcolm, upstairs. Quick."

Malcolm didn't need a second instruction. He avoided the stairs leading to the porch, going to the back of the building instead.

"Listen," Daniel said, "I know what I'm doing."

"Really?" I leaned back just enough to give him a view of the boy's face. "Can you fix that?"

The boy's open eyes caught the streetlight. There were marks on his face that I hadn't noticed before.

"Jesus," Daniel said, his tone completely different now. "He's not—?"

"Go home," I said. "Get Elijah out of here. Now."

But even as I said that, I heard a whimper behind me. Elijah. "That's Brian Richardson. What's wrong with him, mister?"

"Go home," I said to Daniel. "*Now*. The last thing you want to do is get mixed up in this."

"What's wrong with him?" Elijah asked again. But something in his voice told me he knew.

More footsteps behind us. It had to be the undercover cop.

Daniel seemed to hear them too. Or maybe I had gotten through to him. "Come on, Elijah. Let's go."

"But Brian's hurt."

"And Bill'll take care of him. *Come on.*"

They ran across the yard, long loping steps that took them to the end of the block in a matter of seconds. I turned my attention back to the body.

Brian Richardson. I hadn't learned his last name. He was the little boy who had wanted to know where Jimmy was, where Keith had gone. The boy who was afraid he'd have to spend the rest of his summer alone.

"What is this?" The cop. He crouched beside me. His gun was stuck in his belt.

"He's dead. You'd better call it in."

"You just found him?" He sounded like he didn't believe me.

I glanced at him. His beefy face looked tired, his eyes red rimmed. "He's been dead a while. You've been following me. He wasn't here when we left. You put it together."

"I don't have a radio in the car."

"Sure you do," I said. "It's under the dash. Go turn it on. I'm sure it'll work."

He glared at me, but got up all the same.

"And get a flashlight too. The porch light hasn't worked since I moved here and the streetlights aren't bright enough."

"You're coming with me. I'm not leaving you with the body."

"Then it's a stalemate," I said, "because I'm not moving."

At that moment, Malcolm came out the front door, Marvella behind him. They stopped on the porch.

"Go call the cops," the cop said to Marvella. "We've got a problem here."

"Who is this guy?" she asked me.

"An undercover cop who refuses to use his radio," I said. "Do you have a flashlight?"

"Yeah."

"Get it for me, would you?"

159

She nodded and went back inside. Malcolm hunkered down above the body, staring. He raised his eyes to me. Even in the dark, I could read him.

"What happened?"

"I wish I knew." I turned toward the cop, who was still crouched beside me. "You going to call for help or not?"

"I got a good look at this kid," he said. "If anything gets moved—"

"I know the drill."

He frowned, knowing he was beaten. Then he hurried toward the car. He would keep me in sight as best he could.

"Open the door wider, will you, Malcolm?" I asked.

Malcolm got up and pulled the front door back. Light spilled out of the building, giving me a clearer view of Brian's face.

It was bruised and blotchy, his lip split. There was dried blood beneath his nose. But that wasn't what had caught my attention. What I found myself staring at were small perfect little circular sores on his cheeks and just below his eye.

Cigarette burns.

"Son of a bitch."

I must have said the words out loud, because Malcolm asked, "What?"

I shook my head. Behind me, I could hear the crackle of a police radio. Then Marvella came out the door, blocking my light. She handed me a thick metal flashlight—an electrician's light.

"It's all I have," she said, crouching just like Malcolm was.

"Would you guys stand back?"

"Bill—"

"Please." I hefted the flashlight. I had a hunch the rest of this wouldn't be pretty.

She took Malcolm by the shoulders and eased him up. She tried to lead him to the door, but Malcolm refused. He moved to the side, out of the light.

No more radio static. A car door slammed.

I turned on the flashlight. Its beam was wide and stark. Brian's damaged face looked unnaturally pale. Marvella gasped. I glanced up. She had a hand over her mouth. Malcolm stood beside her, his eyes glistening. He hadn't moved.

I shone the light down Brian's shirt. It was short-sleeved, checked, a school shirt that looked like it might have been one size too small. The breast pocket had been ripped off and recently. The threads still hung there like an afterthought. Buttons were missing. And there was a rip going down the right side.

All that damage nearly made me miss the entrance wound. A single slit visible only because the shirt's fabric caught in it, bending the slit open slightly. A bit of blood ruined the checked pattern.

A knife wound.

Someone had stabbed this child in the heart.

The cop crouched beside me. "Bring the light toward me."

Suddenly we were colleagues, and I didn't mind. I moved the light down the boy's arm, like the cop indicated.

More cigarette burns, all of them just as fresh as the ones on the boy's face. The cop was staring at them. I wasn't. I was looking at Brian's fingers.

They'd been broken.

This child had been tortured before he'd been killed.

"Holy son of a bitch," the cop said under his breath.

"Yeah," I said softly. I moved the light toward the boy's legs. He wore cutoffs, just like he had when I'd seen him. They were pulled up and zipped, stained with blood. The splatter pattern suggested the blood had come from his nose.

There was blood on his bare legs, but no cigarette burns. There were fresh scrapes on his knees and calves as well as yellowing bruises—the kind a kid got when he played hard on a hot summer afternoon. The shoe that was off seemed to have slipped from his foot; someone had bought the sneakers one size too large in anticipation of growth.

In the distance, a siren wailed.

"We're going to have to secure this area," the cop said.

I nodded, but continued the move the flashlight around the body. Once the rest of the police arrived, I wouldn't get another look.

Footprints in the dry grass, but they might have belonged to Daniel and Elijah. The killer probably used the sidewalk.

"We should move." The cop almost sounded nervous. He wasn't used to homicide. He was bad at undercover work too. How raw was he? Raw enough to let me be senior, at least until backup arrived.

"We're fine." The flashlight caught dark drops near my foot. I hadn't moved since I had arrived. I would wager those drops were blood.

I looked up. There were no drops on the porch or the threshold. The body hadn't come from inside the building, at least not through the front door.

"Marvella, Malcolm, would you make sure no one comes outside, please?"

Marvella nodded. She led Malcolm inside. They blocked the light for a moment, and then they disappeared.

"That's not what I meant by secure," the cop said.

The sirens were getting closer, louder, their wail ominous in the quiet night.

I pointed to the blood drops. "There are none on the porch." I raised the flashlight, shone it down the sidewalk. Drops dotted the cracked concrete all the way to the street.

The cop looked at me, his eyes large in the reflected light. "Son of a bitch," he said again.

A single car rounded the corner. It was a nondescript sedan with a light that could be removed from the roof. Its siren was off now, but its lights cast red-and-blue circles all over the neighborhood.

"What're they doing, just sending one?" The cop stood and headed toward the street, careful to walk alongside the blood trail, not on it.

I aimed the flashlight at the boy. He'd been dumped here. Placed on these stairs on purpose. His good, uninjured hand crossed his belly. His broken hand was open. So that someone could see the injuries? A medical examiner would have found those. Was it merely coincidence that the arm had been left open?

Or did the other arm bear the same marks?

I couldn't raise it and look. I didn't want to tamper with the body. Instead I studied what I could. The boy's fingernails were filthy and there was a cobweb matted in his hair.

Behind me a car door opened and closed.

"Officer Jack Sinkovich," the cop I'd been talking to said, clearly by way of introduction.

"Detective Truman Johnson," said a deep voice in response. Marvella's cousin had arrived.

"Watch the sidewalk," Sinkovich said. "There's a blood trail."

Johnson didn't respond. Instead he walked toward me. I glanced up. He was a big man, broad shouldered, large arms and no neck. He was getting thick around the middle. His build and his tendency toward fat suggested he had once been a football player. He still carried himself with an athletic grace.

"You Bill?" he asked as he crouched beside me. He was careful about where he stepped and how he moved.

"Yeah."

"Thanks for the call." He said that last under his breath. Then, louder, "What've we got?"

I pointed the flashlight at the boy's face, then at his arm. Then I aimed it at the entry point on his chest. "Knife," I said softly. "He was dumped here."

"Fuck," he whispered.

"What?" I asked.

His gaze met mine. "We got ourselves a pattern."

"This has happened before?"

He nodded. "This is victim number three."

TEN

The news of a pattern rocked me. I had thought—perhaps because I'd mistaken the boy for Jimmy—that someone had done this to Brian as a warning, as a way to let me know that I was being watched.

I usually wasn't this self-focused. I usually had clearer vision. Anything was possible at the moment and I had forgotten that. I had also forgotten that Brian Richardson lived in this building.

He might have been dumped here because he lived here.

More sirens sounded in the distance.

"Are you telling me people have been murdering children?" I asked Johnson.

"Boys," Johnson said. "Black boys."

"You gonna get this case?" I asked.

Sinkovich had started toward us. Inside the building, I heard an apartment door open.

"Maybe," Johnson said. "Things are crazy right now."

It took me a moment to understand his words. "You mean you wouldn't normally?"

"Do I look white to you?" he snapped.

I glanced at him. He was still staring at the boy's ruined

shirt. "I thought black police officers had made some strides in Chicago."

"We have," he said, rocking back on his heels. "But interfacing with the FBI is a white thing."

"This is theirs?"

"It will be now. Two victims is a coincidence, or so they tell us. Three, well, the odds against that—"

"Against what?" Sinkovich stopped beside us.

"What the hell are you doing here anyway?" Johnson was not polite or subservient to him. He seemed to resent him and it was clear they had never met.

"Detail work."

" 'Detail work.' Harassment is all it is."

"Not my decision," Sinkovich said. "I'm just doing my job."

"Well, get out of my light so I can do mine." Johnson hadn't looked up at him. "Move that flashlight on those shoes, would you?"

I leaned back, careful not to lose my balance, and aimed the flashlight at the sole of the boy's shoes. The sirens were growing closer, their wails forming a discordant harmony found in Schoenberg. A modern funeral march, played in a key this boy would never have understood.

"Dirt," Johnson said. "It's a start."

But it wasn't the dry brown dirt of the neighborhood. The shoes looked new and the dirt out of place. It was dark and thick, almost like he'd walked through a cloud of ash.

"What I wouldn't give to see that exit wound," I said.

"We're not touching him." Sinkovich sounded panicked.

"Of course we're not." Johnson stood, his knees cracking. He extended his hand. "Mind if I use that flashlight?"

The investigation had just left my control. I couldn't argue with him. I had as much information as I would be able to gather on my own.

166

I handed him the light. He shone it on the blood drops. They were quarter sized, irregular. Something had dripped, not gushed. The dripping had been slow, but steady.

A dead body didn't bleed. But a saturated shirt would drip like that. Or a knife.

Johnson moved the flashlight out like I had done, examining the drops as they moved down the walk. The sirens were so close that I expected to see the lights any moment.

A knife. A personal instrument, nasty, frightening. Deadly. Faced with a knife, I'd do anything to keep it away from me. Anything at all.

I frowned. "Hey, Detective, think we can get a peek at his hand?"

"You already seen it."

"The right hand. I want to see the left."

Johnson cursed, but he turned toward me. He shone the light on the hand.

The fingers weren't broken and there were no cigarette burns on the back.

"Nothing," Johnson said.

"That's the problem." I clenched my own hand to keep myself from grabbing the boy's and turning it over. "He was knifed."

"No defensive wounds," Sinkovich breathed.

"Except maybe on the palm."

I nodded.

Johnson studied me. I saw, in that instant, a respect that he hadn't shown before. "We'll catch it before they zip him up."

Then he went back to examining the blood drops. I wished he hadn't taken my flashlight. I wanted to see if there were more drops in the grass.

Voices rose inside the building. I heard Marvella telling people to calm down.

The sirens screamed onto the street, accompanied by red-and-blue lights. Anyone who hadn't awakened when Johnson arrived was awake now.

In a few minutes, this place would be a madhouse.

Johnson ignored that. He made it to the curb, then shone the light on the grass, the street, and the sidewalk again. He crouched, but said nothing.

Cars pulled up all around his, four squads and another sedan, parking in haphazard positions. Sinkovich watched, arms crossed. He didn't look pleased.

Officers in uniform got out of the squads. Two white men in suits climbed out of the sedan. Johnson gave me a quick glance, a sad sort of vindication of his earlier statement, then walked over to them.

One of the men in suits gave instructions to the officers, making a motion with his hand.

"Guess we've just been dismissed," Sinkovich said.

"You wanted the case?"

He snorted. "Me? In this neighborhood? I'd have as much success as those two guys are gonna have."

He indicated the new arrivals. I stood slowly. I hadn't expected that much awareness of Sinkovich. I had been underestimating him all night.

"You're homicide?"

"I wish. I'm in vice. Most of the bodies I see still have a rubber hose tied to their left arm."

"Must get old." I couldn't believe I was chatting with a white cop over the body of a dead boy. It felt surreal, almost unnatural, and I wasn't sure how to stop the conversation.

"It's why I'm here. I volunteered for this. Johnson's right. In the House, it's called harassment detail."

"You were following Malcolm."

He glanced at me. "I was following his little friends, but they just hang out on street corners. Things didn't get interesting until yesterday when you strong-armed your way into things. Then when you took him today, I thought I'd follow, see what it got me."

He glanced at the boy, his expression a mixture of sadness and disgust. I understood his thoughts. It had gotten him to another dead end.

The crime-scene officers moved us aside. They weren't as cautious as Truman Johnson had been, and I remembered what my old partner Loyce Kirby once told me: More clues were destroyed by careless investigators than by criminals.

I moved to the grass behind the stairs, where I was certain the murderer had not been. Sinkovich joined me. He pulled a pack of cigarettes out of his pocket, but I waved them away.

There was a bang inside the building, a door slamming or something falling. Marvella's voice rose again. "Wait! Wait! Let them—"

And then a woman appeared in the doorway. Malcolm was beside her, grabbing her arm. Over his shoulder, I could see Franklin, his eyes swollen with sleep.

The woman shook off Malcolm and took a hesitant step out of the building. She was fully dressed, which surprised me, her orange cotton sundress wrinkled and stained with sweat. I knew even before I saw that same square chin that she was Brian's mother.

She didn't say a word. Her eyes grew larger. Malcolm reached for her again, and she shook him away. Marvella had come outside, and Franklin stood in the doorway. The teacher from the attic apartment leaned against Franklin's back.

"Sorry, ma'am," one of the officers said to her. "I'm afraid you can't come out this way."

But she took a step closer, her gaze trained on the body covering the stairs.

Johnson was still talking to the other two detectives. The techs were concerned with cordoning off the area around the body. Only Malcolm, Marvella, Sinkovich, and I really knew what was going on.

She extended a shaky hand toward the boy, slowly easing down so that she could touch him.

"Brian?" she said. "Brian, honey?"

The officer who had first spoken to her, a white man with a head full of gray hair, looked up. His eyes closed for the briefest second, and then he reached for her.

"Brian?"

The officer put his arms around her, apparently planning to get her back into the apartment, but she screamed and started hitting him. The shift was abrupt and startling.

"That's my boy! What're you doing to my boy? Lemme go! That's my boy!"

Malcolm raised a hand as if he wanted to help, but the officer kept forcing her backward. She screamed harder. The other crime-scene officers stopped. One of them started up the stairs, stepping over the boy's body.

"Hey," I said. There was more anger in my voice than I expected. What were they thinking, handling her like that? "Let me."

The officer stopped. She was struggling, getting the best of the man holding her. Malcolm had backed away.

I climbed onto the porch from the side. Sinkovich followed me but was wise enough to stay back. The woman was flailing at the officer. I grabbed one of her fists. The other hit me alongside the head with enough force to make me grunt.

"Let me," I said to the officer, and this time he backed away. His movement surprised her, knocking her off-balance. I pulled her the rest of the way toward me, into my arms, burying her face in my shoulder.

"You don't want to see this," I said.

She struggled. The woman was stronger than most men. "You don't understand. That's my boy. That's my Brian."

"Not anymore."

My words were soft, but she heard them and froze. She raised her gaze to mine as if she were assessing the truthfulness of my words. Her expression cleared and then she looked over my shoulder. From her vantage, all she would be able to see would be his side, his arm resting across his stomach, his damaged hand, and his sneaker trailing off his foot.

A shudder ran through her. "No." The word was firm as if she would not allow this to happen, not to her, not to her son. Then she looked at me as if it were my fault.

"No," she said again.

I recognized the emotion. I had felt it not an hour earlier when I had mistaken her son for Jimmy.

I slipped an arm behind her back, turning her, leading her inside.

"It's not possible," she said in a tone that recognized what had happened. "He just hasn't come home yet, that's all. I haven't even reached his dad. He's probably there. His dad's. You know."

They're gone, Brian had said to me. *David's gone. Even my dad's gone. Everybody's going away but me.*

And then he had kicked the ground with a bare foot, a lonely little boy facing an even lonelier future.

I couldn't look back at him now.

"He's there, right?" Her voice was hollow.

"Let's go inside, Mrs. Richardson."

She bowed her head and let me take her through the door. My neighbors crowded the hallway. Franklin leaned against the banister, and the teacher sat on the stairs, head in his hands.

A woman I'd seen around the building took Brian's mother into her arms. I stood there for a moment, feeling useless, feeling guilty, and then my gaze met Franklin's.

I saw fear in his eyes.

I nodded once, just to let him know I saw him, and went back outside.

The sky was pink toward the lake. More cars had arrived while I'd been with Mrs. Richardson. A photographer was taking pictures of the body. The two detectives watched, arms crossed. Malcolm leaned against the building. Sinkovich still stood in the corner and the crime scene officials had cordoned off the stairs.

No one spoke. There was nothing any of us could say.

Johnson was walking the yard in a grid pattern, flashlight trained on the grass. I watched him, knowing I could be helping him, yet unable to move.

An ambulance had pulled up, lights off, no siren. It parked as close to the curb as it could get. One of the orderlies got out of the side, then opened the back. Two others came out with a gurney covered by a black bag.

Malcolm winced.

The men started to bring the gurney up the curb, but Johnson stopped them, pointing to the bloodstains. He called the photographer over, and had him shoot that area before allowing the orderlies to wheel the gurney toward the body.

I stepped off the stoop near Sinkovich. He glanced at me, his mouth a thin line. His shift had probably ended long ago. I wondered where his relief was—if he had any relief. He didn't have to stay, but he had.

I wondered if he had seen anything in his afternoon vigil before he had decided to follow us. I'd have to ask later, when this was all over.

Johnson followed the orderlies to the body. The photographer took a few more shots, then changed his roll of film. He moved to the side so that he could shoot the back of the body and the area it had rested on.

One of the orderlies unzipped the body bag, folding it open. Then he bent down, gently slipping the shoe on the boy's foot, and picked him up.

The body didn't change position. It was in full rigor. There was no blood on the back of the shirt, no obvious exit wound at all. But there was a long copper-colored stain that covered the boy's right shoulder. Rust? Dried mud? Paint? It wasn't blood, that much was clear. But I wasn't close enough to see what it was.

They set the boy onto the bag, and started to zip it when Johnson stopped them.

"Oh, for heaven's sake, Detective," one of the white detectives said. "Let's get this done."

But Johnson ignored him. I moved toward him, not a lot, but enough so that I could see what he was doing. He reached for the arm, but he couldn't lift it—the rigor got in the way—so he pushed the shirt away from the hand and peered at it.

"What're you looking for?" the other detective asked.

Johnson let the shirt fall. He glanced at me, and shook his head so minimally that I doubted anyone else could see it.

No defensive wounds. The boy had been knifed and hadn't defended himself.

Or hadn't been able to.

The sky was even lighter now. "One more thing," I said. Johnson looked at me, and I touched my wrist.

"Who's that guy?" the first detective asked.

Johnson looked at the child's wrists, raised his eyebrows slightly and stepped away. The orderly zipped the body bag. A vibrant boy had been reduced to a small black lump.

The second detective walked toward Johnson. "What were you looking for?"

"Answers," he said.

We were silent until the ambulance left. Then the detectives ordered all the civilians to remain in the building until they were interviewed. Johnson went back to walking his grid and Sinkovich headed toward his car without a backward glance.

I led Malcolm inside. "Let's get some breakfast."

An apartment door at the end of the hall stood open. I could hear Mrs. Richardson's voice, thick with tears, saying, "I don't know how it happened, Barry. He just didn't come home. You can't blame me for this. . . ."

"I'm not hungry," Malcolm said.

"I know. Come upstairs anyway." I owed the boy. He had done much more than I expected, had found Daniel, assisted with Elijah, and then had been a solid presence throughout the long night. I was keenly aware of the fact that his former friends had asked him where he was going to sleep. I didn't want him to be alone, not after this.

Malcolm didn't argue. He gazed down the hall. Mrs. Richard's voice was still carrying.

". . . don't know where they're taking him. Barry, please. He's just a little boy. . . ."

"Come on," I said.

We walked up the stairs together. There were voices coming from inside a number of apartments. Marvella's door was ajar, but I didn't hear her. I suspected she was downstairs with Mrs. Richardson.

I opened the door to Franklin's apartment. He stood in the window, watching the street below. He still wore his robe, although on his feet he wore a pair of dress shoes. I hadn't even noticed in all the confusion.

Malcolm tensed beside me. I hesitated for a split second, wondering how this meeting would go. Franklin had pinned Malcolm to the wall the day before, after all.

174

But there wasn't much I could do. I was already committed.

"Franklin," I said. "Meet Malcolm."

For a moment, Franklin didn't move. It was almost as if he hadn't heard me. He continued to stare out that window as if the fire escape held answers.

I knew what he was thinking. The same thing I had been thinking when I was helping Mrs. Richardson. He had a son the same age as Brian. It could have been any of our boys.

Then Franklin turned. His gaze ran over Malcolm and I think it took a moment for the boy's presence to register. I could feel Malcolm's tension grow. He vibrated with it.

Finally, Franklin nodded. "You were some help tonight."

For a moment, I thought he was talking to me. Then I realized he was talking to Malcolm.

"Good work. I don't think things would have remained calm without you."

Malcolm's hand went involuntarily to his cheek—his bruised cheek—and then he seemed to realize what he had done. He let his hand fall. "Thanks."

"We haven't eaten," I said. "You got pancake fixings?"

"Waffles," Franklin said. "I'm the king of waffles."

It was a statement that sounded practiced, like a joke he had with his family. Then he shook his head. "I'm sorry. I didn't mean . . ."

His voice trailed off. We were all silent for a moment.

"What did they all do to that kid?" Malcolm asked into the silence. "Those marks on his face—"

"Burns." I pushed the door to make sure it was tightly closed. It was.

"Why? Why would anyone do that?"

Such a tricky question. There were a thousand rationalizations, and I was certain that the killer could have given us one. But ultimately, there was no answer. There was no real why.

"Let's get some breakfast," Franklin said, apparently deciding that no answer was the only answer he could give.

He shuffled toward the half kitchen, looking fifteen years older than he had the day before.

"You want some orange juice?" I asked Malcolm. He seemed shaky, as if the nerves that had held him through the night were finally failing.

"I should go."

"Where?" I said. "It sounded like by helping me, you lost your only home."

Franklin looked over his shoulder, startled, but to his credit, didn't say anything.

Malcolm shrugged. "There're places I can stay."

"I'm sure. But it'll take you a while to get there. Have breakfast with us, and then we'll discuss the rest of your day."

Franklin turned back toward the cabinets, reaching inside for a flour canister.

Malcolm was silent for a moment. Then he sighed. He looked as exhausted as I felt. "Can I wash up somewhere?"

I led him toward the bathroom, grabbed a towel and washcloth out of the tiny linen closet, and gave them to him. He took them, then disappeared into the bathroom, closing the door firmly behind him.

Franklin had moved from the half kitchen to the middle of the living room, cradling a large bowl with one arm. In his other hand, he clutched a wooden spoon, using it to mix the batter.

"Still doing it, huh, Smoke?"

My entire body ached. After the meal, I would have to get some rest or I wouldn't be able to function at all. I had a hunch that now, more than ever, I needed to be sharp.

"Doing what?"

"Taking in strays."

I couldn't tell if Franklin approved or not. "I wouldn't offer your home without your permission."

Franklin gave me a half smile. He stirred harder, as if moving quicker got rid of some of his angry energy. "I didn't mean that. I was just wondering how the two of you became partners overnight."

Partners. I guess, in an odd way, we were. "He helped me find a young boy."

"Brian?"

"No." I went to the refrigerator and poured myself some orange juice. It was a thin and unappetizing orange; someone had put too much water into the concentrate. But I drank it anyway, knowing that I needed something in my stomach.

"You're detecting again?"

"Marvella asked for my help. I was able to do her friend a favor. It seemed minor. Still does, after last night."

Franklin nodded. He came into the kitchen and set the bowl on the countertop. Then he rooted in a drawer for a thick silver waffle maker. It looked both expensive and well used.

He set it beside the bowl, poured some oil in the center, closed the lid, and plugged it in.

"That little boy," Franklin said softly. "It could have been Keith or Jimmy or—"

"I know," I said.

"You don't think . . . ?"

"It was the first thing I thought."

Franklin glanced at me. "Sounds like you ruled it out."

"Not entirely. But Truman Johnson says there've been two other deaths just like it."

"When?" Franklin asked.

"I don't know the details. I'll find out."

Franklin bowed his head. "I keep thinking we should

have warned the neighbors, maybe helped them get their kids out when we got ours out."

That thought had crossed my mind as well, and I didn't like its implications.

"I'm going to figure this one out, Franklin, before the kids come home."

He stirred the batter halfheartedly, then stopped and let the spoon drop. "I'm not sure what I want it to be—some crazy out there going after our kids or—God, Smokey. I am so out of my depth."

I nodded. It felt like I was too.

Franklin's waffles were light, fluffy, and golden brown. I ate four of them, covered in butter and syrup. Malcolm ate more, but only because it was the first good meal he'd had in days. Franklin hardly touched his.

We avoided the topic of the dead boy during the meal, but we couldn't seem to manage idle conversation either. The cops' voices filtered through the window from the street below as they finished their gruesome work.

I couldn't make out the words, but I knew they were as unsettled as we were; the death of a child was easy for no one.

Franklin poured me coffee, I gave Malcolm more orange juice, and, when it was clear we were all finished, Malcolm took the plates off the table. Favors and politeness seemed to be the only currency we had.

The knock on the door startled me. I hadn't heard anyone come up the stairs.

Franklin frowned and then glanced at the clock built into the stove: 6:00 A.M. Too early to be a courtesy call.

I was amazed he had a handle on the time. I had been going since the previous morning and so much had happened during that very long day and even longer night that it seemed as if a week had gone by. At that moment, it actually felt as if it were still night and we were getting ready for bed.

The knock sounded again.

I stood before Franklin did, and went to the door. Through the peephole, I saw Detective Johnson. I sighed and pulled the door open.

His gaze met mine. If anything, he looked even more tired than he had earlier. His features were rumpled and his clothes were stained. "Took me a few minutes to find you."

"Marvella knows where I live."

"She's busy." There was a weariness in his voice. Apparently Marvella was still downstairs with the dead boy's family. "You gonna let me in?"

I stood aside, and Johnson entered the apartment. He gave it what seemed like a cursory glance, but in those brief moments, he seemed to take in everything.

The apartment had gotten messy in the short time that Althea had been gone. Newspapers were sprawled on the couch. An empty beer bottle sat on the floor beside Franklin's favorite chair, and dishes were piled in the sink.

Malcolm stood on the edge of the carpet. It seemed like Johnson's presence alarmed him. I mentally willed the boy to sit down and pretend everything was normal.

I closed the door behind Johnson. "So, you're on the case after all."

"For the moment." He ran a hand through his tight curls. "I told them I could interview you better."

"They didn't mind?"

"You could hear this boy being shuffled to the bottom of the pile even before the sun rose."

"I thought you said this would be an FBI case."

He nodded, then walked to the table. "Mind if I eat the leftovers?"

"There's some batter left," Franklin said. "I'll make fresh."

Johnson sat down in what had been Malcolm's chair. Malcolm leaned against the sink.

Franklin tapped him on the shoulder. "Pour yourself some orange juice and sit down. We'll worry about dishes later."

Malcolm did as he was told. Johnson ran a hand over his eyes. I knew the trick though. I had a hunch he was still assessing the room.

"These guys, they'll do the paperwork," Johnson said, answering my earlier question. "But they won't pursue, you know? When they get back to the precinct, they'll rationalize it. After all, who cares about little black boys dying in the ghetto?"

Malcolm grimaced.

"You do," I said to Johnson.

"Yeah," he said. "Like it'll do me some good. I've gotta deal with the damn Democrats just like everybody else. Daley's people did a briefing with the black cops, you know that? Wanted us to keep 'our people' in line. He's afraid we'll have a riot here. The National Guard is mobilizing. They've been training all summer on how to handle public disturbances. We've got new cans of mace and tear gas and brand-new gas masks. No one's thinking about dead kids. They're planning for war."

Franklin poured batter into the still-hot waffle maker. The batter sizzled. It was the only sound in the room.

Malcolm sipped his orange juice, keeping the glass in front of his mouth as if he could hide behind it.

"What will you do?" I asked.

Johnson sighed. "Whatever I can."

I poured Johnson some coffee, then topped mine off. The food had revived me enough to feel up to this conversation. I also wanted Malcolm to remain silent.

Franklin put the finished waffles on a plate and brought it to Johnson. He put syrup on his waffles without buttering them first. He cut the first piece, put it in his mouth and closed his eyes as if he were tasting a little bit of heaven. Then he set his fork down, opened his eyes, and looked at me.

"Quick thinking you did last night."

I put a sugar cube in my coffee, and used my spoon to stir it.

"You knew a lot about procedure."

I tapped my spoon on the side of the coffee cup, then set it on the table.

"You a cop?"

Malcolm raised his eyebrows in an I-told-you-so gesture.

"Nope," I said.

"Former cop?" Johnson wasn't looking at me. He had focused most of his attention on the waffles. Franklin got up and went into the kitchen. I was thankful for that. He was beginning to look worried.

"Nope," I said.

Johnson grunted as if he didn't believe me. "You're not from here."

"My family's in Atlanta." Truth. My family was in Atlanta. I hadn't lived there since I was a child.

"So why aren't you in Atlanta?" He was better than I wanted him to be—at least while he was questioning me.

I shrugged. "Atlanta's changed. It's not the place it was ten years ago, let alone thirty."

"You think Chicago's better?"

"Not at the moment."

That got a grin from him. He ate some more waffles as if they were the only thing that mattered to him. He washed down the food with coffee. The rest of us sat in silence, much as we had when we ate.

Franklin started rinsing the dishes. The running water, the clank of the plates, was comforting.

"There's a flyer at the station," Johnson said. "Two of

them, actually. Came in April. Kinda curious, I thought. Memphis police and the FBI sent out different requests for the same thing."

I took a sip of my coffee, pretending nonchalance. Malcolm was frowning.

"Wanting us to be on the lookout for a forty-year-old black man and a ten-year-old boy. Didn't say what they were wanted for. In fact, the whole thing was vaguer than usual. I was round-filing that crap in June when I remembered Marvella describing her newest neighbor. Some southern black man and his son, and I wondered: any connection?"

"I don't think I look ten, do you?" Malcolm snapped.

I almost spilled my coffee. I wanted to tell him not to do that, that Marvella knew who Jimmy was, but anything I could say would only make this worse.

"You're his son?"

"In all ways that count."

Good boy, I thought.

"You don't share an accent."

"He didn't come to Chicago for the weather." Malcolm was a better liar than I liked.

Johnson grunted again as if he were satisfied. I hoped he wouldn't revisit this. I didn't want to repeat the lie.

"You had Marvella keep an eye on me," I said.

Johnson shrugged. "She gets in trouble with men. She mentioned someone new. I wanted to find out about him."

Franklin glanced at me over his shoulder.

"I'm not involved with her."

"She was interested. When she gets interested, I get worried."

"Worried enough to check the police blotter?"

He grinned. "You haven't met her former husbands, have you?"

I didn't say anything. After a moment, Franklin's rinsing

started up again. I hadn't realized it had slowed down until that moment.

"You're not a cop," Johnson said. "Yet you were clear-headed, and you managed to protect that scene. What is it that you do?"

"I'm a security guard at the Conrad Hilton."

"You're the guy they wrote up in the *Defender*."

" 'Fraid so."

"Why don't you tell me what you did and saw tonight," Johnson said. It was not a request. It was a command.

"If we do an exchange."

Malcolm set his orange juice glass down. He looked like he wanted to bolt.

Johnson gave me an appreciative look. "For what?"

"Information."

"You know it's against the law to interfere with a police investigation."

"I wasn't planning on interfering," I said. "But Brian wasn't the only ten-year-old living in this building."

"Yeah," Franklin said, rescuing me. "My wife and children are due home in the next week. I have boys that age."

"So?" Johnson pushed his plate away.

"So I want to know about the other homicides. I want to know what the pattern was, and why you think the killer struck here."

"All these questions from a security guard, huh?" he asked.

"Yeah," I said. "All those questions from a security guard."

He shook his head. It was clear he didn't believe me. I wouldn't have believed me either, but to his credit, he didn't push it. "You know I'll only tell you what you need to know to keep those other children safe."

I nodded.

He handed Malcolm his coffee cup. "How about a refill, son?"

Malcolm glared at him, then took the cup with a swipe of his hand. Getting Malcolm away from the table wasn't going to do a lot of good. He could hear from anywhere in the apartment. But the symbolic value of the gesture was probably enough to prevent Malcolm from sitting right next to us again.

"First one happened in Washington Park," Johnson said. "Some college students found the boy leaning against a tree. Knifed, like our boy here, posed, and left for someone to find him."

"Would a family member have found him in the park?"

Malcolm brought Johnson's coffee cup back, then beat a hasty retreat into the half kitchen. Johnson used the opportunity to think about his answer.

Finally he said, "Never looked into that part," and I could tell the admission embarrassed him. "He was the first, you know. We didn't have a lot to go on."

"Same kind of entry wound?"

Johnson nodded, cradling his cup. "One simple cut, right through to the heart."

Franklin stopped washing dishes and bowed his head. Malcolm bit his lower lip, then grabbed a towel and turned away.

"The other marks the same?" I was purposely vague about those. I didn't know how much the police wanted to reveal.

"There were signs of a struggle, just like on this kid. But tonight's looked like an escalation to me."

In other words, no. I nodded.

"When was this?"

"April sixteenth, day after tax day. I remember for a couple of reasons. I hadn't had a lot of sleep that month. First there were the riots, then the cleanup. Then I had to stay up all night the fourteenth so that I could come close to having my taxes done on time."

Taxes. I hadn't given them a thought. I obviously hadn't filed mine this year. I sighed.

Johnson didn't seem to notice. He continued, "So I was exhausted and I remember thinking this was the last thing we needed, something like this, some animal carving up a kid. I thought it was a one time thing. My captain thought it was connected to the riots."

"I suppose all the other white cops did too," Franklin said. It was the first real indication—to Johnson at least—that he'd been listening.

"Yeah. You got it." Johnson sipped his coffee. "The second one was around the Fourth of July. Boy's body found at the Forty-ninth Street beach. He was up near the grass, far enough away that the water wouldn't get him. Posed again. The knife wound in the same place. Different kid, different neighborhood. No obvious connections. That's when the chief filed the forms, just like he's supposed to."

"But it was still your case."

"That one was never really mine, but I looked into it. I had to. It was related. And it happened on my turf."

"Defensive wounds?" I asked.

He shook his head. "Bruises, just like the other one, but no other cuts."

"Both of them ten-year-old boys," I said, confirming.

"Ten-year-old black boys," he said. "You can imagine the manpower we've expended on this one."

At the sink, Franklin shook his head.

"In other words, you're the only one who's been paying attention."

"And now it looks like you are too." Johnson put his hands on the table and pushed himself up. He moved like an elderly man; he wore his weariness as if it made him one hundred pounds heavier. "Just do me a favor. Don't make me regret telling you this."

"You haven't told me much more than what I can find in the papers."

"You expect to find this in the papers?" Johnson asked. "You are an optimist."

I knew he was pushing me away from the case. The *Defender* would cover this even if no one else did.

"I'm confused," I said. "Brian's the only child killed in a residential neighborhood."

Johnson shrugged. "It's an escalation."

"He was dumped. Were the other bodies dumped?"

Johnson stared at me for a moment, as if he was debating. Then he nodded.

"It seems odd that the killer would know to dump him here," I said. "If it were a random pickup and murder, then why would he leave the boy on his mother's front porch? Why not put him in Jackson Park or some other public place?"

"I find myself wondering the same thing," Johnson said. "Makes me wonder if he's circling in on a target, maybe the kid he's really angry at, the one he really wants to get. Or maybe his impulses are too hard to control. Maybe he took someone he knew because the kid was convenient."

I was silent for a moment. If Johnson's theory was correct—and I had no reason at the moment to doubt him—then the killer knew this neighborhood.

"Have you spoken to Brian's mother yet?"

"The woman's hysterical. Husband walked out on her last week, and now she's lost her only kid." Johnson sighed. I did not envy him his job. Then he pointed a finger at me. "You leave her alone, you hear?"

"I promised not to interfere with your investigation," I

said. "I meant it. I simply wish you could give us all more reassurances, more ways to avoid this guy."

Johnson looked at Franklin. Franklin had turned, a towel draped over his arm as if he were a maître d' at a fancy restaurant.

"You warn those kids of yours to stay away from strangers," Johnson said.

"You're implying that this guy isn't a stranger." Franklin's voice was soft.

Johnson's lips pursed as if he'd swallowed something sour. He had no answers. None of us did. "You make sure those kids are never alone. Always keep 'em with an adult or an older kid or a group of kids. No going off without calling you or checking with you. Give them a curfew and have them meet it."

"That's all?" Franklin asked.

"It isn't enough, I know." Johnson shook his head. It almost seemed as if he were looking at something none of us could see, maybe something none of us wanted to see. And then, without saying good-bye, he let himself out.

No one spoke. It was as if Johnson had taken what little energy there was in the room with him when he left.

Then Malcolm set his towel down. "If you're not a cop, what are you?"

"I'm not your father," I said, a little more harshly than I intended.

"So?" Malcolm snapped. "You should thank me."

"Why?" I asked. "For making more trouble? Marvella's his cousin. She already knows about me."

"And that ten-year-old kid of yours?" Malcolm crossed his arms. I was surprised. I didn't realize he knew about Jimmy. "If she knows, you can bet that cop knows. He already thinks you lied to him. Why shouldn't he think I'm your kid?"

I shook my head. "It's complicated, Malcolm. And if Marvella knows you, then she knows your history."

"So it should work just fine." He said this so softly I barely heard it.

"Your father's not here, son?" Franklin asked.

Malcolm's back straightened. He hated being called "son." Not that I blamed him.

"Left before I was born," Malcolm said. "Went south. Didn't like Chicago."

"What about your mother?" I asked. "Won't she object to her instant pairing with me?"

"No." Something in the way he said that word made me shiver. Franklin's gaze met mine over Malcolm's head.

"Where's your mother?" Franklin asked softly.

Malcolm's head bowed deeper. All I could see was tight curls forming a circle around his crown. "Died."

And recently enough to make it painful. "When?" I asked.

"September."

"How'd she die?" Franklin asked.

"Cancer." His voice shook. No wonder he resented Daniel Kirkland. While Kirkland concentrated on his studies, Malcolm was dealing with the terminal illness of his only parent.

"So who's taking care of you?" Franklin was the one asking the questions. I'd remind him of that later.

"I'm old enough to be on my own." Malcolm raised his head, his expression defiant.

Old enough, but still having troubles. "You made an alliance with the Machine so you'd have a place to sleep, didn't you?"

He glared at me. "What's it to you?"

"I told you before," I said, "I'm not going to be responsible for forcing you onto the street."

He shrugged. "You wouldn't have approved of those guys anyway."

Probably not, but I knew that gangs weren't always a bad thing. They helped each other, sheltered each other, and in some instances, contributed to the neighborhood. I didn't know enough about the Machine to know if they did that.

"What I think doesn't matter," I said. "What you think does."

Malcolm gritted his teeth so hard I could see his jaw working. "You said you'd pay me."

I had almost forgotten that. "Yeah, I did, didn't I."

I reached into my back pocket and removed my wallet. I pulled out the last of my cash. Franklin was shaking his head, certain that we made eye contact. He did not approve of me giving Malcolm money. Was he afraid Malcolm would spend it on drugs? I had spent over eighteen hours with the boy and saw no sign that he used.

I handed Malcolm the cash. He pocketed it and headed for the door.

"Wait," Franklin said. "If you have no place to go, then . . ."

His voice trailed off. It was almost as if he couldn't bring himself to offer.

"Then what, man?" Malcolm asked. "Then I could stay here? But you don't want me here, do you? Afraid I'll bring my gang buddies to rob you? You're so fucking rich that you have stuff we might want?"

"Malcolm," I said, trying to calm him.

"And you, Mr. Mystery Cop. You think you're such a goddamn hero, but what did you do? You didn't save Brian, did you?"

He yanked the door open and stalked out. Franklin started after him, but I caught his arm.

"You sure you want him to stay here?" I asked.

"Where else is he going to go?"

"Churches provide shelter. There are some other places."

"He needs more than a bed for the night."

I nodded. "If you go after him, you better be sure you can offer more."

Franklin stared at me. I was getting past his Good Samaritan impulse and speaking to his brain. His own family was coming home soon. That had to be a consideration.

"The kid was real solid all night," Franklin said.

"Yes, he was," I said. "Don't you think that means he can handle this on his own?"

"I think he's been on his own too long," Franklin said, and headed for the stairs.

ELEVEN

I cleaned up the last of the dishes, waiting for Franklin to return. I had given Malcolm quite a head start. I didn't expect Franklin to catch him. I almost hoped he wouldn't.

Malcolm had proven himself the night before, and I sensed the same need, suppressed and hidden, that Franklin had. But I was already being pulled in too many different directions, and this apartment was not my home. Even if I had wanted to, I hadn't had the right to ask Malcolm inside.

So I had given him money, and hoped it would help. I shook my head. Throwing money at a problem, then ignoring it, was very uncharacteristic of me, and a sign that I was feeling overburdened.

I dried my hands, grabbed my keys, and followed Franklin into the hallway. I still had a lot to do before I slept. I wanted to check on the Kirkland boys, and I needed to call Jimmy. Not for his sake—my call wasn't anywhere near overdue yet—but for mine. I needed to reassure myself that he was all right.

I wondered if Franklin had already called Milwaukee, giving in to the same impulse. Or was his sense of loss manifesting in his need to take care of Malcolm? Probably both.

The door to Brian's mother's apartment was closed and her place was silent, eerily silent. I couldn't quite comprehend what she was going through. I had experienced devastating loss when my parents were murdered, but I had a feeling that the loss of a child was worse. The death of hope, maybe, as well as the end of possibilities.

The main door to the building was open. Malcolm and Franklin were standing on the porch, the stairs before them blocked by police tape. Franklin had his arm around Malcolm's shoulder. Franklin's instinct had been surer than mine. Malcolm's shoulders were shaking, the tears that had been suppressed for a long and frightening time finally breaking through.

Franklin seemed to know what to say, what to do. Any attempt I made to join them would be an intrusion. I hesitated for just a moment, feeling oddly excluded, then turned away. They needed their time and I had things to do.

I went out the back door and cut across the yard to the Kirkland's.

As I walked, I scanned the dry brown grass for anything unusual. I had a hunch the killer hadn't come back here, but I didn't know that for sure. I had no idea how he had found the boy and conned him into leaving with him.

I did know that Brian hadn't remained a willing participant in his death. He had rope burns around his wrists. He had been tied while he was being tortured—and if he was conscious when he'd been knifed, he wouldn't have been able to sustain any defensive wounds. He would have been unable to fight back.

The ground was so hard that footprints didn't register in it. The grass was so trampled—either by the kids over the last month or the cops last night—that individual prints were impossible to distinguish. There was no blood back here, although bits of glass sparkled in the early morning sunshine.

192

I crouched near one pile of litter, a broken Coke bottle, but the glass was dusty and caked, probably from the last rainstorm weeks ago. Nothing new here. At least, nothing obviously new.

I left the glass—I wasn't going to touch anything at this point—and continued on my way. The morning air was cool, almost refreshing, but it had a heaviness to it that I was beginning to recognize. It would be another scorcher today.

The neighborhood was quiet. I was rarely up and about this early; I had no idea if this was normal. I didn't see my shadow. I didn't see anyone else on the street at all. If I turned back, I would probably see Malcolm and Franklin still on the porch, but even that felt like an invasion of their privacy.

I went inside the Kirklands' building and knocked on their apartment door. I heard nothing from inside. For a moment, I felt a horrible fear that I'd let the killer follow them home. But I knew that was the effect of too little sleep and too much going on. It had been a long night for them too, and they were probably in bed.

Then the door opened. Grace stood before me. She was fully dressed, and she had a glow, a strength that she hadn't had when I first met her.

She smiled and I realized what a stunning woman she was. "Bill." For a moment, I thought she was going to hug me. Instead, she slipped a hand around my elbow and pulled me inside. "I was hoping I'd see you today. I owe you so much."

Her voice trembled just a little, and I knew what she was thinking. If I hadn't found Elijah, he might have ended up like Brian. Only what had happened to the two of them were very different things.

Brian hadn't had a chance.

Grace hadn't let go of my arm. "Would you like something to drink?"

I shook my head. "I just came to make sure everything was okay here."

"Come on in."

I followed her into the living room. Elijah was on the couch, wrapped in a blanket despite the heat, his head on a pillow. His eyes were open, but bleary. He'd clearly fallen asleep at some point during the night. Two empty cups sat on the coffee table, and two bowls with some milk at the bottom and cereal still floating in it sat beside them.

Obviously Daniel and Grace had been talking all night.

Daniel was in the kitchen, closing a coffee can. The percolator was on the stove, and the scent of coffee grounds filled the air. He kept his back to me.

"You come to tell us about Brian?"

"There's nothing you don't already know."

"Who would do that?" He turned. "Brian was just a normal kid, you know? He wouldn't hurt anyone."

"No gang ties?" I asked.

"Hell, no."

"Daniel." Grace was admonishing him for language. Apparently she'd forgotten that he was an adult now.

"Parents involved in anything they shouldn't've been?"

Daniel looked at his mother. So did I. She shook her head. "I hadn't heard anything. I didn't know them well."

"There's been weird guys all over the neighborhood." Elijah's voice was scratchy and muffled, tired. He sounded as if he hadn't spoken in days.

We all turned toward him.

"What kind of weird guys?" I hadn't come here to interrogate the family, but I wasn't going to lose my chance at gaining information.

"I don't know. White guys. People watching everybody."

Elijah rubbed his eyes with his fists. "Can I have some cereal?"

Grace went into the kitchen. The coffee was boiling and she moved it off the burner, a simple, habitual movement that spoke of routine.

"White guys?" Daniel was looking at me. "Like that cop last night?"

"Like that cop," I said.

Elijah leaned against the pillow. Something in his expression—an exasperation with grown-ups, a sense that maybe he hadn't been heard—crossed his face.

"Why'd you bring that up now, Elijah?"

He shrugged and closed his eyes.

"The man asked you a question, Lij," Daniel said.

"I don't know."

"Yes, you do." Daniel sat in the chair next to the couch and shook his brother's shoulder. Elijah opened one eye and glared at him. "This could be important."

Elijah sighed. "Last week, there was a guy watching the kids play in the fire hydrant."

"White guy?" Daniel asked.

"No." Elijah sounded irritated. "Black guy with a 'fro."

I felt cold. "Where was he, Elijah?"

"Across the street, hidden kinda. He moved when he saw me."

"Moved?"

"Walked away. Like he hadn't been doing nothing. But he had. It was creepy, you know."

I did know. "Did you see him again?"

Elijah shook his head.

"Could you recognize him?"

"I don't know. I didn't see him real good. It was kinda quick. And weird. I wouldn'ta remembered if it hadn't been weird."

"You should have told me." Grace put the cereal in front of him.

"Tell you what, Mom? I saw some guy on the street? Nothing happened."

"We don't know that, do we?" Grace sat in her chair. I remained standing, not willing to sit on that blanket-covered couch.

Daniel grabbed his cup and walked into the kitchen. He poured himself some more coffee and didn't offer anyone else any. "This is where you get in trouble, Mom. You worry too much."

That felt like the continuation of a conversation I hadn't been part of.

Grace's hands clenched. Elijah ducked, turning away from her. It was the only warning I had before I felt the force of her anger—however indirectly.

"Too much worrying?" She didn't yell. It probably would have been better if she had. All that pent-up rage wouldn't have felt so powerful. "A little boy gets murdered on our block and you tell me I worry too much? You lie to me, your brother runs off, and you tell me that I worry too much? Don't you know there are cops everywhere? They're just looking to start something and you boys would have been in the middle of it."

They had been in the middle of it, even though the radio this morning had called the events in Lincoln Park peaceful.

Daniel brought his coffee back into the living room. He didn't seem distressed by her anger, although Elijah clearly was. "I'm going back this afternoon."

"No, you're not."

"Yes, I am."

"I didn't send you to a good school so you can play at white-boy politics."

"White-boy politics?" Daniel had also mastered the art

of speaking softly while angry. "It's our people who are dying over there, Mom. White boys get out of it. I'm lucky. I'm in school, so I get a deferment. Most guys from my high school class are heading over there or are there. They couldn't get a scholarship. I'm not fighting for some white boy's vision of the future. I'm fighting against it."

Elijah set his bowl down. It was empty. He hunched against the corner of the couch as if that could take him out of the conversation.

"You're better off getting a good job when you're out of school. That's how you show the white man he's wrong. You show him you're as good as he is, right, Bill?"

I wasn't going to get involved, not in the middle of an argument that had clearly been going on for a very long time.

"Mom, we're not talking about me and jobs. We're talking about guys dying for no good reason."

"Yes," she said, crossing her arms. "We're talking about you dying for no good reason."

Daniel harrumphed and flopped in his chair, somehow not spilling his coffee.

"I'm not letting you go back there," Grace said.

"You can't stop me."

"Bill can stop you."

I raised my hands. "I brought Elijah back. I just came to make sure everything is all right. I am not getting involved in this."

"Because you agree with my son?" Grace's voice was as cold as her eyes. All her gratitude appeared to be gone.

The hell of it was I agreed with both of them. I saw the numbers coming back from Vietnam and could read them as plainly as anyone else. When I joined up for Korea, it was because I thought I'd find equality in the service. Truman had desegregated it just a few years before.

What I hadn't realized was that they'd find a new way to segregate us, to make us the ones who did the dying while the rich white boys got off, just like they always did.

"Bill?"

I looked at her. I knew, just like she did, that the number of police, the National Guard, the kids would all make a bad combination. I knew that someone was going to get hurt this week, and I had a hunch it wouldn't be white kids. It never was.

"I'd like to use your phone," I said. "I need to make a call. It's local."

Grace stared at me as if she hadn't heard me correctly. I certainly hadn't responded the way she thought I was going to. Daniel's eyes narrowed. I had probably lost a bit of respect in his eyes—zealots always hated it when someone failed to agree with them.

But I would gain nothing from entering this argument and I'd only make matters worse.

"It's over there." She waved her hand toward the wall phone beside the refrigerator.

"Thank you." I walked over to the phone and picked up the receiver.

"You're still my son," Grace whispered. "I still decide what you do."

"I'm eighteen, Mom. Old enough to be drafted. Old enough, I think, to make my own choices."

I leaned against the refrigerator, wishing I could shut out the voices, and dialed Laura's number. No one would trace this call. I was safe, for the moment.

"Let's go outside," Grace said.

"Mom—"

"Let's give Bill some privacy. Outside."

The phone was ringing. Grace stood, and so did Daniel. Only Elijah remained, huddled on the couch. Grace glanced at him. He stood reluctantly.

"Hello?" Laura answered, her tone fresh and cheerful. I clung to the receiver. I hadn't realized until that moment how much I needed to hear her voice.

"Laura."

The Kirklands stepped through their patio doors into the garden. I could hear their voices, muffled, Grace and Daniel still arguing.

"Smokey! You're early. Is everything—"

"Is Jimmy there?"

"Yes, you want to talk to him?"

I leaned against the wall, feeling a deep relief. "In a minute. I need to talk to you first."

"What's going on?" Her tone had changed. The cheerfulness was gone.

"A ten-year-old boy was murdered in the neighborhood last night."

"Jesus, Smokey. Do you think they were after Jimmy?"

"I thought so at first. Now I'm not sure. There seems to be something else going on. But I had to call. I had to—" My voice broke. I cleared my throat, swallowed, got control again.

"He's right here, Smokey. I'll get him for you." She set the phone down. I couldn't even tell her to wait. I wanted to talk to her, to make sure the security was going well, that she hadn't seen any suspicious men with afros hanging around the building. I wanted to make sure that nothing was going to happen there.

"Smoke?" Jimmy. He sounded so normal. "Can I come home?"

"Not yet," I said.

"You sound funny."

So much for my ability to mask my emotions. "I haven't slept all night."

"You find the guy?"

"No."

"Then why did you call?" To the point. Jimmy was always to the point.

"Just to talk to you. I miss you."

"I miss you too. I want to go home."

"In a week or so, Jim. No one's home except me and Franklin right now. Everyone's in Milwaukee."

Voices rose outside, followed by a loud shush. I leaned around the wall. Elijah was standing near the fence, his hands in his pockets, staring away from his family. Grace and Daniel were arguing in low tones now, their faces inches apart.

"Where's that?" Jimmy asked.

It took me a moment to come back to the conversation. "Milwaukee? Just north of us. Althea took the kids to visit family."

"To get them out of the house."

"Yes." I wasn't going to lie to him.

"I want to be with you."

"You will be very soon."

"Laura's finding us a place to live."

I leaned my forehead against the plasterboard. It was cool against my skin. "We don't take charity, Jimmy."

"I told her that. She laughed. She laughs a lot, Smokey."

I closed my eyes. I could see her face, with its delicate white skin, the smile that lit up everything. I could see it in the bright sunshine flowing into my kitchen on a March morning, when I actually had hope for a future.

"She said it wouldn't be charity, Smokey." Jimmy sounded subdued now, as if he took my silence as a rebuke.

"That's good, Jim."

"If she finds us something this week, can we move?"

There was the trap. I'd been waiting for it. "No."

"Why not?"

I had told him. I had already explained it, but he was getting desperate. "I want to find this guy, Jimmy, before we do anything. Please let me try. And you promised you would stay there."

"I know." He sounded sullen.

"Remember everything we talked about."

"Okay."

"Now, let me talk to Laura again."

He set the receiver down with a clatter. I waited, heard his voice, so faint that I couldn't make out the words. The tone was comfortable, though. He was getting used to Laura, and that was good.

Then, in the background, I heard canned laughter. The television had started up.

Laura picked up the receiver. "Smokey?"

"Still here," I said.

"What happened to the boy?"

She could have asked that before, but she hadn't. She had known that I had called to hear Jimmy's voice, that I needed to hear him. She knew me that well, and we had hardly spoken all summer.

I suddenly felt very tired.

"Stabbed, then dumped like a package on our front step."

"A warning?" Her voice was low.

"I don't know. He lived there. And apparently there've been other deaths like it. I have no idea what it means."

"But you're going to find out."

"Yeah."

She took a deep, audible breath. "I can find you some other place to live, get you out of the neighborhood."

"That won't solve it, Laura."

"But then you won't be in as much danger."

"I'm not." At least, I didn't think I was.

"You and Jimmy—"

"Laura," I said. "Franklin has two sons. One of them is ten. There are children all over this neighborhood. I'm going to figure this out."

"Oh."

I should have said something sympathetic then, that I understood how hard it was to take care of someone else's child, that I knew how moody and emotional Jimmy could be. But I couldn't find those words. I wasn't sure they were in me.

"I'll call tomorrow."

"I didn't mean to be insensitive, Smokey."

"I know," I said, and hung up.

I stayed in the kitchen for a moment longer. Jimmy wasn't the only one who was moody. My emotions were all over the place, and when they settled, they settled on the image of a boy, left like a bag of garbage on a front step.

I ran a hand over my face. I had to work that night and I was tired. I also wanted to dig into the other killings, the ones that Johnson had mentioned.

There wasn't enough time in the day anymore. I wished, not for the first time, that I could quit my job. I didn't even feel secure enough to call in sick. If I quit right now, they'd investigate me, thinking maybe I was involved with the demonstrators. That was the last thing I wanted.

I made my way across Grace's living room. She and Daniel were still arguing. Elijah was still in the corner of the yard, staring over the fence.

I pulled the patio door open. The morning air smelled spicy and green—Grace's garden had a welcoming scent of its own.

"I didn't mean to kick you out of your own living room," I said.

Grace and Daniel both started as if I'd caught them doing something wrong. Elijah didn't even turn around.

"Thank you for the use of the phone."

"You're welcome," Grace said. All sweetness and politeness to me now. The woman who'd gotten angry at her son was lost beneath the surface mask she had just put on, the mask the stranger—me—was supposed to take away with him.

My gaze met Daniel's. I could still see anger in his eyes. He was old enough to make his own choices, his own decisions. I had done so at his age, and I would wager that Grace had as well.

Instead, I walked between the rows of vegetables to Elijah, and put a hand on his shoulder. "Can I talk to you for a moment?"

He jumped as if he hadn't even heard me approach. Then he looked over his shoulder at me, eyes tired and old. "I guess."

"We'll meet you inside in a minute," I said to Grace and Daniel, dismissing them from their own yard. Apparently that was my function this day, to take over their home.

They went inside, Daniel first. Grace left the patio door open, probably so that she eavesdrop. I spoke softly enough so that she couldn't. "Were you and Brian friends?"

Elijah shook his head. "He was too little."

"But you knew him."

"Yeah."

I put my hand on his shoulder. He didn't flinch. He leaned into me as if he had needed someone to acknowledge him.

"I know you agree with your brother and you want to be part of the protests, but stay home. Help your mom."

His body tensed. "Why?"

"Because I think there's someone crazy out there, and you need to protect her."

He was silent for a moment. "I thought this guy was going after little kids."

"He is, so far as I know." I worked to keep my voice level. I didn't want to patronize him. If I patronized him, he wouldn't listen. "But if you disappear again, what's your mom going to think?"

Elijah's breath caught, and I knew I had him.

"The cops I spoke to said that the best thing to do is to stay inside or if you have to go out, stay in groups. Warn your friends about that, okay? Make sure no one is alone."

"The cops gonna catch this guy?"

I nearly said, Probably not, but caught myself just in time. I could be honest with Elijah and then I could be too honest with him. "They're doing everything they can."

Elijah was silent for a long moment. I stood beside him, sensing that the conversation wasn't entirely over. After a moment, he said, "You never answered Daniel."

"About what?"

"About the war."

So someone noticed. I sighed. "I was in Korea, Elijah."

"So?"

"That was a war, kinda like this one. Only it was a U.N.-sanctioned action."

"Yeah?"

I was in new territory. I didn't know how to talk about any of this. "Chicago's ready to explode. Someone's going to get hurt here, and it doesn't matter whether the protestors are right about the war or whether they're wrong."

"You think they're wrong because you were a soldier." He said it matter-of-factly. I envied the tone. It had been a long time since I'd seen the world so starkly.

"I think the protestors are probably right. I'm not sure I agree with their methods, but I generally agree with them."

"So I can go to the park."

I shook my head. "Stay home. Take care of your mother. It's safer."

"I don't want to be safe!"

I'd never heard anyone who lived on the edge express that opinion before. But then, from Elijah's perspective, he wasn't on the edge. He lived in this comfortable apartment with a mother who cared for him and a brother who was going to Yale. From what I'd seen of Grace, she made certain that her boys didn't know how hard she had struggled to keep them comfortable. They probably had no idea about all her sleepless nights, her struggles to pay bills, her desire for them to do better than she ever could because she knew how hard it was to live life her way.

And then I understood what he was saying.

"Do you think you can protect Daniel?"

Elijah looked down. "It's not about Daniel."

"Isn't it?"

He didn't answer.

"When you're eighteen, you can make your own choices, just like he is. But until then, your job is to stay here, get good grades, and take care of your mother."

"She can take care of herself."

"Can she?" I lowered my voice even more. "Look at the garden. What do you see?"

He scanned it. "So?"

"Does it normally look like this? Does the apartment?"

He glared at me. "You saying this is my fault?"

"I'm saying this is what happened when you were gone."

He opened his mouth to answer but I turned away from him and headed inside. I'd done enough interfering for one day. I doubted I would have said anything at all if it weren't for the image of Brian that still dominated my brain.

I stepped through the patio door and left it open just a crack. Both Daniel and Grace were watching me, expecting me to tell them what I'd said.

I looked at Daniel. "You watch your back."

He nodded.

"Thanks for the use of the phone," I said to Grace.

"I owe you for what you've done. How much—?"

"Nothing," I said. "A favor for the friend of a friend."

And then I let myself out.

I stood for a moment in the hallway, letting the tiredness

take me. In Memphis, I would have charged her as much as she could have afforded. Or maybe I would have asked for some of that wonderful produce from her garden.

But here, I didn't dare take the chance. I'd revealed too much about myself already.

I hoped my momentary generosity wouldn't come back to haunt me.

TWELVE

I got no sleep that day. I went back to the apartment to find Franklin and Malcolm still deep in discussion. I lay down for a few minutes, but the sun beat down on the twin bed, and even with the shade drawn it was too hot.

Besides, I kept seeing Brian's body, fingers broken, skin dotted with cigarette burns, the shoe half off. And Johnson's words—*You could hear this boy being shuffled to the bottom of the pile even before the sun rose.*

I got off the bed, showered, and made myself a crude lunch. Malcolm was watching me as if he expected me to throw him out. I nodded to him, waited for him or Franklin to tell me what was happening, and when neither did, I acted like it didn't matter.

I picked up the phone book, scanned the white pages. There was no Jack Sinkovich listed in Chicago, but I knew he had to live here. He was on the police force; residency was required. I found a John Sinkovich on Eighty-seventh. I showed the address to Franklin and he grunted.

"The Bush," he said.

I waited. He knew the question I would ask next.

"Pretty tight neighborhood. Mostly Polish." Franklin frowned. "Don't do anything stupid."

Malcolm was watching me. I could see that question in his eyes again as he tried to figure me out.

"I'll be back after work," I said.

"Let me know if you need help."

I didn't answer Franklin. I just let myself out.

The front stairs were still covered with police tape. I didn't know if that meant the police planned to return or if we were just meant to live with the reminder. I went out the back.

Brian's apartment was still silent. His mother was probably taking care of all of the business of death—the funeral arrangements, the burial, the family.

The midday heat was as stifling as I'd thought it was going to be. There was no breeze, no hope of relief from the lake. The air had weight, oppressive weight, and the sun added to it. My shirt stuck to my back, the effect of my shower instantly gone.

As I made my way around the building, I scanned for unfamiliar faces. Elijah was right; there were more white faces than I'd seen when I moved in. But there were no black men lurking in the shadows, no watchers with afros who kept to the darkness and spied on this house.

My rusted Impala looked even more decrepit in the sunlight. I'd need to get it serviced again soon. I'd tinkered with it as much as I could. The interior was good—the car had power—but it was held together by a wish and a prayer. A few weeks ago, I'd worried whether or not the car would make it through this next winter. Now I worried whether it was strong enough to get me out of tight situations.

I slipped behind the driver's seat and checked the rearview mirror. Reflex. I checked all the cars behind me, a couple of white Chevys, a mustard-colored truck, and two dark blue sedans. I pegged the sedans for undercover cops.

No one was hiding anymore, that was for certain.

This time, I didn't care. This time, I wanted the son of a bitch to follow me, and I wanted him to catch me. I wanted to know what the hell was going on.

I pulled out and headed south, staying close to the lake. The city changed down here. The skyline lost its elegance. Tall chimneys dominated, belching multicolored smoke. On any given day, the stench ran from a harsh metallic odor to rotten eggs. The heat was worse here, too, trapped in the air along with particles sometimes big enough to see with the naked eye.

Jimmy and I had looked at a few apartments near the steel mills. Mixed in with the white working-class neighborhoods were some black neighborhoods as well. But I couldn't stand the stench or the desolate look of the buildings. A lot of this part of Chicago seemed to have lost hope.

Sinkovich's neighborhood was nothing like the places Jimmy and I had looked at. Trim houses with small, neat lawns gave the impression of small victories won at great cost. The pride the neighborhood took in its houses reminded me of my neighborhood in Memphis. None of us were rich, but all of us maintained our homes.

Here, the streets were tree-lined, and a park made the western edge of the neighborhood seem welcoming. A large Catholic church, a block long, sent a spire into the sky. Somehow that building spoke of more power than the steel works, which blocked the view of the lake.

I turned onto Eighty-seventh and parked in front of a tiny two-story house. It was at least sixty years old, with a design I hadn't seen outside of Chicago. The front door was on the second story. Stairs led to it and a small covered porch. Beneath the stairs was what builders were now calling a daylight basement, but in the period when the house was built there had been no such term. There was also no way to enter on that level. Two windows hid in the darkness, and above the porch's roof another window revealed an attic room.

Maple trees lined the front lawn and they looked healthier than they should have, given the sickly air. Sinkovich's car was parked on the street, along with a number of other Fords, mostly trucks, which seemed to be the vehicle of choice in the neighborhood.

My Impala looked as alien as I did.

I glanced into my rearview mirror and saw none of the cars from my block. It appeared that no one had followed me. I felt a vague disappointment.

I got out of the car and the hair rose on the back of my neck. I was being watched. Without seeming obvious, I glanced around. Faces peered at me from windows all over the block—white female faces, most of them, and all of them watching, I assumed, with one hand on the phone.

I had expected this, but I still didn't like the feel of it.

I crossed in front of my car and mounted the front walk as if I had done it every day.

A flower garden struggled to survive on the side of the house. The summer heat had destroyed most of the plants and obviously Sinkovich's family hadn't watered like Grace had. It seemed odd to me that Sinkovich lived in a place like this; I had pegged him for a loner in a messy bachelor apartment. No furniture, empty pizza boxes, piles of unwashed clothing.

But this house was neat, newly painted, and obviously well loved. The wooden stairs, as I climbed them, didn't even strain under my weight, nor did the porch groan when I stepped on it.

I rapped on the door, my skin crawling. I didn't like having my back to all those eyes.

A phone rang inside, and a female voice rose, complaining. A male voice—Sinkovich's—answered and then I heard footsteps make their way to the door. Someone picked up the phone in the middle of a ring.

Sinkovich pulled the door back. "What the hell do you want?"

"A civil conversation."

"You should have called me."

Through the door, I could see a thin woman with very large breasts holding a baby in one arm, a phone cradled against her shoulder. She was swaying, keeping the baby happy, and watching me as if she thought I would shove past her husband and take everything of value from her house.

"I didn't think we could talk on the phone."

"I don't got no good choices here. We go on the porch, the whole neighborhood watches. We go inside, and . . ." He waved a hand toward his wife and child, as if that explained everything.

I waited, forcing myself to keep my expression neutral. Laura had spoiled me. Before her, I never would have come here, never would have thought Sinkovich could have told me anything of importance. If I had seen him again on the block, maybe I would have talked to him. But I wouldn't have subjected myself to this.

"All right." He opened the door wider. "Come on in."

"Jack!" His wife dropped the phone and put a protective hand around her baby's head.

"Shut up, Charlene."

I walked in, although it went against all my instincts. Sinkovich's wife backed away, still clutching her baby, as if my skin color were contagious. The phone squawked. Apparently there was still someone on the line.

Sinkovich reached down, grabbed the receiver, and, without speaking into it, hung up. "Get us a couple beers."

"Jack—"

"Charlene." There was anger in his voice.

She ducked through the door, which I assumed led into the kitchen.

"Come on," Sinkovich said to me. He led me into the living room. It took me a moment to realize the air was cooler here. An air-conditioner stuck out of a side window, rattling, and dripping water onto an ancient gray carpet. Someone had placed a pan beneath it, but the pan was overflowing.

The house smelled of cigarettes, cooked cabbage, and dirty diapers. The air was stale, as if the windows hadn't been opened in a very long time. A console television played a baseball game in black and white, the sound turned down.

Sinkovich hovered near a leather recliner, so old that the back was ripped and stuffing tumbled out of it. He wasn't going to invite me to sit down.

His wife came into the room clutching two Old Styles. She handed one to Jack and mouthed something at him. He glared at her. Then she brought a can to me, but she couldn't bring herself to hand it to me. Instead, she set it on the coffee table, as far away from me as she could get.

"Charlene," Sinkovich said in that same tone, only she ignored him, and disappeared into the kitchen. His gaze met mine. "She don't like strangers."

I didn't respond and I didn't reach for the beer. "There's still police tape on the front porch, but I don't think anyone's coming back to take it down."

Sinkovich's shoulders slumped. "That kid—"

"Was an only child."

His gaze flicked toward the kitchen. "You screwing with a police investigation?"

"I don't expect there to be a police investigation."

"Not even your friend Johnson?"

"What do you think, Sinkovich? All of you seem to be

sitting around watching all of us. There's no time for investigation."

"So you think you can do it? What the hell kinda guy are you, anyway?"

I struggled to keep my voice level. "Why don't you just tell me what you saw yesterday afternoon."

"I don't get interrogated by nobody. Especially not some"—the pause was too long; he was obviously groping for a better word than the one he'd originally come up with—"civilian."

That was it. I had wasted a trip. I had thought that Sinkovich and I felt the same way about the murder. I had thought he cared. But apparently he cared about the good opinion of his wife and neighbors more. Or maybe I had embarrassed him in Old Town last night. Harassment detail usually didn't allow itself to get harassed.

I turned and headed for the door.

"Wait." The posturing tone was gone. "Look, this ain't usual, you know?"

I knew it. I had my back to him. I could see his wife through the door to the kitchen. She sat at the table, feeding the baby in his high chair, her hand shaking.

"I been goin' over it in my head. Maybe if I'd've stayed instead of followin' you . . ." His voice trailed off.

This was the man I had seen the night before. The one who hid beneath the tough-guy surface. The one who still felt things. Sometimes guys on the street lost their ability to feel anything.

I faced him. "I don't think it would have made any difference. Some of those burns were old enough to scab."

"Jesus." He breathed that, then fumbled in his breast pocket, pulling out a pack of cigarettes. He tapped it, letting one slide forward, and offered it to me. I shook my head.

He picked it out with his lips, then replaced the pack

and found his lighter. It took two attempts to get the butane to ignite, and then it barely lasted long enough for him to light up.

"I never seen anything like that, you know?"

"I know." I recognized the response. Nicotine to calm the nerves. Beer to keep the memories down.

"I thought with all the guys there . . ." He took a drag, then tapped the cigarette out in a tin ashtray on an end table. "I went back to the house, wrote up a report before I came home. Dog tired, but I haven't been to sleep yet. Can't seem to close my eyes."

"I haven't slept either."

"Nobody's been here. Nobody's called. Nobody's followed up." He reached for the cigarette pack again, stopped himself, took a sip of beer instead. "Just you."

We both knew that most murders were solved in the first forty-eight hours. Investigators usually worked around the clock the first twenty-four on egregious cases, just to hedge their bets.

"It wasn't the kids, the ones I was watching. They were harassing that boy you took north. Malcolm?"

I nodded.

"They made it real clear. He wasn't nothing to them no more. It was almost like a sport, you know? Pick on the kid, see if he comes back. It was kinda pathetic, the way he just kinda stayed close, maybe to see if they changed their minds."

I still didn't say anything. I was afraid that if I did, this stream of consciousness would end, and Sinkovich would remember who he was talking to.

"There was at least one other unit on the street. And the guy I replaced. I'll see if he saw something. But I didn't. I didn't even see the boy. I didn't see any boys, you know? No kids at all. I figured it was too hot. Everyone was inside."

214

Where it was even hotter. He had said the night before he knew nothing of the neighborhood. That last comment proved it.

The phone rang. Sinkovich blinked, as if the sound brought him to himself. He held up a finger, then went around me and answered it, listened for a minute, and gave me a surreptitious glance.

I suppressed a sigh and stepped deeper into the living room, even though I didn't want to, just to give him some privacy.

The recliner wasn't the only old piece of furniture. The couch had claw feet, and the coffee table had been refinished several times. Family photographs hung on the wall behind three high school football trophies with Sinkovich's name on them.

The house was in all the photographs. Long rows of people, a number of them with a variation on Sinkovich's features, lined up before the stairs. The newest photos were in color and closest to the trophies. But it was the old ones that held my attention. They were posed. The women wore long skirts and starched blouses, and there was a fence where the maples were now. The road was dirt, and there were no houses nearby.

This place had been in Sinkovich's family for generations, just like the furniture. Somehow I hadn't expected such poverty in a cop's house—especially in a town like Chicago, where extra money had to be easy to come by.

"Sorry." Sinkovich was behind me.

As I faced him, I said, "Did you reassure your neighbors that I haven't robbed you blind yet?"

He had the grace to flush. "They know I'm a cop. They worry."

"I'm sure they do."

He looked away. "I don't know much about this stuff,"

he said, "but that looked like a pro job to me. Calculated, you know?"

"Either that," I said, "or we have a hell of a sadist on our hands."

He winced. "This isn't my case, so there ain't much I can do, official."

"I know."

"But maybe if I hear something, I can pass it along."

"I'd appreciate that."

"Is that all you come here for? To find out about yesterday afternoon?"

"No." This was the gamble. I had to watch him closely and hope I could read him well enough to recognize a lie. And hope that he trusted me enough to give me an honest answer. "I need to know the name of one of your undercover guys."

He stiffened.

"He's black, has an afro, does his job real well. Undercover's probably his specialty."

Sinkovich's eyes narrowed.

"I know it's not procedure to give me the name of an undercover cop, but I think this guy may know something about the murder."

"I told you last night, it's not my normal neighborhood." Sinkovich held my gaze.

"If you don't want to tell me, maybe you can ask him directly. A few of the neighbors saw him watching the house. He might have seen something."

"Our orders were pretty plain. See and be seen. A little intimidation was okay, but don't start nothing. That's why they sent in white cops. They figured if we dogged the right people, they'd stay away from the convention."

I frowned. "You're saying he's not one of yours?"

"If he is, I don't know about it. He's not doing the same job I am."

Sinkovich seemed sincere, and I didn't think he was a

good enough actor to fool me. "What kind of job would he be doing?"

Sinkovich shrugged. "Undercover usually just don't watch places. They become part of it. If that's what he's doing, somebody in your neighborhood knows him."

I hadn't thought of that possibility. "I'd appreciate hearing anything you find out."

"You think you can solve this?"

"Not without help."

Sinkovich took another sip of his beer. His hand strayed to his shirt pocket, patted the cigarettes, then eased back as if he were reminding himself not to smoke. "How come you know so much about this stuff?"

Asking me that question made him nervous. It was almost as if he was afraid of me. "What stuff?"

"Procedure. Most people, they don't know about cop stuff. They just know to call us or they're afraid of us. Guys like you usually don't like us."

In the kitchen, the baby let out a wail, and his mother's voice cooed at him.

He'd been honest with me. I owed him the same in return. "I didn't call the cops. You did. I called Truman Johnson."

"Like he's gonna do something."

You could hear this boy being shuffled to the bottom of the pile even before the sun rose.

"I seem to remember you didn't think you'd get anywhere in my neighborhood."

He rocked on his feet for a moment, then nodded. "You still didn't answer my original question."

A point for Sinkovich. Most people would have let my answer distract them and would have forgotten the question until I left—if they remembered at all.

I didn't know what to tell him. On this one, I couldn't tell him the truth. "Where I come from, people take care of themselves. They don't expect others to do it."

He gave me a small, understanding smile, then nodded. "I'll see what I can find out for you."

"I appreciate it."

He set down his beer and extended his hand. I stared at it for a moment, surprised by the gesture. A look came over his face at my hesitation, an embarrassment, almost an anger, precisely the way I had felt at the front door when he refused me entry.

I took his hand and shook it. Then I nodded at him. He nodded back, and I headed for the door.

"Hey," he said, picking up his beer again and following me.

I turned. We stood in the entry. He closed the door to the kitchen.

"I did see something kinda strange, but it wasn't yesterday. It was a coupla days ago."

"What was that?" I tried not to sound too eager.

"You mentioning the afro got me remembering." He sipped his beer, frowning, as if drawing on his memory. "I had some business on the West Side before I started that day's harassment duty. I followed a blue Olds all the way to your neighborhood."

A blue Olds had followed me to Lincoln Park the night before, just like Sinkovich had. Only I had lost the blue Olds.

"Parked it about five blocks away from your place and a guy with an afro gets out."

I waited, holding my breath.

"I didn't think nothing of it, but then later, I seen him lurking, you know? In the shadow of one of the buildings, like he was watching something."

"Near my apartment?" I asked.

He nodded.

"That didn't seem unusual to you at the time?"

"Hey, I don't know the neighborhood that well. I don't know what people do."

"Then why'd you remember it?"

He shrugged. "I thought it was kinda weird."

"What was?"

"The car. It had New York plates. I seen it a couple of times after that, parked in the same spot, but I never seen him again."

"Would you recognize him?"

Sinkovich shook his head. "He wasn't my business. I didn't think of it until now. I wouldn'ta remembered if you hadn't said something."

"Where'd he come from?" I asked.

"Near the old *Ramparts* office. You know where that is?"

Ramparts was an underground publication. I didn't know, but I could find out. "Sort of."

"Shit area, if you pardon my French, and that's one of the things that made it kinda weird. The car was pretty new."

I felt a chill. Had Sinkovich been harassing this driver because he looked out of place?

"Think this is your guy?" he asked with undisguised enthusiasm.

"I don't know," I said, "but I'd appreciate it if you checked on who is working undercover anyway."

He nodded. "Let's hope they seen something."

"Let's hope," I said.

I didn't have time to check on the lead before work. I had started the week of twelve-hour shifts. I would have to be very organized or I wouldn't have time to do anything.

The hotel was crazy that night and I was grateful for it. I was too exhausted to do a good job. If it had been a long, dull evening, I might have fallen asleep leaning against the wall.

Instead, I watched celebrities go to the Haymarket Lounge and get lost in the haze of cigarette smoke. Paul Newman's eyes really were a fantastic color of blue. Walter Cronkite was shorter than I expected. Eugene McCarthy seemed cold and distant and out of place.

Mixed among all of them were the delegates, most of whom seemed starstruck, especially around Newman, though he was a delegate too. He seemed gracious enough, signing autographs, talking politics, but he looked as out of place as I did.

There were dozens of police around the entrances, and the Secret Service had taken over the extra elevator, which went only to the presidential level. The Hilton was the only hotel in Chicago that could house a president because it had one completely isolated floor.

The rooms there had originally been reserved for President Johnson, but he wasn't coming to the convention. The Secret Service had put Humphrey up there instead, maybe afraid he might not survive his nomination.

My job was to repeatedly check the entrances, and tail people who looked suspicious. No longhairs were allowed in, so the suspicious folk were mostly press. Their press badges protected them—at least from me.

I found myself keeping out of the way of the police and Feds, my mind wandering to Brian's body lying on the steps. I couldn't get past the feeling that I was wasting my time here, and yet I couldn't figure out a way to leave.

I was so exhausted I didn't remember driving home. I passed out on the twin bed, fully clothed despite the heat, and dreamed.

The chop-scrape-chop of shovels, the Chinese digging, despite the frozen ground. My mittens were threadbare, my feet blocks of ice in my boots. I rubbed my hands together, bracing my rifle against my chest, peering over the edge of the trench at the snow-covered hills. The light of the full moon gave everything an eerie silver quality. We could almost see the enemy, digging, half a mile away.

We hadn't been relieved. We should have been relieved an hour before, but something was happening. When we radioed in, we were told to hold our ground.

But there was no fighting. The Chinese were digging. We should have been too, improving our poor trench. But we were cold and tired and ready for a warm meal, an uncomfortable bunk. Our sergeant was moving, patrolling the line, trying to keep our morale up. He didn't chastise us for failing to shovel; we'd barely made any progress in the hard dirt and I guessed he didn't want us to feel bad about not making any more.

A figure appeared on the hill, dark against the snow. I caught him in my sights, a clear shot, my finger on the trigger.

"Weapons down," the sarge said.

All of us had been aiming, ready—eager—to fight an enemy we'd been listening to on still nights. Anything to break the monotony and the cold.

I blinked myself awake, shivering and sweating at the same time. My shirt was twisted around my chest, binding my arms in place. I sat up, my breathing harsh and strained.

I peeled off my shirt and my shoes, then padded barefoot to the kitchen, my heart still racing. I opened the refrigerator, and in its thin light, I saw Malcolm asleep on the couch. I hadn't even seen him when I stumbled in. His face was scrunched up and he was twitching, as if he too were having bad dreams.

I poured myself a glass of water, drank, then poured some more. This time, before I sipped, I put the glass against my sweaty forehead, but the chill seemed weak against the cold of my memory, those days in Korea that I thought would never end.

The same feeling stifled me now, the sense of being trapped in events bigger than I was. I was an insignificant player on a vast team, in a game none of us entirely understood.

I finished the water, set the glass in the sink, and went back to bed. This time, no dreams found me, and I actually got some sleep.

THIRTEEN

Monday morning, I awoke to a phone call from Grace Kirkland, panicked and angry. Franklin got me out of bed with an apology, handed me orange juice while I stood in the living room, listening to her soft voice on the other end of the line.

Apparently there had been some sort of riot in Lincoln Park the night before. She wanted me to go back there and find Daniel.

"He's an adult, Grace," I said. "He's free to do what he wants."

"But he could be in trouble!"

"He already knows how you feel. He also knows that I'm around. If something's going on that he feels he can't handle, he'll call."

"Are you sure?"

"Yes." But I wasn't. I had felt responsible for Elijah. I didn't feel responsible for Daniel. I wasn't going to get in the middle of this family battle any more than I already had. "Is Elijah still at home?"

"Of course he is. Why?"

"He's the one you concentrate on now, Grace. Let Daniel be Daniel." And then I hung up.

"Aren't you the wise one?" Franklin said, grinning at me.

I shook my head. "It's not my fight."

"Daniel would disagree." This from Malcolm, who was still lying on the couch.

"Daniel would be happy to know that I'm leaving him alone," I said. Then I excused myself and went to the shower. I had had a bad night, and I had a hunch the day wasn't going to be much better.

I drove to the West Side to investigate the tip that Sinkovich gave me. Along the way, I checked in with Jimmy and Laura from a pay phone near the University of Chicago. They seemed to be fine. Laura reported their first racist incident— she'd managed to avoid them up until that point by frequenting places where she was well known. She'd made the mistake of going to a restaurant she wasn't familiar with and having the waiter refuse to serve Jimmy. Apparently Laura created enough of a scene that the owner promised her free meals for life.

She told the story as if it amused her, but she was still angry. I was too tired to be angry, and too preoccupied. Besides, the incident wasn't unexpected. I was amazed it had taken this long for something to happen.

I hung up, and got in the car, refusing to dwell on impossibilities. The drive to the West Side took more time than I had planned because I had to detour several miles around the Amphitheater. When I finally reached the old *Ramparts* offices, I had lost an hour to traffic delays.

Franklin had known where *Ramparts* had been, but he didn't know where they had moved to. He said they were still publishing out of their Chicago branch (it was a California-based operation) and he gave me the special convention broadsheet for the day before. I hadn't asked where he had gotten the protest newspaper or why he had held on to it.

The neighborhood was on the fringes of the streets burned in the riots after Martin died. Several buildings a block north were charred, and many looked abandoned. Most were covered in graffiti. Burned-out and broken-down cars hugged the curb. In this area, the Impala fit right in.

I parked in front of the address Franklin had given me and got out. The door to the former *Ramparts* building had been torn off its hinges, and inside there was a layer of dust.

"Whatcha doin'?"

The voice came from behind me. I turned. A man about twenty stood behind me. He was wearing a fringed vest with no shirt beneath, frayed blue jeans, and sandals. He wore his hair in an afro so large that it seemed to overpower his head.

"I'm looking for *Ramparts*."

"Moved," he said.

"Where?"

He shrugged.

"I'm also looking for a man who drives a blue Olds, New York plates. He'd be dressed something like you."

He grinned. "The Professor?"

I felt a shiver run through me. "Yeah."

"I haven't seen him in four or five days. I figure he's in Lincoln Park."

"Why aren't you?"

My informant shrugged again. "Not my scene, man."

"Is there anyone else around here who might know where he is?"

The friendliness was leaving his face. I was asking too many questions. "The students he brought. You'd find them at the park, I'm sure."

"Students?"

"He brought a carload from Columbia. For the protests."

"All black?"

My informant looked at me as if I were crazy. "You think he'd bring white kids here?"

"*Ramparts* has a white staff."

"And is *Ramparts* here anymore?" he asked.

"Good point," I said. "Who would I be looking for in Lincoln Park? Have any names?"

"What're you? A narc?"

I shook my head. "I'm just looking for an old friend."

"Sure. And I'm Muhammad Ali."

I sighed. "Is the Professor staying nearby?"

"Like I said, I ain't seen him or his car in days." The kid had started backing away from me. I only had a shot at one more question.

"You ever hear anyone call him anything besides the Professor?"

"Nope." And his tone said he wouldn't have told me even if he had. He turned away and headed down the street, his walk fast, his head down.

I went inside the building, but found nothing except locked doors and dust. When I came back outside, no one was on the street. I wondered if the kid had warned people away from me.

By then, it was time for work. Work, which felt like it was interfering more and more. The last thing I wanted to do was stand in corners and watch rich white people discuss the future of the country.

I hadn't gotten half of my chores done that day; I hadn't managed to question any neighbors, not research the old cases or talk to Truman Johnson. I hadn't found my shadow, although I had some more information about him.

If this Professor was the man I was looking for, then he had come with a carload of ringers, people who would disrupt the demonstrations. Whether they were from New York or not was impossible to determine.

But there would be no reason for a man from New York to hang out on street corners in our neighborhood.

I resolved to come back here and see what else I could find.

I got to work at one, and by four I had caught three college-age women who had facial tissues dipped in butyric acid stuffed in their purses. The tissues made crude stink bombs that the women clearly planned to dump in the hotel. Butyric acid smelled like rotten eggs, and that was what clued me. As they walked past, the stench followed them.

I took them to a cop who arrested them—on what charge, I didn't know and didn't care.

Apparently the protestors were using women to get into the hotels because the cops usually didn't stop them. The women had cleaned up nicely and looked as if they belonged. I caught another group outside of the downstairs ladies' room, spray painting Pigs across the door.

The message was lost on me, and I thought the entire incident rather silly.

By five, my sense of absurdity had fled. Several hundred marchers had converged on the front entrance, chanting in question-and-answer style:

What do we want?

Revolution.

When do we want it?

Now!

The delegates were at the convention, but the support staff and some of the press watched the entire thing from the Haymarket Lounge. To them, it was just something else to talk about, but it was beginning to anger the cops out front. I could tell from the way they fingered their nightsticks and the flushes that were building on their cheeks.

I went to the other entrances to make sure they were secure. When I got back, the marchers had left the Hilton and were circling the Logan statue in Grant Park. Some idiot had draped the statue in a Viet Cong flag, and that was enough to set off the police.

They started a northward sweep and beat any demonstrators who came near them. We watched all of this from the hotel windows, prepared to blockade the place if we had to. There were at least a thousand protestors in Grant Park, most of them listening to speeches and cheering.

But when the police started their action, everything stopped until the streets were clear. It took about an hour to get everyone quieted down.

My boss, Walt Kotlarz, watched from beside me. When the demonstrators started heading north, toward Lincoln Park, he sighed.

"I hope to hell we can continue dodging these bullets," he said.

The twelve-hour shifts cut into my time. I got home at two in the morning, went to bed, and was up by seven. By eight, I was back on the West Side. I spoke to an elderly man who didn't remember anyone and some children who had seen the Professor. They believed they had heard someone call him Tim.

Besides those people, though, no one else would talk to me. No one knew where the Professor had gone and no one had seen him in last several days. No one knew who his companions were or where they had gone.

It was a dead end.

I still had some time before work, so I went to the library to search the newspapers for articles on the previous murders. The librarian, a dried-up little old white woman, frowned at me as I pawed through the newsprint—most of the issues I wanted weren't yet on microfiche—but she didn't interfere. I wasn't the only black face in the research area, although mine was probably the oldest.

The *Defender* covered the stories in depth, but told me nothing more about the murders than Johnson had. The paper's stories did give me family names and addresses, though, and I wrote them down diligently, not sure how I was going to use them.

The *Tribune* and the *Sun-Times* both gave the deaths an inch in their city sections and then never returned to the stories. The neighborhood weeklies didn't cover the murders at all.

It took the rest of the morning to find all of that. Then I drove past the places where the other two bodies had been left. Both were public, both were open, about as different from Brian's death site as they could possibly be.

I wanted to talk to Johnson, but I didn't have time. All I had time to do was check in with Jimmy and Laura before I went to work.

The first thing that greeted me at the Hilton was the stench of rotten eggs. Apparently my colleagues hadn't caught other protestors who brought in stink bombs. The smell pervaded the first three floors of the hotel.

That day, I was just as busy as the day before. I caught a clean-cut white boy lighting campaign literature on fire at the top of a lobby stairwell. He'd been trying to burn down the hotel.

Around midnight, I found a homemade bomb made of plastique in one of the elevators. Apparently the bomb hadn't gone off as planned—a good thing, since the delegates had just returned.

But the worst moment for me that day came shortly after my shift began. The remains of Martin Luther King's Poor People's Campaign sponsored a mule train to draw the attention of the world to the plight of the impoverished.

The train stopped outside the Hilton's front entrance, and Kotlarz sent me to keep on eye on everything. I went through the main doors, and immediately melted back inside them. Ralph Abernathy had been standing near the entrance. Ralph had worked with Martin for years and was trying to keep Martin's dream alive, by leading the Poor People's Campaign. I'd known Ralph casually for years, and we had seen each other just six months before at Martin's disastrous last march.

I didn't dare let anyone notice me. They couldn't know that I was here.

Fortunately none of them were staying at the Hilton, but I didn't know how long I could continue hiding.

Only luck was keeping me from being found out.

Brian Richardson's funeral was held on Wednesday morning at the First Presbyterian Church. I borrowed a suit from Franklin—his winter suit, made of black wool. The pants were too short and the coat too big, but I had nothing better. I wore my work shoes and resigned myself to being uncomfortable for the entire day.

I drove alone, even though Franklin and Malcolm planned to attend. I wanted to talk to people, if possible, follow a few leads if I got them, and see what I could discover.

Franklin and Malcolm left for the church before I did. I wanted to see if they were being followed, but no one tailed Franklin's dusty sedan. I didn't see anyone in my rearview mirror either as I drove into the heart of the Woodlawn neighborhood.

The church was the most dominant feature in the triangle formed by Washington Park, Jackson Park, and Oakwoods Cemetery. I'd driven past the church a number of times in my months in Chicago, but I'd never had occasion to stop.

It was a grand stone building with a tall bell tower done in the Gothic tradition. I'd never seen a black church quite like this one—as large, yes, but not as classic. I parked in the spacious lot and followed a well-dressed family toward the church.

As I got closer to the building, I realized some of the stained-glass windows were broken. Blocks of wood covered the damaged panels. The stone exterior had been riddled with bullet holes.

A shiver ran down my back. In Memphis, people didn't shoot at churches. Unlike other places in the South and, apparently, the North, the people of Memphis still believed that God's house was sacred.

As we went inside, a white woman wearing a shapeless black dress and small black hat with veil greeted us. She took our hands in her tiny gloved ones, and said, "The service will be in the chapel today. I'm so sorry for your loss."

I must have given her a startled glance, for she responded by patting me and pointing down a hallway.

I followed the family toward the swelling piano music playing hymns I didn't recognize, all of them in minor keys, appropriately somber for an extremely somber day. The piano music was beautiful, but I would have expected a church like this to have a pipe organ.

As I walked, I realized we weren't heading to the sanctuary but to the chapel. The sanctuary was quite large. Apparently someone had thought a funeral for a child wouldn't need that much room.

But when we reached the chapel, it was clear that whoever had made the decision had miscalculated. The wooden chairs sitting on the stone floor were full, and people were standing in the back. A white minister in full black robes sat in a high-backed chair in front of the stained-glass windows.

Brian's coffin stood in front of the minister. The coffin was polished but clearly cheap, and it was closed. On top of it lay flower garlands that trailed to the floor. A picture of Brian sat on the wooden table beside the minister, right in front of a large white cross.

The piano I had heard was a baby grand. It seemed dwarfed by the room, which was not small by anyone's measure.

An elderly white man in a black suit handed me a program and apologized that there were no chairs left. I gave him the same startled glance I had given the woman. I hadn't expected to see any white faces here.

But there were dozens of them, many of them seated on the wooden chairs. Brian's mother was in the first row, surrounded by family. She wasn't sobbing now. She was sitting with her back straight, her proud face staring at her son's coffin. A man who must have been her estranged husband sat on the aisle, all alone. His face was blotchy with tears, and he held a crumpled program in his left hand.

Malcolm and Franklin had both managed to get seats. I stood in the back left corner and leaned against the curtain-covered wall. A young black man, also carrying programs, approached me.

"Sorry, sir," he said softly, "but that wall's not real sturdy there. You want I should find a chair?"

I shook my head, the feeling of unreality still with me. The young man who had spoken to me was no older than Malcolm. This congregation was mixed and comfortable with it.

I had never seen anything like it in my life.

The piano music rose to a crescendo and then stopped. The minister stood and walked toward the small podium on the right side of the chapel. He was slender, and younger than I was. The podium looked like a portable lectern my professors had used in college.

"Today," he said, "the Lord has visited upon us unimaginable sorrow. . . ."

And that was the moment I turned my attention away

from the service. Christian funerals, white or black, it seemed, were fundamentally the same, made up of platitudes that tried to make some sense of the horrible death of a ten-year-old boy.

Instead of listening, I watched, and looked at faces, familiar and unfamiliar. The white faces were all unfamiliar. Some of them were elderly, clearly members of the church, but the rest belonged to young families.

The whites mingled with the blacks. No one sat in a separate section. Often white parents and their children sat next to black parents and their children. It was a difficult day for all of them, I knew. It would be some of those children's first experience with death.

Grace Kirkland and Elijah sat toward the front. Daniel was not with them. He had apparently not felt it important to come back from Lincoln Park. Marvella sat near them, and beside her was her cousin Truman Johnson. I didn't see any of the white cops who'd been assigned to the case.

I scanned for afros and found them, all in the same two rows. Teenage boys wearing leather jackets and, incongruously, ties sat shoulder to shoulder with each other. I recognized one boy. He lived upstairs with his grandmother, and he was a member of the Blackstone Rangers.

The other boys had to belong to the same gang, but again, no one bothered them. Not even Detective Johnson gave them a sideways look. I watched as they stood to sing hymns, their heads down, their caps on the floor. They had no weapons and they seemed at ease.

None of them fit the description Marvella had originally given me. As carefully as I could, I looked at the people surrounding me, but none of them fit the description either. Most of them were my age or older, all of them with care marks on their faces, and a look of sorrow in their eyes.

Then I noticed something was different from the Baptist funerals I'd been to in Memphis. This funeral was subdued.

Brian's mother sobbed in the front row, but quietly. There was no wailing, no screaming, only sniffles and tear-streaked faces. The grief seemed more terrible for all that.

No one stood up to speak except the minister, who gave a confused little sermon that tried to find meaning in senseless death. Brian's father attempted to read a passage from Job, but couldn't finish it. A white boy no older than Brian who identified himself as Brian's best friend read the Twenty-third Psalm.

" 'Yea,' " he said in a forceful voice, as if the passage could give them all comfort, " 'though I walk through the Valley of the Shadow of Death, I shall fear no evil for Thou art with me. . . .' "

The passage didn't comfort me. I'd seen Brian's face. As he had walked through that valley, he had feared the evil before him. And he had found no comforting rod or staff, no benign presence. He had died in a way no human should die, and certainly no child. As I stared at that small coffin, I felt my fingers clench into fists.

The service was blessedly short. We were all invited to the Fellowship Room for refreshments, but I didn't plan to go. Instead, I blended into the background and watched the mourners file out. Johnson saw me, though, and nodded in my direction. I nodded back.

Franklin went over to Brian's family and spoke to them. Malcolm came and stood beside me. His eyes were red, and it made me wonder how well he'd known the boy.

The Blackstone Rangers walked out in single file. A few of the elderly parishioners greeted them, and some of the Rangers stopped to talk to a few of the parents.

My amazement must have shown on my face because when Johnson reached me, he said, "Close your mouth. People'll think you've never been to church before."

"Do they know who those boys are?"

"Sure. They're more welcome here than I am."

"What?" I turned toward him. He was watching the mourners leave as just as I was.

His gaze met mine and I could see a bit of anger beneath the surface. "You saw the damage when you came in? My white brothers in blue did that. Cops aren't real popular in this congregation."

"Because they tolerate the Rangers?"

"Because they're trying to rehabilitate them." He shrugged, turned back to watch the mourners. "Long story, and not really relevant."

"So you don't think the Rangers had anything to do with—"

"They see themselves as guardians of this neighborhood. They wouldn't let a child die. I'm sure they see Brian's death as some kind of failure."

Malcolm stood silently beside us. He was watching too, listening. I wondered if he agreed, and resolved to ask him later.

Brian's mother stumbled past, her estranged husband beside her. They were clinging to each other like drowning people.

The minister followed them, staying close, concern on his face. When he saw us, he gave us a sympathetic smile. "There's coffee in the Fellowship Room."

A white midwestern dismissal. I was learning to recognize them. Johnson nodded, and let the minister usher us out of the chapel. But we didn't go to the Fellowship Room. Instead, Johnson and I went outside. Malcolm didn't follow us.

Johnson seemed to know his way around the church and he led us to a garden hidden from the street by stone arches that only added to the church's Gothic majesty. Here too were holes in the stone, broken windows, and evidence that someone had tried to start a fire near one of the doors.

"So," I said when I was sure we were alone, "you were

sent to cover the funeral because you weren't a white boy in blue?"

"Those boys wouldn't dare cross the threshold. I probably couldn't come in here in uniform either, not and sit comfortably in one of the chairs." He sat on a stone bench half-buried behind greenery.

I sat beside him. "I've never been in a place like this before."

He smiled at me, understanding what I meant. "About fifteen years ago, this church decided to be part of the community, not hide from it. They do what they can."

I hadn't heard that tone in his voice before. He admired the people here, maybe even envied them. "You'll have to tell me about it sometime."

"Not on a day like this." He sighed and tilted his head back. The sun caught his face. I could feel it warm against my neck. For the first time in weeks, the heat felt cold. The service had chilled me, not because it lacked warmth but because of that small coffin in the front of the chapel.

"So how's the investigation going?" I asked.

He snorted and sat up. "Just the way I expected it to."

"Nothing new, huh?"

"I told you not to get involved."

"I got involved Saturday night."

He looked at me, measuring me. He wouldn't have been on the scene if it weren't for me, and we both knew it.

"Got the autopsy this morning," he said. "Kid was killed by a single stab to the heart."

"Was he conscious?"

Johnson nodded.

I closed my eyes against the knowledge, saw the body crumpled against the stairs, the cigarette burns, the fingers, and realized it was better to keep my eyes open. The garden didn't give me any peace but at least it didn't haunt me either.

"What else?"

"We have a pretty clear picture of his last few hours."

He glanced at the door we'd come out of, apparently not wanting to be overheard. And I couldn't blame him. Brian's friends and family had suffered enough. They didn't need the exact details of his death.

"He disappeared in the afternoon." Johnson's voice was low. "We know this from an interview with his mother. She fed him a peanut butter and jelly sandwich about noon, called him for dinner about six, and couldn't find him. The coroner says he hadn't eaten anything in the interim."

A bee landed on a bright yellow flower a few yards from me. It walked along the petals, then flew off passing me on its way to something sweeter.

"He was tied up on two separate occasions, in two different ways. First he was tied with his hands behind his back, overlapping, with some kind of thick rope, maybe jute. Fibers got caught in the wounds and they were only on the back of his left wrist and the front of his right. The scrapes were thicker than the later ones. His feet were crossed and tied with the same kind of rope. There seems to be no evidence that he was gagged."

I frowned. "His lip was split."

"He'd been hit a number of times across the face. Backhanded, the coroner thinks."

"So it didn't matter that he screamed."

Johnson nodded. "He was taken somewhere pretty isolated. A lot of evidence points to that."

"The cobwebs," I said.

Johnson looked at me sideways, that measuring look again. "And the dirt. It was dust and grime, the kind you'd find in a basement."

"Or an abandoned building."

Johnson was still studying me.

I shrugged. "You can hear screaming in a basement. Es-

237

pecially in that neighborhood. Those buildings aren't that soundproof."

"There's no evidence he stayed in the neighborhood."

"Is there evidence that he left?"

Johnson's lips thinned and he leaned back. My speculations interfered with his own notions of the crime. It was clear he didn't like that.

"What's the rest?" I asked.

He seemed to gather himself, as if remembering where he was. "The second time, he was tied to a chair. His legs were tied separately around the ankle, and his arms were bound in two places. Around the center of the forearm which gave his hands some mobility, and around the bicep. This time, the perp used some kind of thin rope, maybe clothesline, and tied it tightly enough to bruise. There was no burning because struggle wasn't possible."

I let out a small puff of air. I recognized the position. In my last few months in the service, I'd been assigned to assist the Intelligence Unit in San Diego. They were practicing interrogation techniques they'd learned from the North Koreans.

One of the things they had done was tie subjects twice around the arm, on the bicep to hold the arm in place, and around the forearm to give the hand mobility.

So that the fingers could be broken, if need be.

"You okay?" Johnson asked.

I nodded. "What else?"

"There was also a bruise on his chest in the shape of a belt buckle. We figure the perp used that to bind Brian's torso to the chair."

"What kind of buckle?" I asked.

"Standard, square, open so that the belt can weave through it. We're having it analyzed—at least that's what I've been told."

He didn't sound like he believed it.

"The autopsy sounds pretty thorough. Maybe you're wrong about the way that this case will be handled."

Johnson shook his head. "We've got the Feebies looking over our shoulders now. All the paperwork will be done properly, evidence properly filed, autopsy by the book. Lack of follow-up will be blamed on caseload, the convention. Your choice."

He seemed so sure, and it made a curious kind of sense. Dot the *i*'s and cross the *t*'s so no one looks too closely at the actual investigation. Or lack of one.

"What about the cigarette burns?" I asked.

"Our perp gets off on torture. First he hits the kid, then he burns him over a period of hours. Finally he breaks his fingers." Johnson swallowed. This part clearly made him uncomfortable. "They weren't broken in the same pattern. The little finger was broken at the base. The middle finger at the top knuckle. The thumb was twisted and nearly pulled out of the socket."

His voice was dispassionate. His eyes weren't.

"One at a time then."

He nodded.

I stood, unable to sit with the news. My sudden movement disturbed a butterfly. It left a small purple flower and headed out of the garden.

A monarch. I hadn't seen one of those in a long time.

"Is that it?" I asked.

"Knife wound," Johnson said as if reminding me about it. "Very efficient. Almost no blood around the wound at all. Quick, sudden, and lethal."

"This isn't a quick loss of control," I said. "It was a very methodical torture and kill."

"That's my take," Johnson said.

"Was there anything similar on the other bodies?" I asked. "Indications that this is some kind of escalation, maybe?"

"No. The other bodies had bruises, but no burns, no broken bones." Johnson's response was curt. "I no longer think the cases are related. This one is in a class of its own."

"Because of the torture?" I asked.

"Because of this."

I turned. He was holding a small blue evidence bag between his thumb and forefinger.

His expression was different now, wary, and I realized he hadn't been sharing information out of the kindness of his heart. He'd been setting me up for this moment. He wanted to see my reaction to the contents of that bag.

I walked over to him. The heat suddenly felt stifling. A bead of sweat ran down my spine.

I took the bag from his hand and opened it. Inside was a matchbook.

"You can take it out," he said. "It's already been dusted. It's clean."

I stared at it, still not wanting to hold it. "How clean?"

"Too clean. No prints at all."

My stomach clenched. Very few people understood how fingerprints worked, and those who did often forgot that paper carried prints as easily as doorknobs did.

The lack of fingerprints on a matchbook told us we had a pro.

"Where'd you find this?" I asked.

"In Brian's right pants pocket. Deliberately placed, we think since his shirt pocket and left pants pocket were ripped open. And the right pocket had nothing else in it. Not even lint."

I handed the bag back to Johnson. "I don't feel comfortable touching evidence."

He raised his eyebrows, then reached inside the bag. He took the matchbook out carefully, holding its sides with his thumb and forefinger.

"The Haymarket Lounge" it said on the front. I knew

what the back said without even seeing it. Tiny flowing script read: "A place where good guys take good girls to dine in the lusty, rollicking atmosphere of fabulous Old Chicago."

For the longest moment, I didn't breathe. I could hear the bee buzzing near me, and cars passing on the nearby street. Voices, muffled, came from inside the church.

Johnson was watching me. "You want to tell me," he said, "what Brian Richardson's connection to the Conrad Hilton is?"

A trick of sweat ran down my back. So far as I knew, Brian Richardson had only one connection to the Hilton Hotel.

Me.

FOURTEEN

T he way I see it," Johnson said into my silence, "there's a lot happening here that I don't understand. See if you can help me with this."

I hadn't moved. My gaze was still on that matchbook, my body cold despite the heat.

"Marvella told me you have a ten-year-old boy, but she hasn't seen him for about a week. Yet you don't seem very concerned about that."

I took a shallow breath. At some point I had slipped into my usual passive role, the one I often took with cops. White cops. I had never dealt with a black cop before. I didn't know where his loyalty lay—to his people or to his job.

But he was smart, and he knew I was too.

"Marvella also says that you've been being followed." He put the matchbook into the evidence bag and closed it, slipping it into his pocket. "And then there's that notice I received a while back from Memphis. You remember. I told you about it."

I watched each movement closely, not sure what was coming next.

Johnson put his arm over the back of the stone bench, as

if he were having a dinner party conversation. "So here's what I figure. Brian Richardson, who is ten, gets snatched because someone took him for your kid."

The conversation Brian and I had over the sun tea. From far away, that might have looked a lot more personal.

"The perp finds out pretty quick that he has the wrong kid. Which puts him in a dilemma because he probably snatched Brian out of the yard, tied him up, and threw him in the back of a car. No kid is going to stay silent about that."

I could almost see it. A hand, snaking around Brian's middle, another covering his mouth. But I couldn't imagine throwing him in a car or finding a place to tie him up. Not in that neighborhood. Not that close.

But people carried children all the time, sometimes in awkward positions, especially if the kid had been misbehaving. No one would have had second thoughts about that.

"So he takes Brian to his lair, and tries to find out more about your kid. Where he is, what he's doing. Poor little Brian tells him what he knows—"

He said you saved his life.

"—and our friend double-checks that information by breaking a few fingers. No one—especially a ten-year-old—can lie under those circumstances. Young Brian is rewarded for his honesty by a knife blade through the ribs. What do you think so far?"

I still hadn't moved, hadn't even changed expression. But I thought that Johnson was probably right.

"This is where it gets interesting." Johnson spoke in calm tones. He sounded bemused, as if the entire case intrigued him. "Instead of dumping the body, he brings it back and leaves it on the steps in the middle of the night with a little message for you in the pocket. The message intrigues me. You see, it could go a variety of ways. He could have left it for you to find, which suggests that he didn't know you very well. You were very careful not to touch that body or to tamper with the evidence. Which I do appreciate, by the way."

A car door slammed in the parking lot, and voices carried in the humid air. The meeting in the Fellowship Room had broken up.

Johnson didn't even look in that direction. "Or it suggests that he planned to frame you. Or perhaps he wanted someone, like me, to give you this information. Maybe he knew you'd be resourceful enough to find it out on your own."

More voices. I wondered if Franklin or Malcolm would try to find me. I prayed that they wouldn't. I didn't want them interrupting this conversation.

"I don't think he expected the police to show up as fast as we did. And, frankly, I don't think we would have if Sinkovich hadn't been following you. I think you might have done some investigating on your own before we arrived. Maybe you would have seen the bulge in the pocket. Maybe you would have carefully—using a stick, a pen— pulled that matchbook out."

I swallowed. I just might have.

"My bet is that he expected you to take off then, maybe lead him to your kid. But you're smarter than that, aren't you? You're not going to lead anyone to that kid. Not even me."

I was holding my breath again. I made myself exhale.

"So what I've been asking myself is: Why all the interest in a ten-year-old? Can't be for what he's done. Gotta be for what he knows. Maybe he's seen something. Maybe something illegal. That would get the FBI after him, maybe to testify, and that would get the perp after him too."

My heart rose. A plausible lie.

"But that doesn't entirely figure. If that were true, there wouldn't be a simple notice. There'd be a material witness order, something to let us know that he'd seen a crime. And then there's the torture itself."

More car doors slammed. Female voices, bidding good wishes, floated into the garden. I allowed myself a glance at the church doors, but no one came out.

"It's textbook. Too precise, as if the perp was looking for information, not trying to get his jollies."

Johnson rested his elbows on his thighs, dangling that evidence bag carelessly between his knees.

"And then there's you. You're not an average security guard. You have an education you don't try to hide, and you know way too much about police business. I'll bet your name isn't Grimshaw like Marvella thinks it is."

There was no place for me to go and nothing for me to say. All I could do was wait for the last of it, the part that was going to ruin everything.

"But here's the thing that really bothers me," Johnson said. He was speaking even softer now. "Brian's death had a lot of similarities to the other two murders. Enough so that my white colleagues assume that this is just an escalation. They're not going to pay those similarities a lot of mind."

This wasn't what I expected. In spite of myself, I leaned forward to catch his words. He didn't seem to notice, but I knew he had. He was too good not to.

"I pay them a lot of mind," he said. "That body was placed just like the others. The arms, the feet, the entire picture. Posed, in much the same way. The problem is the detail used in that pose was known only to the members of the Chicago Police Department and the FBI. And I don't like what that makes me think."

I met his gaze. I wasn't going to say anything. I didn't dare confirm or deny.

"You know," he said, "if I was a white cop, I'd have you down at the House for questioning right now."

I knew that.

"I still might do that, if you piss me off."

I nodded, once, heart still pounding.

"But for the moment," he said, "I figure I can use you to close this case."

I wasn't sure he would be able to close the case. I had a hunch he knew that. Maybe he wanted to close it to his satisfaction. Maybe he thought he could be a hero and get a child killer off the streets.

I hoped he could.

"What do you want?" My voice sounded strange, strangled, as if it had come from me reluctantly, which, I suppose, it had.

"An information trade." He stood beside me, close, almost threatening. "Do you know who I'm looking for?"

I shook my head. I didn't know. Not by name, not even by face. But I knew what I was dealing with now. By type.

"Assuming you're telling the truth, I'm going to need your cooperation."

I slipped my hands in my pockets to keep them under control. I didn't like how close he had gotten to me. I no longer trusted him. "For what?"

"You can save me some time."

"How?"

"I need to see the guest list at the Hilton for last week. I need a warrant for that. I doubt I'll get one very soon, considering who is inside and what's going on."

I turned, backed away, nearly stepped on one of the flowering plants. "That's not going to get you anywhere."

"You sure?"

I wasn't sure.

He rubbed his cheek with his right hand. "If you don't know who this is, then I gotta proceed like this is a normal perp. I start with the one piece of information I have. The Hilton."

"A place anyone can walk into. Especially the restaurant."

"Not in the last two weeks, Bill, and you know it. I'll

wager every suspicious person who loitered in front of the hotel last week was documented."

"That matchbook could have been picked up at any point."

He nodded. "If we're dealing with a normal perp, yeah, I suppose. But it's never been used. The edges aren't even dented. It either sat in someone's matchbook bowl for a very long time or it was recently acquired. I vote for recently acquired. And if that's true, then we have a general description of our perp. He's not a young hippie."

"The person following me, according to Marvella, was a black man with an afro," I said. "He wouldn't be too welcome in the Hilton either."

"Then maybe he's not our man."

"Maybe he is."

Johnson shrugged. "The list'll get me started."

"Any search you do based on that list won't hold up in court."

He grinned. "You *are* smart." Then his grin faded as if it had never been. "I've already asked for the warrant, but nobody's willing to fast-track anything this week, especially concerning the Hilton. If I don't get it, I'll figure out another way to cover myself. I expect it to be a dead end, but if it isn't, I want to get moving quickly. Every hour we waste is one that prevents us from solving this crime."

"What if you solve it," I said, "and can't touch this guy?"

His eyes narrowed. "I thought you don't know who did this."

"I know as much as you do."

"I doubt that," he said.

"So?" I asked again. "What if?"

"Seems to me," he said, "if the right things are brought to light in the right ways, no one's untouchable."

It was my turn to smile, but it wasn't a pleased smile. "You haven't been doing this very long, have you?"

"Long enough to know that sometimes you catch a break."

"But usually, you stick your neck out and you get screwed."

"Is that what happened to you?"

"Remains to be seen, doesn't it," I said.

For the first time in our conversation, he seemed uneasy. "You'll get me that list?"

I would get it. The idea was a good one, and the information might help us both. But I didn't want him to think I was happy to do his dirty work.

"Do I have a choice?" I said.

"People always have a choice," he said.

"Yeah, and sometimes it's between bad and awful." I stood up and tipped an imaginary hat to him. "Thanks for the information, Detective. When I bring you that list, I'll consider us even."

I walked down the path toward the arches.

"I'm going to need help with the names," he said.

I stopped. "Anything else?"

"I don't know yet." He paused. "I want to catch this guy."

"Believe me," I said, "so do I."

I got into my car, shaking. Not because Johnson was onto me—he was, but he was smart enough to realize that there was more going on here than he understood—but because of that matchbook.

Brian Richardson was dead because I had chosen to come to Chicago. Because I had found my old friend Franklin Grimshaw and he had offered me help. Because I had chosen to stay in that apartment longer than I should have, because I had been picky about where Jimmy and I were going to live.

I believed Johnson's scenario was right. The man who found us, who had orders to get rid of Jimmy, one of the only witnesses—if not the only witness to the King assassination, had not known us. Or had not known Jimmy.

And that was a plus.

This guy was days ahead of me, true. I let out a small breath. But he hadn't found Jimmy yet. I had just spoken to Jimmy and Laura that morning. Because of the violence, they were planning to stay in all day. Jimmy hadn't liked the prospect, but I had. Laura was keeping him safe.

The last thing I needed to do was drive to the Gold Coast and see him. That was probably what the perp, as Johnson had called him, expected me to do. No phone calls. No visits.

Just follow the plan as we had laid it out less than a week ago.

A lifetime ago.

I put the key in the ignition and shifted to reverse, scanning the area for familiar—or unfamiliar—cars. Except for Johnson's unmarked, mine was the only car in the lot. I backed around him and headed to the street.

The details of Brian's autopsy were swimming in my head. Johnson was right. The torture method the perp used was by the book, and the book had been developed in San Diego just after the Korean War.

We were told we would be subjected to various types of interrogation that would stop short of actual physical torture. Anything else was fair game.

The interrogations were supposed to show how information—anything from patches on flight suits to personal items found in the pocket—could be used against the prisoner. But the process quickly evolved into something else, a contest between the marines and military intelligence.

Intelligence started using real personal information from

files to break the "prisoners" and it usually worked. Only it hadn't worked with me. I had so frustrated my first interrogator, one Thomas Withers, that he had struck me and had gotten pulled off the project. He had hated me ever since.

My second interrogator, George Nichols, fared no better. I was the only prisoner in that unit who couldn't be broken. I gained a measure of fame for that and maybe a bit of fear. I'd learned later that I was used as an example for years to underscore the maxim that some people couldn't be taken apart without brute force.

I had become a legend among the ranks.

I was beginning to wonder if that legend had come back to haunt me.

I continually checked my mirror as I drove to the neighborhood. No one was following me. I didn't even have the sense of being followed, which bothered me. If the shadow, thought I was going to lead him to Jimmy, he'd be on my tail.

He hadn't been—at least not so that I could see. And unlike earlier in the week, I'd been watching for him. So had Franklin.

I hadn't seen anything suspicious since the night Brian died. Then I had seen the blue Olds. I'd had a sense for the last few days that something made this guy drop me. Now I was wondering if it was something Brian had told him. What could the boy know? He certainly hadn't known where Jimmy went. No one knew that but me, Laura, and Jimmy.

Maybe this guy assumed I wasn't going to lead him to Jimmy. Or maybe his time in Chicago was short.

Just like his time with Brian would have been.

He would have killed Jimmy the moment they were alone. But he hadn't killed Brian immediately. So he must have figured out fairly quickly that Brian wasn't Jimmy—quickly enough to change his plans.

Brian had been a well-loved child. His mother had noticed he was missing at dinnertime, had searched for him, and had assumed, reluctantly, that he had gone to his father. The absence of a child as well cared for as Brian would be obvious quite soon. The perp would know that.

And, if he wanted to leave the boy as a warning to me, he had to act fast. Hence the crudeness of the torture. He needed as much information as he could get as quickly as he could get it.

A man like that didn't pick up a boy, bind him, throw him in a car and drive him to a remote section of the city. He'd planned on murder, not torture. He grabbed the child and carried him, just like I'd thought when Johnson was talking.

He had tied Brian up at the last moment, when he realized he had the wrong boy. As he was preparing for the torture.

I pulled onto our street and parked in front of the building, staring at the sidewalk. Drops of blood that led to the street but went no farther hinted at a car.

But the perp was smart enough to keep the matchbook clean, to leave no accidental clues pointing to his own identity. And if he was that smart, then he was smart enough to make up evidence pointing to an imaginary car.

I got out of my Impala and scanned the neighborhood. No strangers with afros. Nothing. I looked at the sidewalk again.

Knife wound, Johnson had said. Very efficient. Almost no blood around the wound at all. Quick, sudden, and lethal.

The broken nose and split lip were scabbing, the blood on Brian's body old. The knife wound would have bled internally for the few seconds that Brian's heart continued to beat. The perp wouldn't have pulled out the blade until the boy was dead.

There was no blood that could have dripped on the sidewalk, no reason for that clue, except to throw the police off the trail, to think that Brian was part of a pattern. The matchbook had been for me, just as Johnson thought it was. No one else was supposed to get the message and the white cops wouldn't have.

Johnson had.

I whirled, looking at the buildings. Basements were too public, especially in the daylight, even if they were soundproofed, which they were not. People were in these apartments during the day. They would have heard something. Brian had not been gagged. He had to have been somewhere isolated enough that his screams wouldn't be heard.

And he would have screamed.

My gaze turned toward the stone steps where I had first recruited Malcolm. That building had been empty for a long time. The windows were boarded up, and the walls were made of thick stone.

Someone screaming in the basement of that place would not have been heard.

For a moment, I toyed with seeing if Franklin was home or Malcolm. Then I decided not to involve them. My shadow had made it clear that he wasn't going to harm me. I didn't interest him. Only Jimmy did.

I opened the passenger door, and reached into the glove box. I got my flashlight and my gun. I didn't like carrying the gun openly on the street, especially with undercover police around, but I felt as if I had no other choice. I wasn't going into the building unarmed. Alone, yes, but not unarmed.

I slipped the shoulder holster on, then put my suit coat over it. It was too hot for wool, but I didn't care. I crossed the street, looking both ways to see who was watching me. I recognized all the faces on the block. I didn't know them by name, but I recognized them.

Part of me wanted him to be there. Part of me wanted to take care of this myself. I wasn't sure how I'd do it, but I'd find a way.

I hurried up the stairs. The door was closed but not locked. I pushed it open and stepped inside.

The floor was made of marble, cracked now, and yellowed, covered with dirt and grime. There were footprints in the dust, dozens of them, most of them old. But I saw what I was looking for. Little sneaker prints, about the size of Brian's shoe, dragging down the hallway.

Dust motes floated around me and I resisted the urge to sneeze. Cobwebs covered the ceiling, but none were low—and they should have been.

I turned a corner, saw stairs leading up and down. The stairs going up were marble also, worn in the center, and covered in dried mud and dirt. But no child's sneaker prints. Only the faint scent of urine. Squatters or maybe the Machine.

The stairs heading down were the ones that interested me. They were wood, rotted and old. The first two, the only ones visible coming out of the darkness, were shattered. I trained my flashlight on them.

The breaks were fresh. Someone had done this deliberately to make the basement seem impassible. Probably the same someone who was smart enough to leave a carefully orchestrated blood trail.

The third step was still intact, as were the others leading down. And while there were cobwebs, they had been broken. They were hanging on either side of the staircase, but not in the middle where they normally would be.

I used the stone wall to brace myself as I reached for the third step. It groaned under my weight, but didn't break. The sound made me freeze. I held my breath and heard nothing.

It felt as if I were alone. But feelings could be deceiving.

That one sound was enough warning for someone waiting to ambush me at the bottom of the stairs.

But why do that? A man who didn't want to be found could hide from any unexpected visitor, and if he was expecting me, he wouldn't kill me. Not right away. He would want to know where Jimmy was.

I reached into my shoulder holster and pulled out the gun. It felt like a feeble defense. I had once told my friend Roscoe Brown in Memphis that a gun was the choice of a man with no imagination or no options. But I had been wrong. There was a third category, a category I was in now, one I wasn't sure I wanted to acknowledge.

I took the fourth step and the fifth. They sagged beneath my weight, but didn't make a sound. Neither did my dress shoes. The wall's grime coated my fingers and the heat was stifling. The air no longer smelled of urine. Just dust and mold—the smell of a place that had been closed up a very long time.

There were only ten steps. The basement was large, the floor covered old concrete that was flaking. A rusted furnace loomed beside me, empty wooden shelves leaned drunkenly against each other. I held my breath, listening for the sound of another human being.

I heard nothing.

I went around the corner, the flashlight playing against the darkness. There were no windows here at all. But at the far end of the room, I saw a thin band of light. I shut off my flashlight, saw that the light floated through the vertical slats of a badly constructed wooden door.

I made my way toward it slowly, shrugging my coat sleeve over my left hand as I walked. In my right, I held the gun. When I reached the door, I grabbed the knob through the fabric and pushed.

The door creaked as it swung open. A single bulb hung in the center of the room, bright against the darkness. The room itself was small, more of a pantry or a walk-in closet. In the very center, stood a rickety table and an old chair with ropes at its base, and more hanging from the arms.

The floor was spattered with dried blood. As I got closer, I realized the tabletop was too. There was another blood-stain against the back of chair, right about the place a child's heart would be.

How many hours had Brian sat here, just a half a block away from home, hoping someone would find him? Or had he given up hope the first time he got backhanded across the face? Or when the first cigarette dug into his skin?

I forced those images out of my mind, and looked—really looked—at what was before me. Table, chair, rope. Old rope, thin, maybe even came from the building. No ciga-rettes. No ashes. The blood spatter was smeared closest to the chair. Someone had swept the floor. There wasn't even dust here and no spiderwebs hanging from the ceiling.

I felt as if I'd walked into a stage, and I felt as if it had been set up for me, but I wasn't sure what message I was supposed to receive. That Brian's death was horrible? I got that, and I also got that he would have been alive if it weren't for me. But what else? That this awaited me as well, unless I turned over Jimmy? Or that this awaited Jimmy, which was a lie.

Or was this message even subtler than that? *I can torture a boy within earshot of you. I'm that good. I'm so good I can kill your boy and you won't even know he's dead.*

A message like that was extremely personal. This torture chamber made the crime feel as if it were about me, not about Brian, and certainly not about Jimmy.

Very few people had reason to direct something like this at me. Nichols was one. Withers another. Withers, who had incited kids to riot in Memphis. Withers, who had been working undercover the last time I had seen him.

The urgency I had felt after Brian's funeral when I was

talking to Johnson rose in me again, and I forced myself to stay rooted. I had no proof that Withers was involved. I had no proof of anything—not even the involvement of this so-called Professor.

I needed something more concrete, and I needed it quickly.

I had the sense that time was running out.

FIFTEEN

I went back to the apartment. No one else was there. Malcolm's bedclothes were neatly folded at the end of the couch and the breakfast dishes were drying in a rack. A fan circulated hot air throughout the room.

I was filthy and still shaking, along with a twisting in my stomach. I was still holding the gun, and the flashlight was weighing down the pocket of my suit coat. I didn't remember placing it there.

I put the gun back in its shoulder holster, sat on the arm of the couch, grabbed the phone book, looking up Johnson's precinct.

Someone answered and promised to patch me through. The wait seemed interminable. I glanced at the clock. It was after four. I was late for work.

I squinted, felt the tip of an anger that had been building since I saw that crumpled body on the step. If I had been less concerned with going to work, making a salary, guarding rich white people in their rich white hotel, maybe I would have seen all of this coming. Maybe I would have talked with Brian's mother, felt that frisson of warning, searched and found Brian while he was still alive.

Maybe. But I would never know.

A female voice came on the line and told me that Detective Johnson was not at his desk and would I like to leave a message?

I left the address of the abandoned building, told him to check the basement. When the woman asked my name, I hesitated.

"Tell him his hotel informant called."

"Your name, sir?"

"That'll have to do."

And then I hung up, still staring at the clock. By the time I got to work, it would be nearly five. Things were probably already getting rough on the streets. This was the night that Humphrey was supposed to win the nomination. The Secret Service had already informed us that the candidate didn't go to the convention hall—it was customary for him to wait in the hotel and watch on television.

There would be more police, federal officials, and demonstrators than I cared to think about. If Johnson hadn't gotten me thinking about that list, I wouldn't go to work at all.

I peeled off my borrowed suit, threw it on the twin bed in the boys' room, and hid my gun beneath it just in case Malcolm arrived unexpectedly. Then I headed for the shower.

I would go to work, but not so much for Johnson as for me. This had become personal. I wanted to see the names on the guest list as badly as he did—as well as the names in the restaurant's reservation book and maybe, if I could find it, the names of the outsiders working security detail at the hotel.

But I had a hunch I might learn something at the hotel. I would stop in, and see what I could find. If nothing panned out, then I would go to Lincoln Park and see if anyone had heard of the Professor.

Getting to work was a problem all by itself. I had to go past the International Amphitheater and Grant Park. My normal route up Michigan was out of the question—it had been periodically closed for the last few days for marchers or delegates or police. Lake Shore Drive was usually my second option, but that required me to cross Grant Park on Congress—and if the park was even more congested than it had been the night before, I might never make it.

So I took the new Dan Ryan Expressway. I had never taken the expressway. Franklin disliked it because it had made so many people homeless—especially through the Black Belt—and I had let his opinion influence mine.

Still, I had to admit, merging into traffic at sixty-five miles an hour felt heady, and I wondered why I hadn't done this before. Chicago politics weren't my politics, and Chicago's problems weren't my problems.

I had let myself get suckered into someone else's way of doing things, into living a life I didn't recognize and didn't want.

I had put my gun and flashlight back in the glove box, and I wore my Hilton pass around my neck. Late or not, I was going to get into the building. As much chaos as there had been all week, I doubted anyone would be paying attention as to when an employee clocked in.

There was a lot of traffic, but it moved quickly. The breeze from the open window was heavy with exhaust and humidity. I had the radio on as loud as it would go, listening to the report from the convention. The delegates were voting on the platform plank about the Vietnam War. It sounded like the peaceniks were going to lose.

I switched stations as I got closer to downtown, heard the voice of WBBM's Jerry Williams urging calm. Williams was an acerbic talk show host who liked to stir up trouble; I had no idea why he was telling people to calm down—until I realized he was talking about rioting in Grant Park.

At that moment, I took the off-ramp into the Loop and found myself in the middle of a fog. I recognized the smells—mace and tear gas mixed. I rolled up my window, kept one hand on the wheel, and reached across the passenger side, rolling up the other window, while trying to keep my stinging eyes on the road. I weaved, missed another car, and then got my bearings again.

Shouting and voices amplified through bullhorns echoed throughout the Loop. White college kids, Yippies, hippies, and sedate-looking demonstrators mixed with the after-work crowd, all wiping at their faces as the cloud rolled over them. The tear gas had to be coming from the park. The cloud seemed thickest to the east of us.

A wall of blue seemed to fill each intersection and police squadrols were parked kitty-corner to block access to Michigan Avenue. I didn't want to go there. I needed to get to the Hilton.

The back entrance and the parking garage would be open. The delegates and candidates would have to be able to come and go. As I made my way down Eighth, I could see the edges of Grant Park in the distance. Crowds and crowds of people filled the park, surrounded by National Guard and police. The tear gas cloud was thinner here—obviously the gas had been deployed earlier and wasn't being used at the moment.

Chants echoed and nearly drowned out the squeal of bull-horns, but I couldn't make out any words. I reached Wabash, and turned north.

The parking garage below the Hilton was guarded by more police than I had ever seen. I lifted my pass as I drove into the garage, and a white policeman wearing a gas mask indicated that I should roll down the window. I plugged my nose and shook my head. He pointed again at the window, and instead, I pressed the pass against the glass.

He bent, his eyes hidden by his mask, and peered at the pass before waving me forward.

I drove down two levels into the darkness, as far from the floating toxic cloud as I could get. The crowd noise grew faint and my radio crackled with static. I let out a small sigh, relieved to be away from the tension in the streets.

Before I got out of the car, I made sure the glove box was locked. I didn't want anyone using my weapon in the heat of the moment. Then I got out, locked the car, and headed to the service elevators.

The smell of tear gas was faint down here, and it mingled with the stench of vomit and gasoline. The service elevator was covered with red, white, and blue confetti, as if a garbage bag filled with it had exploded.

I got out, went down the familiar back corridor to the employee lockers, feeling the weight of the job fall on my shoulders as if it had never left. There was even a part of me that worried because I was late.

I clenched my fist, made myself remember the funeral, that horrible basement, and move on. The locker room was empty—shifts generally changed at the same time—and my uniforms hung side by side on the employee rack. I grabbed the closest uniform, brought it to my locker, and changed quickly, hoping no one would see me here. Then I went to the time clock, grabbed my card, and punched in.

Then I returned to the hallway and walked to the tiny Housekeeping office. To call it an office was charitable. It was a cubicle, and the two women who headed the Housekeeping division did most of their paperwork there—paperwork that included check-in and check-out times per room.

Usually that paperwork was a very faint carbon of the main desk's daily check-in, check-out sheet, complete with names. It had been done like that for years, apparently because it was easier to type one list with half a dozen carbons than two or three lists with two or three carbons. From there, the heads of Housekeeping made the cleaning assignments.

The Secret Service had put an end to that practice at the Sunday meeting once someone had realized it was going on. But that still left the forms from the previous week, if no one had destroyed them yet.

The light was on in the cubicle, but it was empty. I slipped inside. A row of clipboards hung on the wall. I grabbed the closest, saw the typewritten form with no names. The check-out and check-in information was listed by room. I thumbed through the sheets of paper, saw that all of these forms had been specially typed and set the clipboard back on the wall.

Then I grabbed the next one. Under the first sheet was the first faded carbon—the names smudged and some of the letters unreadable. Most of the rooms had no names. Instead there were blocks reserved for delegates from various states. Others had reservations by campaigns.

It was also clear why the Secret Service clamped down on this practice. Senator McGovern's room on the fourth floor was clearly marked on the sheet. I scanned back through the previous day's sheets, looking for familiar names. I saw none, and felt my frustration grow. A lot of rooms simply had "Government" marked across from them—obviously the places where the various Secret Service, FBI, and other authority figures were staying.

I'd have to get to the Haymarket Lounge and see if I could find a way to look at the reservation book without drawing too much attention to myself.

I took the stairs up to the first floor. The green carpet was stained—remains from the acid attacks earlier in the week. The stench of rotten eggs remained too.

As I opened the steel door and stepped into the main part of the hotel, the din assaulted me. Voices in agitated conversation, shouting, and the sound of television sets on full blast, tinny strains of "We Shall Overcome" caught my ears and I looked at the nearest TV screen—a portable set sitting on front desk as a courtesy to the delegates. The set's rabbit ears were extended as far as they could go, and the reception was still lousy.

On the screen, white people in suits were waving hand-made Stop the War signs in the convention hall. That anger that I was keeping tamped down flared—they had no right to that anthem—and then disappeared as the convention's band started playing "Happy Days Are Here Again."

Beside me, a white woman wearing a green dress and pearls snorted. "Happy Days are where again?" she asked me, sweeping her hand toward the windows. "Do they even know what the hell's going on here?"

I glanced at the windows and then froze in surprise. People, most of them wearing T-shirts and blue jeans, stood in front of the building, so many of them that I couldn't see past them to the street beyond. At the moment, they were peaceful, but if they decided to move in any direction, there would be trouble.

The woman continued to stare at them—I wasn't even sure she was aware she had spoken to a security guard—and I moved away from her, toward the Haymarket Lounge. No delegates crowded the hallways—they were all at the convention—but campaign workers did, wearing their bright buttons and cheerful hats. Their smiles were long gone, though, and as I approached the hotel bar, I realized a lot of McCarthy supporters were inside it, drinks in hand.

This was the night their loss would be confirmed, and they knew it. Or perhaps it had been the defeat of the peace plan that had gotten to them.

The waitresses were working hard—several had quit during the week and those who were left were scrambling. Their short skirts rode high, and more than one tugged at her low-cut blouse as she carried a tray toward the drinkers.

Outside, the gas was so thick it looked like smoke. The lounge's patrons watched the windows as if the demonstrators were out there for entertainment; only a handful stared at the television screen in the corner.

The restaurant itself was busy, patrons huddling at their tables. Waitresses were busy here too and the hostess was dealing with a long line of drop-ins, many of them with wet handkerchiefs in their hands. They were refugees from the streets who had somehow gotten past the police barricade at the front door; many wore press passes and all of them had red, teary eyes and blotchy skin from being gassed.

I went behind the hostess desk. The reservation book was open to the middle, the day blocked off in units. I had just turned to the beginning of the book to see where it started when I heard my name.

I turned. Roy Gaines, the Secret Service man who was coordinating everything with the Hilton, stood behind me, arms crossed.

"Come with me," he said.

I expected him to take me outside or lead me to one of the doors, but instead we went behind the main desk to the hotel offices. He led me inside one of the smaller offices and closed the door.

The room was a mass of paperwork. Maps, Yippie posters, and Dump the Hump signs covered the walls. A large map of the hotel behind the desk had areas circled with black Magic Marker. There were no windows. The desk itself was covered with more anticonvention literature and newspapers. On the top was that day's *Chicago Tribune*, headline blaring "Dems Recess in Uproar: Galleries Lead Cry, 'Let's Go Home.'"

264

Gaines shut the door and stared at me for a moment. I saw a coldness in his face that I hadn't actually seen before.

"Who do you work for?" he asked.

Whatever I had expected him to ask, it hadn't been that. "The Hilton."

"I can listen to the bullshit or you can tell me the truth. Who're you working for?"

"The Hilton," I said, letting myself sound a little panicked because that was what any normal citizen would do. I didn't feel panicked. I felt very calm.

"I'm not going to charge you with anything if that's what you're worried about. Just tell me who you're working for. The Panthers? MOBE?"

"I've been working here since May," I said.

He shrugged. "MOBE has had an office in the Loop since February. Some groups plan ahead. What's your mission here, Grimshaw?"

The name startled me. Hardly anyone at work called me by the last name I'd hidden behind. I wasn't used to it.

"I don't have a mission, except to do my job." I nodded toward a poster that read Confront the Warmakers. "And I think you need me to do it right now."

"The last thing we want is you out there," he said. "What were you doing in the restaurant?"

"Didn't you see the crowd in front of the plate glass window? Half the people in line looked like they'd been gassed. How many unauthorized people are in this hotel at the moment?"

"I don't know." His voice was flat. "You tell me."

I felt as if I'd walked in the middle of a dream. I'd gone from being a valued employee to this in less than a week. "What's this about?"

"Tell me who you work for."

"Tell me why you're asking."

"I'm here to protect the candidates," he said, "and I have reason to believe that you're a threat."

"That *I'm*—?" I shook my head. "Why?"

"We've been hearing a lot of questions about you in the last day or so, questions we can't answer."

"Questions?" I felt numb. But this wasn't unexpected. I should have been ready for this from the moment the delegates descended on Chicago. "What kind of questions?"

"You know the drill. Who're your friends? Where do you spend time? We realized that no one knows much about you, Mr. Grimshaw."

"Who has been asking these questions?" This time the urgency in my voice was real.

"I got some phone calls suggesting you may not be who you seem to be. And then today, we had to throw out a man who was questioning some of the security guards."

I felt cold. "What did he look like?"

"Does it matter?" Apparently that last question sealed my guilt in his mind because he continued, "Consider yourself fired. You'll wait here until I can get someone to escort you off the premises."

"Wait," I said. I wanted to keep him there, wanted to keep him talking, to find out what he knew about me. "How do you know this isn't a setup? Maybe someone is trying to get rid of me."

"Why would anyone care about you, Mr. Grimshaw?" he asked and let himself out the door. I heard the lock turn. I was trapped inside.

I paced the room, wondering how long they'd keep me here, wondering how much they knew. Who had been calling? What had the Secret Service learned?

Then I stopped, realized this was my last opportunity to search the Hilton records. I went to the desk and began rifling the papers, not sure what I was looking for. I found duty rosters, dates, names of suspicious persons. I found reports on Tom Hayden, Jerry Rubin, Abbie Hoffman, and David Dellinger. An analysis of the Mobilization to End the War in Vietnam told me that's what MOBE stood for, and I saw other reports on the Blackstone Rangers and the Devil's Disciples.

But I saw no names of officers, no names of FBI officials or Secret Service operatives. I found nothing useful, and I was getting desperate. Someone knew who I was, but I had no idea who they were.

I had been alone for at least half an hour, maybe more, when I heard a key in the door. I backed away from the desk, careful not to knock any of the piles down, and hurried to one of the chairs. I sat there, hands folded, biting my lower lip and trying hard to look terrified when two of the other security guards entered.

One of them, a white man from the day shift, looked vaguely familiar. His name badge read Duffy. He glowered at me. The black man beside him, Donald Lavelle, had worked with me on the July thefts.

"Let's go," Duffy said as he flanked me. Lavelle walked to the other side of me and didn't say a word.

We stepped out of the office and the air got cooler. I could hear conversation still rising from the lobby, but beyond that, there were sirens and screams.

"What's going on?" I asked.

"None of your fucking business," Duffy said.

We went to the service elevator, and as Duffy punched the subbasement for the parking garage, I said, "I have to clear out my locker."

He didn't respond. I reached past him, hit the button for the basement, and he glared at me. I raised my eyebrows at him, daring him to do something.

He didn't.

The doors opened to the employee level and I walked down the hall to the locker room, now leading my escorts.

All I had in my locker was my clothes, but I didn't have many and I wasn't about to leave them. Besides, I wasn't going to make this easy for anyone.

"Sorry, Bill," Lavelle said.

I glanced at him.

He shrugged. "When that creep started asking about you, I knew there was gonna be trouble."

"What creep?"

"That guy. You seen him, didn't you, Duffy?'

"I didn't see no one," Duffy said, apparently still annoyed that I could quell him with a glance.

"What'd he look like?" I asked.

"Undercover, that's what I think," Lavelle said.

We had reached the locker room. I went to my locker and fiddled with the lock. I wanted to hear what Lavelle had to say.

"Better clock out," Duffy said.

"Do it for me," I said.

"I ain't your ni—." He stopped himself just in time.

I glared at him again. Hitting him would have been a pleasure. Apparently that registered on my face because he slunk toward the time clock.

I stopped diddling with the lock. "What did he look like?" I asked Lavelle again.

"Afro," Lavelle spoke softly. "Scarred face. Big guy."

A scarred face. Thomas Withers had acne scars so bad that his face was pockmarked.

I swallowed. "What kind of scars?"

"Acne, I think."

I didn't like how this was going. "Did he give his name?"

Lavelle shook his head.

"How tall was he?" I asked.

Lavelle raised a hand above my head. Withers was taller than me by about that much.

"Was he my age?" I asked.

Lavelle nodded.

"No real discernible accent."

"Yeah," Lavelle said. "You know this guy?"

"I just might," I said.

It would explain a lot. How he managed to seem one step ahead of me. Why he had designed that torture chamber. It hadn't been set up by some intelligence operative responding to a legend. It had been set up by Withers, settling a personal score.

The last time I'd seen him, in Memphis just before Martin died, Withers had said to me, *Knowledge is power, Smokey, and sometimes the right fact can be mighty useful.*

He was right. Knowledge was useful. I had to use mine carefully. I had to remain clearheaded. But I'd been thinking of Withers all day. I couldn't continue to ignore this. If Withers was here, I had to act, and act quickly.

Thomas Withers was one of the few people in the world who knew about my connection to Laura. It would only be a matter of time before he figured out where Jimmy was.

"Ain't you got your crap yet?" Duffy came down the row of lockers, swaggering. "You boys plotting something?"

I didn't answer him. Instead, I made the last twist on the combination lock and pulled it open. My street clothes and my pass were hanging on hooks. Before Duffy got a peek at the pass, I tucked it in my shirt pocket, then grabbed the clothes and pulled them out.

"I ain't waitin' while you change," Duffy said. "There's some serious shit goin' down, and I'm not about to miss it. So let's get you out of here."

I clutched my clothes to me and staggered forward like a drunken man. Lavelle gave me a strange look, but I ignored him. It felt as if my mind had stopped.

But it hadn't. It was remembering Withers.

Withers and I had hated each other since Korea.

In San Diego, he had been supposed to practice verbal

interrogation techniques on me. Even though the torture chamber had been set up just like it had been in that basement, the brass were aware that they were attempting a form of mind control on their own men.

Withers thought he could break anyone. He had wanted to break me.

Duffy frowned at me, then shoved me into the service elevator. I glared at him again and he shrank back, but not as far as he had before, as if he knew that my heart wasn't in it.

I'd met Withers toward the end of the war. Withers was supposed to have brought Korean refugees across the line. Instead, he had arrived alone, claiming the Koreans were dead. I hadn't believed him and had been clear about it.

My disbelief fed my sergeant's, which then trickled to Withers's boss. Withers got sent to San Diego, where I encountered him nearly a year later.

In that torture chamber in San Diego, he'd tried to make me pay for his demotion. Instead, he'd gotten demoted again.

"Bill?" Lavelle asked.

The service elevator doors opened to reveal the parking garage. Screams and shouts from the street, the sounds of running feet, and cries of *Sieg Heil! Sieg Heil!* floated down from above.

We got out of the elevator. Duffy looked toward the street level with longing. Lavelle's lips thinned. He wanted no part of this.

The air still held the sting of tear gas, although I couldn't see it here. Something crashed above us, followed by a chant of *Hell, No! We Won't Go!* and the sounds of a police bullhorn, ordering people back.

"Hurry up, Grimshaw," Duffy said.

I didn't have to be told twice. We hurried to my car. I unlocked it and threw my clothes in the back. By the time

I reached for the driver's door, Duffy and Lavelle were already heading toward the hotel.

I got inside the car and made myself think. Withers had found me, somehow. Maybe accidentally. He'd been working undercover in Memphis, trying to disrupt Martin's marches from the inside. If he was the man I'd heard called the Professor—and I had no reason to believe otherwise— he probably had a similar undercover job in Chicago. I'd already suspected that carload he'd brought to town were undercover agents. This might have gone deeper than I suspected. He had been posing as a Black Panther in Memphis—and there were Panthers in my neighborhood here in Chicago. Maybe that first sighting had been accidental.

The rest hadn't been, though, and he'd tried to figure out, in that mass of children, which one was Jimmy.

He'd guessed wrong.

I reached for the glove box, stopped myself, made myself breathe.

He had stopped following me, figuring I wouldn't lead him to Jimmy, and he'd started talking to my friends. Withers hadn't put Laura into the equation then. He hadn't known where Jimmy was. He'd called the hotel, told them I wasn't who I seemed. He'd figured out that Grimshaw was the name I was using. Then he'd gotten inside the hotel somehow and questioned my co-workers for names of friends and family. He'd go through them first. Maybe even try to figure out where Franklin's kids were, or who Franklin's friends were.

But at some point, Withers would remember Laura, and when he did, he would know where Jimmy was.

I had to go one step at a time, just like Withers was doing.

Another bang sounded around me, followed by more screaming and the squeal of brakes.

First I had to warn Laura, get her to leave town. Then I'd talk to Franklin.

Finding a pay phone in this mess was going to be a problem. The closer I got to the Gold Coast, the less chance I had of finding one that I could use.

I was better off going back into the hotel if I went quickly. With the protest going on, no one would notice if I was in the hotel. No one would probably even care.

I ran for the service elevator and let it take me back inside.

The closest bank of telephones was on the first floor, around a corner. It was also the most hidden.

I still wore my uniform. No one questioned me as I walked across the marble floor and ducked behind the rows of valet carts. There were new pay phones, side by side and in the open, but I entered the old one. It was a wooden booth with a door that closed and a seat worn smooth by time.

I plugged the machine, dialed Laura's number, and listened to the rings. Usually she answered on the fourth or fifth. I let the phone ring ten times and got no answer at all.

My stomach churned. She had said she and Jimmy were going to stay in. She had said she hadn't wanted to expose him to all the violence going on around him. She had said they would spend a nice, quiet day at home.

I hoped she had lied.

I hung up and the dime clattered into the coin return. I plugged the phone again, dialed again, and let the phone ring.

Nothing.

Finally, I called the front desk to her building, and identified myself as someone connected with Sturdy Investments.

"I've been trying to reach Miss Hathaway all day," I said. "Do you know if she has left her apartment?"

"I haven't seen her leave, but that doesn't mean that she hasn't," said the cultured male voice on the other end of the line. "We don't keep track of our residents here."

"This is a matter of some urgency," I said, "and given what's going on in the parks, I don't want to drive across town unless I know she's there."

"Let me ring her, sir. Just a moment." And then I was put on hold.

I tapped my foot, leaning against the wall of the phone booth. There was no one down here. It seemed eerie, given what I knew of the rest of the hotel and the crowds outside. I couldn't hear anything except the clicking of the line, telling me we were still connected, and my own breathing, harsh and ragged.

"Sir?" the male voice said. "She's not answering our pages, but none of the doormen has seen her leave. As I said, we're not obligated to keep track of our residents. If you would like, I can continue trying to ring her and then call you when she returns."

"No, no. No, thanks," I said. "I appreciate your time."

And then I hung up.

I didn't like how this sounded or how it felt. I had to go up there. Now that I knew who I was up against, I at least had a chance.

First I called Franklin.

He answered on the first ring. "Smokey! The radio says there's all kinds of disturbances going on around you."

"Listen, Franklin," I said. "I need you to do me a favor."

"All right."

"I want you to keep calling this number"—and then I gave him Laura's phone number—"until someone answers. If the person who picks up the line is a woman, tell her not to open her door to anyone. You got that?"

"What's going on, Smokey?"

"Just tell me you'll do that, Franklin."

"Sure. I got it. Tell her not to open her door. Is she in danger, Smokey?"

"I'll tell you more tonight," I said. "Just do this for me."

"All right."

I hung up, and let myself out of the booth. As I rounded the valet carts, two security guards got off the service elevator. I turned away from them and went up the half staircase that led to the lobby.

It had grown dark outside. The hotel lights were on, but it was almost impossible to tell. Tear gas had wafted inside the hotel mixing with the cigarette smoke, giving the air a filmy haze. There wasn't enough gas to make people ill, but everyone was coughing and wiping at their eyes.

Young people, bloody and battered, were lying across the marble floor, being tended by hotel guests. The concierge was on the phone with one of the hospitals, requesting an ambulance. Guests stood, horrified, near the windows, watching the display outside.

I could barely see it over their heads—bright lights shining down on the road, cops chasing after kids, battering them with nightsticks. National Guard troops held rifles with bayonets on an advancing line of protesters and everyone seemed to be screaming.

I was torn for just a moment, ready to go into the fray, to help the wounded, pull people back, but I couldn't. If I delayed here any longer, Withers might get to Jimmy.

I sprinted across the lobby and caught a down elevator. A man wearing a press pass held his hand over his eye. He was shaking his head. Beside him, another man clutched a broken Nikon. They shrank away from me as if I were the enemy, and it took me a moment to realize that it wasn't me or my color that worried them. It was my uniform.

They got off at the first parking level. I got off at the bottom. I ran to my car, and climbed in, starting it before I had the door closed. Then I backed out of the parking garage, and headed for the Gold Coast.

SIXTEEN

O r tried to.

The riot was going on in front of the hotel, on Michigan and in Grant Park. But a lot of the problem had spilled onto the side streets, streets the authorities had to leave open to get the candidates and delegates back to the hotel.

I pulled out of the parking garage into chaos. Demonstrators ran in front of my headlights, followed by police, their nightsticks raised. Cops were hitting people and throwing them aside. Others stopped and pummeled them. Demonstrators hit back and were clubbed. A blue-and-white squadrol was parked in the intersection, blocking traffic heading east. The cars still moved west and north. My car was pointed west, and I tried to go in that direction, thinking it would probably be my only way out.

Blue-helmeted cops dragged bloody protestors inside the squadrol, hitting them as they went. Screams echoed around me, screams that would occasionally unite in chants: *The Whole World Is Watching. The Whole World Is Watching.* Bright lights from television vans mingled with the klieg lights brought by the police. Cars heading toward Michigan

Avenue were stopped in the intersections and National Guard troops wearing gas masks bent toward the car windows, yelling at the people inside.

Behind me, I heard singing mixed with more shouting and the sound of sticks hitting heads. A rock bounced off my windshield, and a young white woman, blood streaming down her face, rolled across my hood. She reached for me as two policeman grabbed her by the feet and pulled her off my car.

A procession of people was marching down Wabash and CTA buses stopped alongside them, disgorging police officers who ran into the crowd. The din was so loud I couldn't hear the car's engine.

I eased onto Wabash, and people slammed into my car as they ran. A cop smashed my driver's window with a nightstick, and the glass fell inward. The stick narrowly missed my face. Other cops surrounded the car and one reached for the door. They had pulled other drivers out of their cars, and were beating them on the street.

As the cop bent toward my window, I hit him in the face with my fist, then stepped on the gas. The car sprang forward, and I prayed I wouldn't run over anyone. People got out of my way. I made a zigzag onto Eighth and headed for the expressway.

All along the streets, dazed hippies walked, hands to head. Some had sunk to the ground, leaning on buildings and lampposts. Still others huddled in groups, arms around each other as if they were protecting each other from nightsticks.

More tear gas wafted through the streetlights. I drove faster to get away from it, my eyes stinging, my nose running. More squadrols were arriving, followed by squad cars and police buses, as well as CTA buses filled with cops. It was as if they were all being drawn to the same spot, and it wasn't until I passed a police motorcycle that I heard the code "Ten-one" which meant, at least in Memphis—and I assumed in Chicago as well—officer needs help.

The entire downtown was covered in gas. I could hear the shouts and screams even as I drove away from the mess. It wasn't until I turned north that I let out a shaky sigh of relief.

The radio jabbered about the riot, and I listened to hear what else was going on. I was taking a circuitous route to Laura's, but I figured it would get me there faster than trying to take the mobbed streets in the Loop.

As I drove, I reviewed the evidence as I knew it.

A man with an afro had been watching me. He had probably driven a blue Oldsmobile with New York plates. He had arrived in Chicago's West Side with a carload of young people who called him the Professor. One of the children I'd spoken to had heard someone else call him Tim.

Maybe the child had been mistaken. Maybe the person had called him Tom.

A man with an afro and acne scars, a man who was taller than I was, had interrogated my co-workers. Someone had told the hotel that I wasn't who I seemed.

Another FBI undercover agent wouldn't have been thinking of me or Jimmy. We probably blipped off the mental radar months ago. Undercover agents would have been concentrating on the mission at hand.

But Withers would have recognized me. In fact, he had recognized me, then he had acted. And somehow he had managed to stay out of my sight.

When I'd seen him in Memphis in the month before Martin died, Withers had been worried that I would screw up his mission. He'd done everything he could to keep me away from the young men he'd been trying to corrupt.

At the end, I hadn't been able to stop him. I'd seen him on Beale Street and he'd smiled at me.

I gotta admit, Smokey, he'd said, *I thought you'd be a more formidable opponent.*

That last encounter had made him careless. He was underestimating me this time.

He didn't expect me to figure out who he was until it was too late.

I hoped it wasn't too late.

As I got to the Gold Coast, the streets were silent. All of the expensive buildings were closed up tight, as if they expected to be stormed by troops of angry college students. Security guards and doormen hovered around the front of each building, arms crossed, looking scared instead of tough.

It was probably good that they weren't allowed guns. Men who were scared were trigger happy.

My heart was pounding harder than it had been in the riot. If Withers had found her, he wouldn't have gone in the front door. He couldn't have, not without displaying his FBI credentials. With all the violence in the city, no black man— with or without an afro—was going to get into a high-security expensive building like that, especially at night.

But Withers was smart; if he knew where she lived, he would be able to get in. All he had to do was go around back.

No one expected trouble at the back doors of these highrises.

I parked behind Laura's apartment complex and took my gun out of the glove box. If anyone caught me in that building with a gun, I'd be going away for life, but I didn't care. I wasn't about to face Withers unarmed.

I got out of the car and loped to the service entrance. My uniform helped me—it looked official. The door had been propped open. I saw scratches near the keyhole. Someone had picked the lock.

That more than anything confirmed my suspicions. I

wondered if Franklin had reached Laura, and I prayed that he had.

I pushed open the door to the stairwell and took the stairs two at a time. No one else joined me on the stairs, and when I reached the penthouse level, the door was propped open again.

I burst through it, expecting to find Withers or blood on the floor, but the hallway was empty. Laura's door was closed. I pressed my ear against it, but heard nothing through the thick wood. The weight of my body made the door ease open and I nearly tumbled inside.

The apartment felt unfamiliar. Lights were on, and through the windows on the far end, I could see the city glittering in the darkness. But something was different here. It took me a moment to know what it was. It was the smell. Cigarettes.

Laura didn't smoke.

The phone rang and a shiver ran through me. I knew, without answering, that Franklin was on the line.

I pushed the door closed, careful to latch it quietly. Then I moved down the hallway, gun in front of me, careful to look all around me. A familiar voice spoke softly from the living room.

". . . not your fight, is it? You have all this. Why lose it over a scruffy little street urchin who would probably knife you in your sleep if he got the chance?"

Withers. Sounding so reasonable. Talking about Jimmy. Which meant he had no idea where Jimmy was.

The phone continued to ring. I peered around the edge of the hallway. Laura was tied to one of her ornate metal chairs. Her feet were tied separately and her arms were bound in two places, the biceps and the forearms. The left side of her face was bruised and her mouth was red with blood.

Withers stood behind her, smoking a cigarette, the tip

279

glowing coal red as he inhaled. Another cigarette had been stubbed into an ashtray on a nearby table, and I wondered if its tip had touched her skin at all.

He had once told me that he could make anyone talk. That, if he were given his head, he could remake them in his own image.

I couldn't sneak around behind him, not with the layout of the apartment, and I couldn't risk a direct shot. He was too close to Laura.

He hadn't seen me yet. He had taken the cigarette from his mouth, and held it between two fingers as he ran his hand down Laura's hair.

"How much are you willing to risk for a child that isn't even yours? Your looks?" He brought the cigarette near her eye. "Your life?"

Laura didn't flinch. She kept staring straight ahead as if she hadn't heard him at all.

I leaned back against the wall, completely out of Withers's view. The ringing phone became a backdrop. I had to ignore it and concentrate on Withers's voice.

I slipped my left hand in my pocket, grabbed one of the dimes, and clutched it between my thumb and forefinger. Then, crouching, I pitched the dime toward the window as if I were skimming stones across a lake.

The dime clattered against the glass and tumbled to the ground. Withers looked in that direction and I launched myself at him.

Laura screamed and ducked her head away from his hand.

Withers started to turn toward me as I tackled him. He stubbed the cigarette into the back of my neck, the stench of burning hair mixing with the smell of tobacco. Then the pain hit me, running all along my nervous system, making me tremble.

He used his knees to get me off him and rolled away from

me. I yanked his shirt, pulling him toward me. His fingers scrabbled toward an end table, knocking down a hunting knife. I reached for it, and so did he. He found it first, and slashed at me, missing.

I grabbed him by the collar and pulled him into a sitting position.

He slashed at me again, cutting through my shirt and nicking my belly.

I shoved my gun against his heart.

"Drop the knife," I said.

His gaze met mine. To my surprise, he smiled.

"Don't threaten me, Dalton. We both know you can't go through with it. Just tell me where the kid is and I'll be on my way."

His hand still clutched the knife. I saw his fingers tighten, felt the muscles in his arm move to start the thrust, and I pulled the trigger.

The sound was impossibly loud in the space, an explosion times fifty. His blood splattered the floor behind him. He jerked once, his face having no time to register a reaction, and then his entire body collapsed.

I held him up by his shirt collar, staring into his lifeless eyes. His weight pulled on my arm.

"Smokey?" Laura sounded as if she were speaking through a deep tunnel.

I let him go. He fell backward, slamming against the floor, sliding on the blood, smearing it.

There was blood on my hand and arm, my chest and face. His blood, still warm.

"Smokey?" Laura said again.

I turned to her. She looked terrified. Of me? Of everything? I didn't know. "Where's Jimmy?"

"He's okay." The wounded side of her mouth didn't move. "Are there others?"

It took me a moment to realize what she was asking.

Other people who were going to come after Jimmy. Other threats on this long and horrible night.

"I don't know." I looked at Withers. His mouth was open, his eyes staring at nothing. The scars that pockmarked his face made him look vulnerable.

I hadn't asked him anything, hadn't found out the extent of his investigation, hadn't found out who he told.

"He came here alone?" I asked Laura.

She nodded, twisting her body toward me. She was still tied.

I stood and undid the ropes on her arms, my fingers staining the cord. There was a belt wrapped around her chest, just below her breasts, a standard black belt with an open gold buckle. I glanced at Withers. His dark pants had no belt at all.

I went to the front of her, untied her feet as her hands struggled to unbuckle the belt. She was shaking too.

Logically, Withers wouldn't have told anyone he was coming here. His job was to kill Jimmy, and the fewer people who knew that the better.

But had he informed his superiors that he had found us or was he only supposed to contact them when he got the job done?

"What did he tell you?" I asked.

"Nothing." She got the belt off and flung it across the room as if it burned her. The thought made the back of my neck throb. I didn't feel the cut on my stomach, though. I looked at it, realized it was just a flesh wound, and decided not ot worry about it.

We had a much larger problem.

Laura was staring at him, her face a greenish white. She had obviously never seen a corpse before. "We should call the police."

"Laura, for chrissake. He's an undercover FBI agent. How do you want to explain that?"

"Would they know?"

"They'd know."

Her eyes, wide and blue, met mine. "He used your name."

"Yeah."

"This isn't about Jimmy?"

"It's about Jimmy." I glanced around the apartment. There was no sign of him. "Where is he?"

"Safe," she said again. The word sounded rote, and that was when I realized she had used the same word in answer to Withers. She hadn't told him anything else.

"Laura, you can tell me. Where's Jimmy?"

She blinked, glanced at Withers, and then stood, slowly. Her legs buckled and I caught her. She was shaking so hard I thought she was going to come apart. I pulled her into my arms.

"I didn't think anyone was going to come," she said against my chest. "I didn't think you'd come. He was so strong, and he would tell me what he was going to do to me. I didn't know how long I would be able to stay quiet. I thought maybe I could survive the burns, but I'm not good with pain, Smokey. I was afraid he'd find a place that I couldn't tolerate, and I'd tell him."

I wrapped my arms around her tight, holding her as close as I could. "You did fine."

"No, I didn't. He got in and he got me, and it was only a matter of time—"

I grabbed her elbows and pushed her back so that I could see her face. It was smeared with the blood from my shirt.

"Yes, it was only a matter of time," I said. "It doesn't matter who you are. Everyone breaks. That's why torture works. He set out to torture you, Laura, and he would have continued until you finally told him what he wanted to hear."

Her lower lip trembled.

"But that's not a failing for you. You did wonderfully. You got Jimmy out of his way. You held him off, and I got here. You did what you had to do. You did better than most would have in this situation."

"I was so frightened, Smokey."

I nodded, then held her again. This wasn't over, not yet, but I wasn't willing to let her go. She had nearly died because I had asked a favor of her. And she was worried that she had somehow failed.

"Where's Jimmy?" I asked again.

She let out a small sigh, and remained against me for a brief moment before standing up. Her clothes were ruined, the blood on her face streaked even more than it had been a minute before.

"My father built this place," she said. "For me."

Her father was a small-time crook who had moved up to become a wealthy businessman. Obviously I was supposed to find some significance in that.

"There's a false wall behind my closet. It leads into a big storage room. For my important papers, he said. I put Jimmy in there, told him to be quiet."

A closet. I had hidden in a closet the night my parents had been murdered. "How did you know that Withers was coming?"

"He picked the lock." Her voice got stronger as she spoke. She was coming back to herself. "I heard it. I'd already showed Jimmy the closet. I pushed him there, got him inside, and went for the phone. That's when he got in. Withers. Him."

She gestured toward the body and winced.

The phone. It was still ringing. I turned away from her and found it, picking it up. "Franklin?"

"Smokey?"

"It's okay. Thanks for the help. I'll talk to you soon."
And then I hung up.

Laura was frowning at me.

"I called you too late," I said.

"It started to ring after he already had me. I tried, Smokey. I threw things at him, I tried to get past him. I figured if I could get to the stairs I'd be all right. I made it to the hallway and that's when he got me and I couldn't get away."

Her voice broke.

"He do anything else to you?"

"Hit me, threw me in the chair. I think I passed out."

I was certain she had passed out.

"We need to get Jimmy," she said.

I looked at her, blood covered and bruised, and knew I looked no better. The living room was a mess—shattered table, the knife, and blood all over the marble floor.

And the body in the middle of it all. Jimmy had seen one death. He didn't need to see another—and he didn't need to know that I caused it.

"We need to take care of this first," I said.

"But he would have heard everything." She was right about that. I remembered how it felt to be tucked up in a small space, listening to the violence—and then, even worse, the silence.

"All right," I said. "Tell him you're fine. Tell him he can come out as long as he doesn't leave your room. I don't want him to see this, Laura. I don't want him to see the body or the blood."

She nodded, looking at Withers. "What are we going to do about him, if we can't call the cops?"

I had the beginnings of a plan. But it was going to take a lot of work, and it was going to be a very long night.

"You could leave," she said. "I could call them, say he broke in here. Say I shot him."

"With my gun?"

She shrugged.

"And what about Jimmy? Certainly people in the building saw you with Jimmy. They'd wonder if Withers was connected to him somehow."

"I don't know, Smokey. I'm just trying to figure out what to do."

"We don't bring in the Chicago police, and we certainly don't lie to them." I could feel her rising panic. The reality of what happened was finally hitting her. "Talk to Jimmy, but don't let him see you yet. Wash your face and put some iodine on that lip. Get some clean clothes, but don't change into them. We have some cleanup to do."

Her lips thinned, but she didn't say anything. As she started down the hall, I said, "Is that rug in the entry the only one you have?"

She stopped, glanced at Withers again, and swallowed. "It's the widest."

"It's not some priceless antique, is it?"

"No. It's not priceless."

"But it's traceable?"

"It's just an oriental rug, Smokey. It's expensive, but it's not that unique." Then she walked down the hallway, looking as haughty as she had when she had first come to my office six months before. Her defense mechanism: look imperious. It probably worked most of the time. Once I got Withers out of here, it might work again.

I crouched and examined the mess. The blood had spattered to the front and back, but very little of it had gone to the side. There was the smear, but so far neither Laura or I had stepped in it. There were no telltale tracks away from the body.

Blood had hit the wall and part of an ornamental table, but nothing else. I had probably gotten blood on the phone. Cleanup would be hard, but we could do it.

I took off my shoes and examined the soles. There was

no blood on them at all. I set them far from the body and took off my socks, putting them over my hands. Then I rolled up my pants legs and went to work.

First, I searched him. He had fifteen dollars in his front pocket. I unrolled the money to see if anything was hidden inside it. Just an unidentified receipt, printed from an old cash register, with yesterday's date on it. I left the entire wad plus some miscellaneous coins in the pocket. All I wanted to remove was anything that identified him, the city, or me and Laura. Everything else would remain on him.

His other front pants pocket was empty. His breast pocket had been ruined by the gunshot—bits of cigarette were mixed with the blood, and the package of Pall Malls had crumpled oddly. I didn't touch that at all.

I slid my hands under his back and propped him on his side. Blood dripped off his shirt into the pool on the floor. I reached into his back pocket, found a wallet that contained a hundred dollars and a New York driver's license with Withers's photo, claiming his name was Earl Cameron. Tucked farther back was a staff parking permit from Columbia University, and a professor's university identification.

So he had posed as a professor. It made sense, considering the unrest at the university in April. Perhaps he had been involved with that. He certainly seemed to be in all the hot spots this year.

His other pocket contained a small notebook. It was soaked with blood, but I opened it anyway. The first few pages were hard to read. Careless notes with July dates. At the end of some of them, he wrote, "Report filed." The farther into it I got, the more I realized what I had.

These were his case notes.

He had infiltrated the local Panthers at the end of July, and by August, had this notation: "No plans—checking

Rangers." If he had been investigating the Rangers, that would have brought him to my neighborhood. I thumbed forward, and found what I was looking for.

"8/21: Surprise, surprise. S.D. in Chicago."

No further notes like that, although my address had been scribbled down, and so had the Hilton. Then there was a list of last names that read like a Who's Who of my acquaintances in Chicago, a checkmark beside each.

Laura's name was not there, although one notation from the day before chilled me. It was a list of all the residents of the building at Randolph and State. Had he followed me into the Sturdy Investments office last Saturday? I hadn't seen him do it. Or maybe someone else had seen me. I was in the Loop, after all. Any one of my co-workers could have seen me enter the building.

And then the last notation in the book was that day's date and Laura's address, followed by exclamation points. He had figured it out, maybe through the connection to Sturdy Investments.

And that had led him here.

I thumbed through the notebook again, searching for all the "Report filed" notations. He had marked the last one on August 15—and he hadn't found me until August 21. He had been waiting, just as I figured.

He hadn't told anyone he had found us. No one knew we were in Chicago.

I let out a small sigh of relief, then forced myself to continue. I stuffed the notebook in my pocket, patted Withers down to see if he had anything else on him, and found nothing. Then I picked him up and carried him to the rug.

He was heavier than he looked. I dumped him on the rug, but didn't roll it up yet. Instead, I stood, found Laura's utility room, and washed my hands, drying them on a rag, which I threw in the sink. She was rich. She had a washer and a dryer in that room. Both of them would come in handy.

I went back and rolled up the rug, careful not to get any blood on the outside of it.

Laura returned just as I was finishing. Her face was bruised and swollen, and the side of her mouth was a comic orange. "Jimmy wants to see you."

"He will," I said. "Just for a moment. When we're done."

She looked at the rug, then at the mess on the floor. "I'll get a mop."

"Rags first," I said. "We need to wipe down some surfaces."

She nodded, got me some cleaning rags, and we set to work. It took longer than I expected to get the blood off the floor. I kept carrying the bucket back to the utility room and dumping it in the sink. If I got caught getting this body out of the building, we were in trouble. The traps would be full of blood.

Laura found something that made the marble shine. She was wiping across the spot where Withers had lain when I came back into the living room.

"I'll finish up," I said. "Go take a shower, put on some clean clothes. We'll see Jimmy in a few minutes."

She frowned at me, but didn't question any further. She walked down the hallway, disappearing into the darkness.

I inspected the room. We'd gotten the splatter and the droplets and the spray. I'd cleaned off the phone. There was no blood that I could see. I moved some furniture, double-checked beneath rugs. Nothing.

Now I had to find the bullet.

I sat down, eyed the area behind Withers. The bullet would have gone straight through him and it wouldn't stop until it hit something hard.

That something was the concrete wall beside the china

cabinet. A hole the size of my fist marred the surface. The bullet was embedded in the back, flattened by impact. I was able to get it out with my fingers and I put it in my pocket.

I didn't have time to fix the hole, not if I wanted Withers out of the place and safely gone. So I grabbed the cabinet and moved it sideways. The damn thing was heavier than I expected. The dishes rattled, but nothing broke—at least nothing that I saw. I got the hole covered, just barely. I would come back and fix it in the next day or so, and then I would repaint.

I found paper sacks under the sink, plus the day's kitchen garbage, which hadn't been taken out. I had just put the ropes under the wet coffee grounds when I heard Laura say, "Now what?"

I turned. She was wearing a blue shirt and navy shorts. Her hair was wet and dripping on her shoulders.

"You got a robe?" I asked.

She frowned.

"I'm going to shower and wash my clothes. While they're drying, I want to see Jimmy." I sounded like an automaton, but I knew our time was very limited. I had to keep us moving, and I couldn't let us think about what had just happened.

"I've got a robe," she said. "You might look a little silly in it, but . . ."

Her voice trailed off. That was the least of our worries and she knew it.

I headed toward the bathroom. Like the rest of the apartment, it was large and spacious and extremely clean. It still smelled of soap from Laura's shower, and the air was full of steam.

I took the bullet and the notebook out of my pocket and put them on the sink. Then I took off my name tag, and placed it beside the bullet. I stripped, set my clothes outside the door for Laura, and climbed into the shower.

I leaned against the tile, letting the hot water run over me. I scrubbed, feeling as if I could never get clean.

I had known that this could happen. From the day Jimmy and I left Memphis, I had known. Hell, I'd known from the beginning of my career. Loyce Kirby had warned me.

We don't live in the white world, he said on the very first day of my training. *We got our own rules, and sometimes the rules clash. Sometimes you gotta do things your way, even if it ain't the lawful way. If you can't do that, then you don't belong here, doing this work. You got that?*

I thought I had. But I hadn't realized exactly what he meant until now.

When I got out of the shower, I found a robe crumpled just inside the door. Laura had left it for me. It was white terry cloth with a hotel's logo embroidered on the breast pocket. All that mattered was that it fit.

I stepped out into the hallway. Laura was hovering near the door, waiting for me. "Let's go," I said.

She led me down the hall. The black marble floor glistened, and individual lights lit the artwork hanging on the walls from beneath. Big, elegant, and beautifully apportioned. Violence shouldn't have touched this place. Nothing should have.

As we got to the end of the hall, I heard the tinny sounds of the television. Laura opened the door. Through it, I saw the lights of the city, and a large television. David Brinkley was sitting high above the convention floor, looking serious.

Jimmy was sprawled on a king-sized bed. He jumped off it when he saw me and ran toward me. I grabbed him, lifted him, and he hugged me tighter than I'd ever been hugged in my life.

"I thought you died," he said.

I put my hand on his back, attempting to comfort him. "I'm all right."

"That was a gun. I knowed it was a gun. I know guns."

Yes, he did. "It was a gun."

"What happened?"

For a moment, I debated telling him. On the screen, Brinkley's image cut away to the police, pouring out of squadrols, billy clubs raised, hitting protestors. I was stunned to see it; the riot felt as if it had happened years ago.

"We had a scare," I said. "But everything's all right now. In fact, I think we solved our problem. When I come back tomorrow, we can go home."

"We can?" He raised his head, then saw Laura. His entire expression changed. "Who hit you?"

She brought a hand to the side of her mouth. Then she looked at me, clearly not sure what to say.

"There was a man here tonight," I said. "We got rid of him, Laura and I."

That was as much truth as I would give him.

"Is he coming back?" Jimmy asked.

"No," I said.

"You sure?"

I nodded.

He buried his head back in my neck. "Can't you stay?"

"Not tonight. Tomorrow. I promise. We're going home."

"I was so scared, Smokey," he said, his voice muffled.

"I know, kiddo," I said. "Believe me. I know."

SEVENTEEN

I made Laura stay in the bedroom with Jimmy. The hardest part was ahead of me, and I needed to do it alone.

I went to the laundry room, took my uniform out of the dryer, and put it on, even though it was still damp. Then I went to the bathroom, got my name tag, the notebook, and the bullet, and put them back in my pocket. I wrapped the gun in wax paper and put it in the paper garbage bag, along with a well-used garden trowel I found in the utility room.

I did a final check of the main room, saw no blood and nothing that looked out of place. Then I put on my shoes, got the garbage bag, and went into the hallway, where the rolled rug was waiting for me.

No blood marred its outside, and no blood would drip from it. The inside nap would absorb any blood that was on Withers's clothing or body. I set the garbage bag on a table near the door, and pulled the door open.

No one was in the hallway. Not that there should have been anyone up there without Laura's permission. The main elevator was on the third floor. I pulled her door mostly closed and pressed for the service elevator. It arrived, empty, a moment later. I pushed the red stop button that held the door open and went back for my load.

My heart was pounding. The next few moments would be the most difficult ones. I slipped inside the apartment, bent down, picking up the rug in a fireman's carry.

I staggered under the weight. Withers was heavy enough, but the rug added extra pounds. I managed to get it balanced, then grabbed the stained paper bag, and walked to the service elevator. Then I hit the red button with the heel of my hand, and the elevator started down.

It moved damn slow, and I stared at the numbers, waiting for another one to light up, afraid some building employees would get in. If they did, I would continue to watch the numbers, and hope that they would think my uniform was for some delivery or pickup service.

But no one got on. The service elevator stopped on the ground floor and the doors eased open, revealing no one. I crossed to the back door, and let myself out.

The night was hot. Moths played around the building's exterior light. The street was eerily silent, no cars, no people, although I saw lights streaming through closed windows across the street.

I was in the back parking lot. The building's large metal trash cans were only a few feet from me. I made my way toward them, sweat pouring down my back and stinging the burn on my neck. I set the rug and the paper bag down beside the cans, and made myself walk to my car.

The last thing I wanted to do was look suspicious. I wanted someone to think I had just gotten off work, I was carrying garbage out of the building, and then I was going home. A dog barked a few blocks away. In the distance, I heard sirens, but they were heading away from me, toward downtown where, I assumed, the riot was continuing.

I made it to the car, got in, and started it. The car rumbled to life, a sound as loud as the gunshot in Laura's apartment. A man's voice came through the radio, saying, "Mr. Chairmen, most delegates to this convention do not know that thousands of young people are being beaten in the streets of Chicago. And for that reason, I request the suspension of the rules to relocate the convention in another city—"

I flicked the radio off. I scanned the street for signs of life, but no one walked outside. The curtains remained drawn over the windows, and doors remained closed.

I was all alone.

I drove to the parking lot, backed up near the trash, and shut off the car. Then I opened the trunk, using it as protection against the watchful eyes of the neighborhood. The only way anyone could see what I was doing would be if they came out of Laura's building. And that door remained closed.

I picked up the rug, grunting under its weight, and tossed it into the car. The Impala's ancient suspension bounced. I made sure everything was tucked in, then I grabbed the paper bag and set it beside the rug.

I resisted the urge to glance over my shoulder, as I reached inside the bag and unrolled the .38 from the wax paper. I stuffed the gun into the waistband of my pants. Then I unwrapped the trowel, set it beside the rug, leaving the wax paper with the garbage. I tossed the paper sack into the nearest trashcan, wiped my hands on my pants, and closed the trunk.

I got back into the car, put the gun in the glove box and drove away.

So far, so good.

I couldn't go south. South was Grant Park, the riots, and the Amphitheater. I turned north and west, going out of my way to avoid Old Town and Lincoln Park. I didn't want to get caught in another riot, and I had no idea what was happening in that part of town.

I had no real destination in mind. I had never been north of Chicago, but I knew that I had to do a few things.

First, I had to take the body away from Chicago. I had to hide it near a black community so that the body wouldn't seem that unusual if it were found. I also wanted to divert any suspicion Withers's superiors might have. If his body was found, and they did, somehow, know he was on my trail, I wanted them to think it had taken him away from Chicago. I could plant false clues as well as he could.

Second, I had to work in darkness and I had to work quickly. The longer I waited, the more chance there was of being discovered.

I finally settled on Milwaukee. I pointed the car in that direction, and just drove.

It was nearly one o'clock when I found a wooded area off the highway. I parked the car under the protection of some trees, then got out, and wandered toward the drainage ditch like a man who needed to pee. I didn't turn on the flashlight until I was well into the trees. It was dark and loamy back there. The earth smelled damp from the summer's humidity, even though the ground was dry.

I found a suitable spot and left the flashlight there, turned on. Then I went back to the highway and looked for my light. I couldn't see it.

I had found the perfect place.

I got the trowel, and went back into the leaves. And as I started to dig, I realized I had come full circle from the night I had met Withers.

An image rose in my mind, a memory mixed with a dream. The scrape-scrape-scrape of my trowel mixed with the scrape-scrape-scrape of Chinese shovels on frozen earth.

I'd learned to dig in Korea, fast, in all conditions, with a shovel not much larger than the trowel I held now.

I could almost feel the chill, how I had stood in that narrow trench, my feet blocks of ice in my boots, and saw a dark figure climb the rise between the enemy trenches and our own.

I'd braced my rifle on the side of the trench, finding the figure in my scope, aiming at his chest. I had thought he was a crazy enemy soldier, coming toward us.

Withers, as I had first seen him, so long ago.

The sarge had stopped me from shooting. He had waited until Withers was on the dark side of our hill, then sent me after him.

I brought Withers back to our territory and I had told him he was safe. He had looked at me oddly then and I had the sense that he didn't believe in safety for anyone, especially for himself.

It took me hours on my hands and knees to dig a hole deep enough. The eastern horizon was turning pink when I opened the trunk and hefted the rug-wrapped body for the last time. There were still no cars on the road. I closed the trunk with my free hand and headed into the woods.

There I unrolled the body into the hole, and carried the rug back to the trunk. I grabbed my change of clothes and brought them into the woods, then went to work, covering the body with dirt.

I'd saved the grass-covered sod as best I could and replaced it, stamping it in place. Then I used the trowel one last time to distribute the extra dirt over the ground so that the grave wasn't obvious.

I changed into my street clothes from the day before, hoped there wasn't too much dirt on my hands and face, and returned to my car, tossing the uniform in the backseat.

The hard part was over. But I didn't dare get complacent. I had a few chores left.

I dumped the bullet, the notebook, and the rug off a narrow bridge going over a winding river. The river water would get most of the blood off that rug or at least make it unrecognizable at first glance. No one would know where the rug had come from, and if the body was found, no one would find a telltale expensive oriental rug beneath it.

I tossed the uniform in a garbage can behind a Howard Johnson in Kenosha. I kept my name badge, tossing it under the front seat of the car.

In Waukegan, I used a pay phone to call Franklin. He yelled at me. He'd been frightened by the riots, by my tone, by the strange incident with Laura's phone.

I told him I was fine and that I would be bringing Jimmy home later in the day. Franklin started to ask a question, but my change ran out and the operator cut him off.

By the time I made it back to Laura's, I was swaying with exhaustion. I hardly remembered the drive from Waukegan into the city. I parked in the building's lot, half expecting a cop to stop me, but there was none to be seen.

The door to the service entrance was shut. I didn't want to go in that way anyway. I didn't want to call attention to my knowledge of it in the daylight. I went back to the front door, and this time, the doorman let me in.

The elderly elevator operator nodded at me as if I were an old friend. I nodded back, thankful for the silence. He opened the elevator door on the twentieth floor and I peered at the hallway as if I had never seen it before.

It looked just as clean and normal as it had been every other time I'd visited. There were no bloodstains, no bullet holes, no dents in her door, nothing to show the violence from the night before.

I knocked, and I heard her rustle behind the door, then the dead bolt turned and the door opened.

"Oh, God, Smokey," she said, letting me in. She had a bandage over the left side of her face, and there were shadows under her eyes. "I was so worried."

I nodded. I had been worried too. But I wasn't any longer. The notebook, the fact that Withers had found me, was somehow reassuring. I had a hunch the secret wasn't out.

No matter what, I was done running. From now on, I would stand my ground. I wasn't ever going to run again.

EIGHTEEN

Sinkovich was parked on the street when Jimmy and I pulled up in front of our apartment building. He got out of the car as we drove past, and was waiting on the curb when I stopped.

He looked tired, and he had bruises all over his arms. His knuckles were scraped.

It was clear where he had been the night before. He hadn't been on harassment detail. He'd been in uniform, beating demonstrators.

"Got news for you," he said.

I didn't want to hear it. I didn't want to talk with him. But I didn't want to cut him off entirely.

I was about to say something when Jimmy got out of the passenger side, and walked toward us. I didn't stop him from joining us. His presence might keep the conversation civil.

"Jack," I said, "you ever meet my son, Jimmy?"

"Nope, don't think so." He crouched. "How're you, sport?"

Jimmy raised his eyebrows at me. I didn't think he'd ever been called "sport" in his life.

"Can I go in?" he asked me, ignoring Sinkovich.

"No," I said. "Wait for me just in case Franklin's not there."

Jimmy leaned against the car. Sinkovich stood, his smile gone. "What the hell was that?" he asked under his breath.

"What's your news?" I asked.

He put a hand on my shoulder, led me a little way down the sidewalk. "That boy you was looking for, he definitely ain't one of ours."

"Oh?" I asked. I had forgotten I had asked for Sinkovich's help. Everything seemed so long ago.

"Yeah. I checked. We didn't send no . . . black . . . cops down here. Just white guys, to put on the pressure, you know."

"Thanks," I said, moving away from his grasp.

"There's been some FBI down here. I could get their names, maybe. They tell me there's, you know, guys like him on the force. Maybe—"

"That's all right," I said.

"I mean, anything to catch this guy who done that to that kid, right?"

I looked at him. As far as he was concerned, the Richardson case was still open. "Right," I said. "But you'd better work quick. The convention ends today. They'll be going home."

"If I find him, I'll ask him a few questions, okay?"

"Sure." I looked around him to Jimmy. "You ready?"

"Yeah," he said.

"You don't seem too enthused." Sinkovich sounded belligerent. "I mean, I went out on a limb for you."

I looked pointedly at his bruises, his scraped hands, and realized that I couldn't keep quiet any longer.

"Did you really go out on a limb?" I asked. "Or did you just ask a few of your friends in the squadrol as you drove down to Michigan Avenue last night?"

"Hey!" Sinkovich said. "Them kids are a bunch of spoiled brats. They just wanted attention, playing for the cameras, and it got outta hand."

"Really?"

"We don't believe in playing. They gotta know what real life is like."

"So they deserved it."

"You betcha."

Jimmy sidled up beside me, and took my hand.

"You ever been hit with a nightstick, Jack?" I asked.

"No," he said.

"I have." I smiled thinly at him. "No one deserves to get hit with a nightstick."

"Now wait a minute," he said. "I thought you and me, we was on the same side."

I stared at him, at the scrapes on his knuckles, probably caused by birdshot inside his black gloves. Birdshot made punches particularly lethal. Using it was a trick favored by the Chicago police.

"Maybe we were on the same side for a moment, Jack," I said, "but I don't believe in beating people for exercising their constitutional rights."

"Hey!"

I squeezed Jimmy's hand and led him toward the building. Sinkovich continued to yell after me, but I ignored him. I had nothing more to say to him.

For the first time since I'd come to Chicago, the apartment building looked like home. The police tape was gone. I had a hunch Franklin was behind that, and I appreciated it.

When we stepped inside, Jimmy ran up the stairs and I followed, so tired that every muscle in my body ached. I heard a door open upstairs, and then Jimmy yell, "Franklin!" and laughter come out of the apartment.

I was smiling as I walked through the door.

The smile faded when I saw Truman Johnson sitting at the kitchen table. He was watching Jimmy, who was hugging Franklin and exclaiming happily about being home.

"Found what you were looking for, huh?" Johnson asked.

I froze. Franklin heard the tone and looked at us over Jimmy's head.

"Hey," Franklin said. "Let's make sure your room's okay."

"I got stuff in the car," Jimmy said. "Laura, she—"

"Why don't I help you get it?" Franklin said. "Then you can show it all to me."

"Okay!" Jimmy bounded out as easily as he had run in. He had no idea how close we had come to losing it all last night and I hoped he would never find out.

I turned to Johnson. Maybe I could trust him. He knew how things were. He was black.

But he was also a cop.

"What do we owe this visit to?" I asked.

He was staring at the open door, as if he could still see Jimmy. "I went to the torture chamber, and I wanted to find out if you had any ideas. But I think you already figured out who killed Brian."

I walked over to the fridge and pulled it open, looking for something to drink. "How do you get that?"

"You wouldn't bring your boy back here if you hadn't."

"Really?" I grabbed a can of Coke.

"You said the events were connected."

I closed the refrigerator door, and leaned on it. "No, you said that."

He crossed his arms. "I thought you were going to help me solve Brian's death."

"I tried," I said. "Looking for your lists got me fired."

"I thought you were going to share what you knew."

I pulled the ring top. The can hissed open. "I don't know anything."

His eyes narrowed. "I'll bet that cigarette burn on the back of your neck just happened by accident then, huh?"

I sipped, hoping my hand wouldn't shake. He knew. We both understood that. But I wasn't going to tell him anything. I didn't trust him enough.

After a moment, he sighed. "You leaving Chicago, then?"

"No."

"I could still take you in, ask you some questions."

"You could," I said. "It won't help you, though, not on those old cases."

"So you'll admit this one was different."

"No, Detective," I said. "I won't admit anything."

He smiled. It was a cool, twisted smile. A smile of defeat. "Something else happens, I'm going to come to you."

"For help, I trust."

"Yeah," he said softly, "for help."

His gaze met mine. He nodded once, a gesture of respect, and then he left the apartment.

"What was all that?" Franklin stood in the doorway, his arms full of Jimmy's new clothes. Laura had gone overboard with him, saying that shopping was one of the few things they were both able to enjoy together.

Jimmy came through the door, carrying a pile of games almost as tall as he was. He balanced them precariously as he made his way to his room.

I took the clothes from Franklin. "You can call Althea now."

"I gathered as much." He peered at me. "You don't look too happy about this."

"A lot of things changed in the last few hours, Franklin," I said. "It'll take some time for me to work through them."

"Going back to Memphis?" he asked.

"Can't. But I think it's safe to stay in Chicago."

"What did you do, Smokey?"

I met his gaze. There was no humor on his face at all. I'd never seen him look so serious.

"I did what I had to, Franklin," I said. "I had no other choice."

NINETEEN

Six days later, I sat on the metal stairway leading to the elevated train. Thousands of people filled the Loop, all of them silent. The scene was different from a few nights ago—except for the number of police. Their blue helmets were everywhere and a few tapped nightsticks against their hands, as if reminding us that any sign of trouble would not be tolerated.

We weren't about to give trouble. The city was tired of it. The riots had ended, the Democrats had gone home. Humphrey was nominated, and everyone knew he couldn't win. The convention had destroyed the Democratic party and the only one who didn't know it was their nominee.

I felt like the city—superficially intact, but shattered somehow. On the surface, things were coming together. Laura had offered me and Jimmy one of her company's houses. The house was huge—six bedrooms plus an attic and a basement. She made sure the rent was reasonable.

I turned her down, unable to accept her charity, and then I'd seen Jimmy's face. Franklin's apartment had gotten even more crowded with the addition of Malcolm, and after the last week, Jimmy and I needed some time to put our lives in order.

So I compromised. I asked Laura if Franklin could have the house. She agreed. I took Franklin's apartment as a sublet, and Franklin took Malcolm. Suddenly Jimmy and I had all the space we needed.

I still had to contact Henry back in Memphis. It was time to sell my furniture, put my important belongings in storage, and rent out my house. I needed income and that was one way to get it.

The other way was simple. I was already known in the neighborhood for being able to solve problems. I'd continue doing that, for a price. Just like I had in Memphis.

It all sounded so easy. Even my nightmares were gone, although Jimmy's remained. For all his pretense, the experience in Laura's apartment had left him shaky and bewildered.

It left me feeling as if I hadn't known myself at all. Withers had said that he could remake anyone in his own image. I wondered if, through all of this, he had remade me.

The year of assassinations continued.

In the distance, I heard horns honk. The crowd stirred. The people in front of me stood. I had to stand too.

A motorcade rounded the corner, a series of black limousines with tiny American flags waving on the hoods. A battalion of Secret Service agents ran alongside the cars. Others rode inside.

The windows were down in the second car, and Richard Milhous Nixon, the Republican nominee for president of the United States rode by, waving, his mouth drawn in his famous Grinch-like grin.

A shiver ran down my back.

This was what we had chosen for ourselves—with bullets, riots, and a war that was tearing the country apart, this man who had accused innocent people of being communists, who had chosen a vice-presidential candidate who used the word "nigger" in public, who used any stepping-stone he could find to climb toward the highest office in the land.

This was what assassination had brought us. This and a little boy who couldn't sleep without dreaming of blood, a woman who still had a bruise on the side of her face, a child tortured to death for information he didn't—he couldn't—have.

A man buried in an unmarked grave.

I'd been wondering if Withers had a wife, children, parents who were still alive. If they would want to know what happened to him. Or had he become a shadow in all ways?

I would never know. But I couldn't stop brooding about him. Thinking about how his eyes hadn't really changed when that shot rang out. They had already been empty.

They had to have been, to murder Brian that way. To do all the things Withers had done.

He would probably have cheered this motorcade.

I did not. I could not, even though people around me were waving signs. I didn't know what they saw in this man. He couldn't promise anything except darkness, a continuation of the violence, a world where men like Thomas Withers flourished and boys continued to die.

I leaned against the metal railing, watched the motorcade disappear down the street, and wondered if the year of assassinations would ever really end.